*To Lucille and the kids
...always there,
...always watching my back*

Jezebel in Blue Satin

The Hollywood Murder Mysteries

PETER S. FISCHER

THE GROVE POINT PRESS
Pacific Grove, California

Also by Peter S. Fischer

THE BLOOD OF TYRANTS
THE TERROR OF TYRANTS

ISBN 978-0-9846819-9-0

CHAPTER ONE

She is dead.

I can tell by the small black hole in her left temple just next to her slate grey eyes which are fixed on the catwalk high above the nightclub set on Stage 5. I'm not a detective but I know a corpse when I see one and this beautiful, vulnerable young woman from the plains of South Dakota is as dead as they come. I stumbled upon her around eight p.m. when I went back to the stage to retrieve my briefcase which I'd left behind after a particularly aggravating meeting with the movie's director, Kingman Krug, a pompous no talent ex-agent with one accidental major hit to his name. Now when I say stumbled, that's what I mean because she was curled up by the water cooler and in the dim light I tripped over her protruding leg and went down hard on one knee. I thought she'd just passed out and it wasn't until I looked closely that I spotted that little black dot on the side of her face.

I pick up the phone and call Russ Parmalee, head of security for the studio. Between Russ and the city cops and their fish-eyed questions that are sure to be asked, I know it is going to be a long, long night.

Her name was Margaret Louise Baumann, at least that's what

it said on her paychecks. Around the studio she was known as Vivienne Devereaux. Nice name. I ought to know. I gave it to her along with a bio that made her seem as if she were a real person. She wasn't an actress, not yet, but she was working toward it. Ten months of bumping into locked doors and dealing with so-called agents and casting directors with big ideas and even bigger hands had turned her into something of a realist which is why she took the job of standin for the movie's leading lady, May Britton. They were both buxom but petite, knockout blondes with curves that defied description. Neither had a straight line anywhere on their frames.

I met Maggie her first day at the studio, three days before I had to head off to Arizona to plug one of the studio's cheesy sci-fi programmers. It's my job to meet and greet the newcomers. I'm the company flack. That means press agent or feather merchant. I weave dreams and create fantasies. I'm as honest as my peers at the other studios which isn't saying a lot but the people we deal with have come to expect a certain amount of insincerity. As for the studio help, I give all the newbies my irresistible smile of welcome, chat a little about their background, hopes, aspirations. I resist asking "What's a nice kid like you doing in a dump of a city like this?" In Maggie's case, I really want to say it and spare her the heartache, but she's got a dream and I'm not going to quash it. I gave her a new name because the one she had wasn't going to cut it. Nothing official. Not yet. We were just trying it out around the lot to see how it fit.

She came from a little town in South Dakota. (I change it to Muncie, Indiana. Nobody knows where South Dakota is). Her father is a barber, her mother waits tables at the town diner down by the bus depot. Her older brother left for Columbia to study journalism when she was sixteen. At seventeen she left the house one day and grabbed a Greyhound for Phoenix, hot on the trail of her high school sweetheart. She looked, never found him and never went back home. In my version, my official studio biography, her father becomes a banker and the mother the high school principal. Maggie is transformed into a self-sacrificing little heroine who had been saving her pennies since she was seven years old so she could pay for acting lessons. I have her being discovered by a well known Hollywood character actor passing through town who caught her "Emily" in "Our Town" and was so impressed he paved her way to Hollywood. There was no Emily and no "Our Town" and the actor in question had just died a few weeks back and was in no position to refute my elaborate albeit deceptive confection. There are other frills, other bells and whistles. I can create them in my sleep. These aren't lies, they are personality enhancements. In this town everybody needs them.

I don't kid myself. I know that most of the kids who first walk through the studio gates will be gone in a matter of months. Some will try to hang on, deluding themselves. Others will slink back home and blame their failure on the "system". Still others will switch gears and catch hold somewhere near the bottom of the industry's social ladder. Kept boy for some rich socialite, maybe female, maybe not. Drug gofer for a limited clientele, a career that lasts until the first arrest or the first OD, take your pick. Professional escort, high class at the start, degenerating over the years into something a lot more tawdry.

Still, with Maggie Baumann, I thought she might have had a chance. Sure, she was fresh off the baggage car but there was a wholesomeness about her that was complemented by a goodly amount of steel in her backbone. She was sweet and smart and I never caught her kidding herself about who she was and where she fit in. If anybody had deserved a break it was her and I had been determined to help her get one. Why anyone would want to kill her was beyond me, but dead she was and nothing was going to change it. Whatever break she might have gotten was going to somebody else.

It takes Russ twelve minutes to show up and when he does, his normally ruddy complexion pales to the color of an oyster shell. He peers at the body, at me, back to the body. For a guy who's supposed to be tough, he looks like he is about to toss his supper.

"What happened?" he asks.

"She got shot."

He glares at me. "Jesus, Joe, I can see that." He looks at the body again. "I called the cops," he says.

"Good move."

He shakes his head in frustration. "Jesus Christ," he mutters along with some other words under his breath, none of them fit for polite company. He turns and walks away a few steps, staring up at the rafters. Pushing 40, a draftee in the waning months of the war, he seems to be out of his element. A year in the Sea Patrol in San Diego rousting drunken swabbies fresh from the Pacific theater hasn't prepared him for anything like this. Around the studio, excitement is finding some fan who has sneaked onto the lot and tossing him or her out the front gate with a stern warning. The rest of the time it is filling out security clearances or assigning parking spots. A dull easy job of which homicide is not a part.

Most people like Russ. There are a few who don't. Gossipmongers who had crossed him and then gotten crossed in return. They say he'd been booted out of the Navy when he'd nearly killed a drunken sailor taking him into custody. And it hadn't been the first time. I knew Russ had a temper which he kept well hidden and he was as tough as they come, something that he didn't hide. I asked him once about the rumor. He shrugged it off. He had a job to do and orders to follow. You didn't get to pick and choose which ones you liked and which ones you didn't. As for the drunken sailor, he was a boozy bosun with a dirty mouth and a lousy attitude who was just begging to have the crap beat out of him. "I didn't even have to use the stick on him," Russ had said with a smile. "Just these," he continued as he held up two fists.

As I watch him pace, checking his watch every few seconds and throwing panicked looks toward the stage entrance, I feel sorry for him. I am in the group that likes and admires him and I am pretty sure the feeling is mutual, but he doesn't understand the politics of his job. He is a man of action, not thought and I know, too, that he is worried about his future. He is also tired. We both did our time for Uncle Sam during the war, now we are just looking for a place to keep our heads down and recharge our batteries.

The cops arrive a little past eleven. I'd been there an hour and Maggie was still laying there, like nobody cared. I wanted to cover her up and keep her warm and safe from prying eyes, but I knew I couldn't. This was a crime scene. Do not touch. So she continued the lay there, cold and alone for the gawkers to see.

There are two uniforms and a couple of guys in suits and fedoras who I take to be homicide detectives. I don't like the looks of them but that's okay because I don't like cops. Never have.

They make a beeline for Russ who is in his security uniform. Words are exchanged. They look over at me as if inspecting a Klan member with a stout rope in his hand. The shorter of the two, Kleinschmidt, bellies up to me, invading my space and tries to back me into a wall. He does everything but throw the cuffs on me while his partner Johansson, keeps saying "You'd better believe it" every time his partner makes a point, invariably stupid or obvious. Johansson is a balding beanpole with a sharp needle nose and bad teeth.

Kleinschmidt is built like a barrel, kind of on the short side and he reminds me a lot of William Bendix but not as good looking. His suit needs pressing and his shoes need shining and there is a grease stain on his tie. He seems not to care about any of that as he looks me up and down.

"Name." Kleinschmidt says, mostly a statement, not a question.

"Joe," I tell him.

"Joe what?"

"Joseph F.X. Bernardi," I reply.

"How do you spell that?" he asks pencil poised over a small notepad.

I tell him.

"So, Mr. Bernardi, do you own a gun?" Kleinschmidt asks me.

"No," I say.

"Have you got a permit?"

Is this guy deaf? I tell him again I don't own a gun. He smiles.

"Maybe a souvenir from Berlin? A Luger, maybe. This is L.A., my friend. Everybody has a gun. If they don't they should."

Gritting my teeth, I repeat myself. I speak slowly so he will understand. Maybe English is not his first language. He nods. "We're looking. If it's here, we'll find it."

It goes like this for another twenty minutes. They ask a lot of questions but mostly what they want to know is where I have been all evening. Out of necessity I make up a bullshit story which they seem to buy. Then they move away and start talking quietly to each other. I catch scraps of their conversation and a few minutes later when the coroner and the evidence gathering team show up, they hustle over to fill them in.

I sidle up to Russ.

"I think I'm going to be all right," I say. "The short one looked over at me and said I like him, and the other guy said I do, too."

Russ smiles. "That means they think you did it."

My stomach suddenly twists into a big knot as I look over at the cops. So that's how it's going to be. Great.

At that moment I am distracted by a bright flash off to my right. A guy in a herringbone sport jacket holding a speed graphic camera is ripping off shots of Maggie's body. Russ goes after him like a shot and grabs him by his tie. He starts to drag him away when Kleinschmidt stops him, whispers in his ear and then slips Russ a greenback. Could have been a fiver. It sure wasn't a Washington. Russ pockets the bill and backs off as the photographer scoots out of the sound stage.

It is well past midnight when they finally let me go home with the admonishment not to leave town. I am starting to feel like a character in a George Raft movie.

I hop into my '38 Studebaker, race for home as much as the old heap is capable of racing and finally fall into bed at quarter to two. I am dead tired but sleep won't come. I keep seeing Maggie's corpse curled up on the floor, remember how she'd been: all smiles and beautiful teeth and a cute laugh that wouldn't quit. I want to cry but I can't do that either and the last thing I remember is staring at the clock as it reads 5:08.

A minute later it is reading 6:55 and my phone is ringing. Groggily I reach for it and mutter into the mouthpiece. A voice on the other end screams at me.

"Schmuck!"

I know immediately who it is. Leo Blaustein, studio VP in charge of operations, hatchetman and all-round no-good son of a bitch. He knows very well that my name is Bernardi but his pet name for me is "Schmuck" and I humor him by answering to it.

I mumble something into the phone. He screams at me again.

"Dumb fuck! My office. Eight o'clock. Don't be late!"

He hangs up. Hmm. Dumb fuck. He's found a new name for me. I should be flattered but I'm not. I struggle out of bed, ill prepared to face the day. Later I am to realize how really ill prepared I was.

CHAPTER TWO

t's seven minutes past eight. I'm tooling down La Cienega fighting the morning traffic. It's bad but I've been stuck in worse. The sun is starting to rise in the east and already I can feel the humidity start to wrap its arms around me. It's only May but spring is fading fast and it smells like an early summer. My armpits are already starting to dampen. Maybe it's the heat. Maybe it's the idea of having to face Leo Blaustein on an empty stomach.

I think about what I told the cops the night before and I'm thinking I may have screwed up royally. I told them I was on the lot strolling around, getting some night air. I hadn't logged out at the main gate, I wasn't in my office, I hadn't met with anybody who could vouch for my presence. So I was strolling. It was the best I could do on the spur of the moment. The truth is, I wasn't strolling. I wasn't even on the lot. I'd driven out through the rear delivery gate unobserved. It was guarded by a studio relic known as Scotty who was pushing seventy and had been transfered from the main gate to make way for a snot nosed martinet half his age. I waited until Scotty headed for the men's room to empty his ravaged bladder (he went twice an hour, sometimes more). As he disappeared into Stage 7, I made my move and zipped through the gate, heading for Lydia's house on Highland Avenue.

Lydia's my ex. We've been divorced for six months That's almost as long as our married life together. We met in '43 at the Hollywood Canteen. She was hot and so was I and three weeks later, we got married. Two weeks after that I was shipped out to England to join the Great-fucking-Crusade. When I finally managed to get home in early '46, she didn't even know me. I'd been writing to her but she'd moved and the letters never got forwarded and she figured I must be dead so she felt bad for a couple of weeks and then got on with her life. I'm pretty sure that included a lot of guys but I didn't ask because I didn't want to hear the answer. Whatever the case, the marriage was a joke, she said. I was a nice guy, she said, and even though she never said it outright, I knew she didn't want to be tied to a nickel and dime fiction writer the rest of her life, especially one who had two chapters of the great American novel in the drawer and not the foggiest notion of how to get to Chapter Three. Besides, I'd looked good in a uniform but in civvies I looked like an Okie who hadn't had a square meal in a week. She hopped a bus to Reno and six weeks later, she was back to being Lydia Grozny, single person and available to anyone but me.

How did I like it? I didn't. Maybe she had no use for me but the torch I was carrying was big and bright and hot. I couldn't get her out of my mind which is why I'd always be driving to her place at night, watching, hoping for a look at her. This proved to be a mistake when last week this big Cadillac pulls up and she gets out along with this guy in a shiny silk suit with slicked back hair and a Robert Taylor moustache. He oozes snake oil. He doesn't walk her to the door, he slithers, and then they both go in and he doesn't come out. Not for an hour or two or five or ten. I know what they're doing and it's killing me. I have an urge to beat the crap out of this pervert but I remember that my last fight was in elementary school and I lost. Still I can't stay away. Call me sick or demented, maybe even desperate. She's gone but I can't give her up which is why, when Maggie was taking a slug to the head, I was sitting outside Lydia's little ranch house hoping to get another look at that Caddy, maybe get a plate number and find out who the guy is and then maybe give a few bucks to one of the stunt guys to rough him up enough so he'll stay away. I think like that. When I say I am demented, that's what I mean.

The entrance to Continental Studios looms up on my right. I turn in and pull to a stop. The new guy steps out with his clipboard. His name is Bruno and he looks good in his uniform. I know that under that visored cap, he sports a close cropped G.I. haircut. He says he's a veteran but from his first day on the job I've wondered which army he fought for. His American is impeccable but still, I think, he may be a kraut. He sure as hell acts like one.

"Guten tag, my friend," I say. "You probably want to see my studio pass." He's been demanding to see it every day for the past two weeks. This time I beat him to the punch. He looks at it, grunts, writes something on his clipboard and waves me through. Gestapo maybe. More likely SS.

As movie studios go, Continental is small and it isn't much to look at. It was started right after WWI by Sam Harvey and his brother Lew who bought up several acres of orange groves, invested in a few cameras and started cranking out third rate melodramas and comedies, all of which made money because a war weary country just wanted to be amused. In 1929 they invested in seven sound stages, buildings to house equipment and wardrobe and a few cramped offices for their working stiffs. Out back they erected some false front buildings that sort of looked like New York City or a Mexican village or a Hungarian town square if you didn't look too closely. And throughout they continued to make cheesy melodramas and comedies that now made noise. Little was spent on maintenance and the stages and offices slowly started to deteriorate. Roofs sagged, paint peeled, water pipes burst, and furnaces quit at the least provocation. Revenues started to dry up and just when it looked like the doors would have to be shut, the Japanese attacked Pearl Harbor. Suddenly America was ready for plenty of entertainment to take their minds off the reality of war and since there was a shortage of everything, the key to success was cheap production. And nobody knew cheap production better than Sam Harvey and his brother, Lew, who sadly did not make it to Christmas of 1942. Then in 1946 the studio was sold and one new, and some say self-indulgent, building was erected just inside the main gate.

The nerve center of Continental Studios business operation is a three story edifice nicknamed "The Palace" by just about everyone on the lot. The entire top floor is occupied by the new owner and CEO, Buford DeSalle. His personal office is massive and the walls are decorated with the heads of various wildlife which he murdered in his home state of Louisiana. Each of his two secretaries has her own office. There is also a conference room with a table that can accommodate sixteen flunkies, and beyond that, a decent sized chapel where Buford DeSalle prays for guidance, the Lord's love, and substantial box office receipts every weekend. He has also been known to pray for clear weather at his locations and an absence of scrutiny by the Internal Revenue Service. Hidden under the chapel's mahogany altar is a safe which houses two sets of books, one to show the tax man and the second to keep him apprised of how much dough he is actually rolling in.

Leo Blaustein's office is on the second floor which makes him important, just not that important. He is a ferret of a man with an overblown opinion of his management capabilities. I do not like him and it is no secret, he has never liked me. I came to the studio in early '46 and my first assignment was to publicize a Tim Holt western that was shooting in Mexico a few miles south of Tijuana. Cheap labor, cheap extras, cheap everything. At least that's how Blaustein saw it. The trouble was, the Mexicanos suffered from mananaism. Everything took twice as long and the quality of the work was half as good. On top of that the federales were constantly showing up with their palms out, making threats about needed permits and possible shutdowns. These were the minions of el presidente Manuel Avila Camacho who never made an honest peso in his life and when I got back to the states, I said as much to the press, describing in great deal the backbreaking rigors of dealing with Mexican officialdom. I was big news and a hero to the local working stiffs who wanted the jobs kept in L.A. but Blaustein was after my scalp. The only thing that saved me was that Camacho got tossed out of office and replaced by Miguel Aleman who said that, yes, indeed, corruption had existed but it would never happen again, not on his watch. Aleman singles me out as a man of honesty and integrity and Buford DeSalle gives me a raise. Blaustein seethes and awaits his opportunity.

I arrive on time and then squirm in one of his overstuffed easy chairs for the next twenty five minutes before his secretary directs me through the doors into the inner sanctum. Blaustein is sitting behind his massive desk. In size it is second only to the desk of Buford DeSalle. Leo is on the phone pretending not to notice me. I approach the desk, trudging through thick piled carpet so lush that small vermin could hide there. The walls are a deeply stained wood. They are covered with artwork that Goering would have killed for though I am not sure they are genuine. In a land of make believe you can never be sure of anything. I reach the desk and stand at attention, then slip into "at ease". Finally he hangs up and glares at me,.

"Schmuck!" he says, tossing the morning edition of the Los Angeles Times at my head. I manage to catch it and look at the front page. There I see the photo that the hustler took at the murder site the night before. The headline screams: STARLET MURDERED!. Beneath that in slightly smaller type: VIVIENNE DEVEREAU SHOT TO DEATH, and below that STUDIO EXECUTIVE QUESTIONED. I look down into the body of the story to see that the studio executive is me. I peer up over the fold of the paper and see Leo glaring at me.

"Let me ask you a question," he growls. "What the hell is going on? What were you doing at the set at that time of night? Were you screwing this babe? Did you kill her? I swear to God, Bernardi, I will have your ass for this."

This is more than one question and I don't know which one to answer first but I decide on the most important one. "I didn't kill her," I say.

"Then why do the cops think you did?" he demands to know.

"They don't," I respond.

"The hell they don't," Leo says. "Read the story. I'm surprised they didn't throw the cuffs on you last night."

I quickly scan the first four or five paragraphs. Each time I see my name I see a word like "devious" or "suspicious" or "unsubstantiated".

"This little tootsie from South Dakota, we get 'em coming through the gate all the time and all the time, they are trouble. Big trouble, looking to be stars, looking to fuck a director or a producer, but they don't get murdered and if they do, they don't get murdered on one of my sound stages!" Leo is turning a bright shade of red. "Your job, Mr. Bernardi, is to see that this studio does not suffer adverse publicity. Dead bodies are bad publicity or did they not teach you that in Press Agentry 101?"

I repeat myself. "Mr. Blaustein, I did not kill her."

He shakes his head. "You've been spending time with her. A lot of time. Probably fucking her."

"No," I try to say.

"That's not what this story says!" he shouts, slamming the newspaper down on his desk

"The story is wrong," I protest. "You know these newspapers, Mr. Blaufeld. Anything to boost circulation."

"And who else around here even knew who she was? She's here, what, a week and a half?"

"Actually a couple of months---"

He doesn't stop for a breath. "I don't know her, Mr. DeSalle doesn't know her, nobody knows her. You know her. So what happened? She give you the old heave-ho. Huh? "

"I didn't kill her and I wasn't fucking her," I insist, my voice getting louder. "I was--- trying to give her a hand, you know, some kind of a break. She was a nice kid and she doesn't deserve the kind of crap that's being written about her."

"You say," Leo says.

"I say." I face him down, unwavering. This may cost me my job but at the moment I don't give a crap.

He gives me a hard look back, but his watery eyes are all squinty and it doesn't quite work. He's a runt of a man, balding, with a large nose and a pointy chin. If he has a sense of humor he takes great pains not to show it. His chief function in life seems to be to bully and intimidate all those beneath him and to kiss the rosy ass of Buford DeSalle at every opportunity. He lights up an Old Gold from the pack on his desk and leans back in his chair.

"I am speaking now for Mr. DeSalle," he says, wheezing. "Mr. DeSalle, who is an early riser, called me at home at 5:45. You are aware, Mr. Bernardi, that Mr. DeSalle is the most moral of men. He lives by a strict Christian code and expects those around him to do the same. Scandal is anathema to this man. He will not tolerate it, not at all. Not for a moment."

"I'm sure he---" I start to say.

"Quiet! When I wish you to speak I will let you know. Mr. DeSalle suggested that I fire you immediately. I suggested to Mr. DeSalle that such an action might reflect unfavorably on the studio's image. After all, you have not been convicted of any crime, you may very well be innocent and beyond that, you are a war veteran. Even two years after VJ Day, firing a veteran is not something you do casually."

"Thank you, Mr.-----"

He glares at me. I shut my trap.

"So this is how it will be, Mr. Bernardi. You will cooperate with the police and with our own security people. No request will be too onerous. With luck they will find out who killed this unfortunate young girl and after a few days, all of this will be forgotten. If they do not discover the perpetrator, if this continues to drag along day after day and week after week in the daily press, Mr. DeSalle will be very unhappy and when Mr. DeSalle is unhappy, I am miserable. Do I make myself clear?" He waves his hand absently. "You may speak."

"I understand," I say.

"Good. Cooperation, Mr. Bernardi. Cooperation. Think of nothing else."

I leave his office and think of nothing else. I'm steaming because I have to work for this unfeeling reptile of a man. A young life has been snuffed out and he couldn't care less. Image. The studio's good name. That's all that matters. Am I the only one who cares?

I realize I haven't eaten breakfast. I hustle over to the commissary where breakfast is still being served. Cookie Fryberger, who had been head chef at Ft. Sill for three years, is still cooking up scrambled eggs floating in grease, grits, undercooked pork sausage, pone and undrinkable coffee from a vat that hasn't been cleaned in weeks. I opt for toast and marmalade and a tall glass of tomato juice and sit down at a corner table to consider my options. I don't have many. Matter of fact, if I read Leo right, he is telling me that if the killer is found I just might keep my job and if not, I will be out on my ass and probably blackballed in every studio in town. In other words my future is in the hands of Detective Sergeant Kleinschmidt and his partner. A very depressing thought. I am perusing the newspaper story in detail when I hear:

"Hey, man, what the hell happened?"

I recognize the voice and look up as Brick Baxter slips into the booth opposite me. Brick is the leading man on our picture, entitled, incidentally, "Jezebel in Blue Satin", playing a two fisted private eye. It is a part he is used to playing. He's been doing nothing else for the past five years. He shakes his head.

"Hard to believe. Nice kid like that. Not that I knew Vivienne or anything but she really seemed, what would you say--uh, nice."

I nod. "Nice."

"Sounds like the cops were all over you," he says, hoping to get a little something that maybe the papers don't have so he can show off for his buddies down at the Blue Parrot Cafe.

"The paper got it right," I say, "except for trying to dump it on me. On that they're fishing in the wrong pond."

"Of course you didn't do it," Brick says. "Who would think a thing like that?"

He smiles. He is trying to be nice. To tell the truth, he is a pretty decent guy. Not too swift upstairs but basically without ego and that makes him an anomaly among the town's leading men. He'd been on top for a couple of years, '44 and '45, but when the real stars like Gable and Power and Stewart came back, heroes all, his career started to tank and now he has been reduced to starring in a 60 minute programmer for Continental. It could be worse. It could be Monogram.

"I really didn't know her," he says for the second time to make sure I get the point. He flashes his pearly whites. "Good looker like her, most times she'd be all over me and I'd have her in my dressing room by day three at the latest. But this time, I don't know, it just didn't happen."

I smile knowingly. Two alpha males sharing a hetero point of view. Trouble is, Brick is anything but hetero and the Blue Parrot is a watering hole for every limp-wristed homo in Hollywood. He doesn't know I know. Hell, he thinks nobody knows. It is the worst kept secret since Al Capone tried to pass himself off as a used furniture dealer.

Brick sighs. "Yeah, I was home last night studying the script, getting a handle on my characterization."

I look at him oddly. He is giving me his alibi. Why? Who asked him? And what is he telling me for?

"So, Joe, what do you think?" Brick asks me. "You think maybe they'll shut the picture down?"

"I don't know, Brick, they don't usually consult me about things like that. Why? You got someplace to go?"

He gives me a funny little smile which looks odd on a guy as big as he is. "You never know." Then he unlimbers, standing and stretching. "Well, better get to makeup. I've got a ten thirty call."

I look at him in disbelief. "They're shooting?"

"Sure. Whatdayathink? We got a picture to make."

I shake my head. "You'd think they might show a little sensitvity."

"Yeah, you'd think so," he says almost bitterly. Then he glances at his watch just to make sure it isn't already past ten thirty. He grins, again revealing the pearly whites.

"See you later, bud. Don't take any wooden nickels," he says, then off he goes and back I go to the newspaper story. I start to count the malicious references attached to my name. When I reach ten, I throw the paper down and head for my office.

I'm furious. It isn't just Blaustein. Last night there's a dead body on Stage 5 and this morning, they're busy as little beavers back on stage filming the movie as if the kid from South Dakota had never existed. Well, hell, it's a dollars and cents business, isn't it? Not much room for sentimentality. Even as I am thinking it, something is starting to bother me but I can't think what. Something I've seen or something someone has said. By the time I sweep into my office, it is really starting to eat at me, like a song you've known all your life and suddenly you can't remember the title.

There is a note on Phyliss's desk. She's gone for a manicure. Phyliss does things like that. She's been around since the days of the silents. Rumor has it she'd been one of Joe Kennedy's trophies. Whatever. She has studio clout and she uses it. I find myself flattered whenever she finds time to actually do her job. I go into my so-called private office.

Russ Parmalee is sitting at my desk drinking a cup of coffee and scanning my appointment book for the past several months.

"See anything you like?" I ask, shrugging off my suit jacket and hanging it on the standing rack by the door.

"I'll let you know when I do," he grins. He points toward my percolator that is sitting on top of a filing cabinet. "I made coffee. Help yourself."

"Thanks."

He taps the book. "You sure spent a lot of time with the Devereau dame."

"Baumann. Her name was Baumann. Maggie Baumann."

"No kidding," Russ says. "Never would have guessed. Were you fucking her, Joe?"

"Why is everybody suddenly so interested in my sex life?"

"I'm really not unless you killed her which I don't think you did. On the other hand, if you were and some guy got ticked off about it, well, he might have done something about it. That is, if you were fucking her which apparently you weren't."

"We were just friends. I was just trying to help her get ahead."

"Which is why you got her a job at the studio, so you could play Svengali."

"I didn't get her the job. Hell, I'd really only known her for ten days. It was the Monday before last when I got back from Arizona and found she'd been assigned to stand in for May Britton."

"Well, somebody got her the job. Kids like her just don't walk in off the street."

"Casting, probably," I say.

"Right. Casting. Who else?"

And then it hits me. That song title that had been evading my memory bank for the past hour or so. Leo Blaustein called her a tootsie from South Dakota. But her studio bio, which I wrote, puts her home town in Indiana. Who told Leo? Had to be somebody because Leo said he didn't know her. Made a big point of it. My brain starts turning over like the wheels on a slot machine. Maybe it wasn't studio casting that opened the door for Maggie. Could be she slipped through the gate courtesy of Leo Blaustein. Maggie had never mentioned Leo whenever we'd chatted but then we really never talked about how she got the job on the picture. I look at Russ. Should I say something? What if I'm out in left field on this? Accusing Leo of playing footsie with the hired help and getting it wrong could cause me severe career difficulties. I decide to keep my suspicions to myself.

"Look, Russ, I know I might be getting in the way but Blaustein laid it on the line. If this killer isn't caught real quick, my ass is in a sling so if you don't mind, I'd like to pitch in."

He looks at me strangely. "Pitch in with what?"

"The investigation," I say.

"What investigation?" Then he catches on. "What? You mean me? You think I'm getting involved with this? No, no, amigo."

"You're in charge of security, Russ. I would think----"

His eyes turn hard and cold. "Don't think, Joe!" he snaps. "I'm not a detective. I'm a traffic cop. You remember Bogart in Casablanca. I stick my neck out for nobody. I don't know what's going on, I don't know who's involved so I'm going to mind my own business and I suggest you do the same."

"Yeah, well, I may not have much to say about that," I tell him.

He nods, almost apologetically. "Yeah. You're right. Sorry. Look, if there's anything I can help you with on the QT, you let me know but it's strictly under the table. I like this job and I was lucky to get it. I do nothing to jeopardize it. Got it, my friend?"

"Got it," I say. I shake my head in frustration. "So how about a look at her employment application."

"Can't help you."

"Come on, Russ. I need help here. Things just don't add up. She's been in town for months. Living where? Working where? She had to be supporting herself somehow."

"Joe, I didn't say I won't help you, I said I can't. There is no employment application."

I frown. "Then how'd she get a job here?"

"Martha Brodsky."

"Casting again."

"She told me to put her on the payroll, paperwork to follow. It never followed. All I know about that kid is her name wasn't really Devereau, It was something like Bauer or Brauner. Something like that." He shrugs. "Sorry, Joe, that's all I've got for you."

I nod. No help here.

"Thanks for the coffee," Russ says as he heads for the door. He starts to say something, then thinks better of it and goes out.

I go to my desk and settle into my chair leaning back. I look at my options and they are bleak. If I am going to pitch in on the case, it would mean working with Detective Kleinschmidt and somehow I don't feel that is really in the cards.

I reach for the phone and dial the interstudio number for the casting department. Brodsky is in but she is tied up all morning with readings. The secretary says she'll leave a note. I thank her and hang up.

There are seven memos on my desk. Two from genuine friends concerned over the story in the Times. Another from a kid in the mailroom who's had his eye on my job since the day he arrived. He, too, is concerned, probably that I might somehow evade a long prison term. Jimmy Fidler, the gossip guy, is proposing lunch. Anxious to get my side of the story. Also Louella. Ditto. And Hedda. Also ditto.

Near the bottom I find one from a successful screenwriter. I mean two Oscars successful. Even bar flies on skid row know this guy's name. My curiosity is piqued and Phyliss gets him on the phone.

"Joe!" he exclaims as if I am a long lost relative, or better, someone who owes him money. "Thanks for getting back to me, sport. I know you have your hands full." I allow as how that is the case. "Bizarre," he says. "This whole megilla. Wow! I mean, you can't make this stuff up, right?" I allows as how that is also the case. "I hear the cops have been busting your balls pretty good." Indeed, they have, I tell him. It goes on like this for a few minutes before he gets to the point.

"Here's the deal, Joe. I want to work up an original screenplay based on the killing, but I need an in, a point of view, a central character if you will, and I'm thinking maybe I could write it from your angle. What you've been going through and how you're feeling and how you've been treated and then after a while, when we get to know each other a little better, we can get into that whole thing about why you did it."

I hang up on him.

The last memo is from Kleinschmidt who wants me at headquarters at two o'clock to give a complete statement and don't bother to bring a lawyer because you won't need one. That was a sure tipoff that a lawyer was the first thing I was going to need. I pick up the memos, crumple them into a giant ball and toss them into the wastebasket. I am about to leave the office without telling Phyliss where I am going. If she wants me she can come looking for me. The phone rings. I look back at it, hesitate, then reach for the receiver.

"Press Relations," I say.

For a moment, there is silence, then a woman's voice. "I'm trying to get in touch with a Mr. Bernardi."

"This is Joe Bernardi."

"Oh. I---uh---I saw your name in the paper this morning. The article in the Los Angeles Times."

"Yes?"

"It was the picture. That awful picture of Margaret. The story said her name was Vivienne but I knew it was Margaret and I thought I have to call somebody and there was your name so I called you."

In my line of work you get a lot of crank calls. This babe is no crank. She knew Maggie. Or rather, had known Maggie.

"Who am I talking to?" I ask.

"My name is Natalie Bloom."

"And you were a friend of Margaret's?"

"We roomed together for several months late last year."

"I'd like to talk to you about Margaret," I say. "Would that be all right?"

"Sure. Any time," she says.

She works at a Woolworth's on La Brea in West Hollywood and she gets a fifteen minute break at 10:30. I walk in at 10:28 and she spots me right away. She is with a customer but she gestures me toward the soda fountain. I grab a stool and in a couple of minutes she joins me. Natalie is nothing to look at, plain, tending toward plump but she has a nice smile and as I discover, a warm heart. She is genuinely torn up by her friend's death.

"It was just the two of us for maybe four months. We split everything right down the middle. Rent, utilities, food. She was nice. Easy to get along with."

"Did she have a job?"

Natalie laughs. "Sure. They don't pay you for doing nothing. Mostly she waitressed but toward the end, the last six weeks, she got herself a cashier's job in a diner in Van Nuys. That's in the Valley."

"I know where it is," I say.

"She didn't like the drive much but the pay was better than what she'd been getting."

I nod. "How about boy friends?"

Natalie shakes her head. "Nope. Strictly single-o." She hesitates. "No, wait. The last couple of weeks, she told me she'd met this guy. She said it like it didn't mean a lot. Romantically, I mean. I think he was an older kind of guy but he was involved in one of the movie studios and that's what interested her. She really had her heart set on getting into pictures."

"She mention any names?" I ask.

Again, Natalie shakes her head. "No names. I never found out what came of that because my Mom got sick and I had to go back to Fresno to take care of her. She lasted a few weeks before she died and when I got back to L.A. Margaret was gone. Matter of fact, she'd run out on the rent. Funny, that wasn't like her but, hey, you think you know somebody and maybe you don't, you know what I mean?"

Yes, I knew what she meant. Kids like Maggie come to Movieland from all parts of the country, full of hope with stardust in their eyes and after a while they're just trying hang on.

"I felt bad about the rent even though I hadn't been there but you know, I felt a little obligation. I gave Mrs. Feeley twenty dollars. She owed more but Mrs. Feeley thanked me. Guess not too many people would have done what I did. Anyway, she gave me a small suitcase Margaret had left behind. There wasn't much in it, just stuff that had been in drawers. Nothing of value anyway."

"Do you stlll have it?" I ask.

"Sure."

"I'd like to take a look at it if you don't mind," I say.

"Sure. I'll bring it to work tomorrow and put it in my locker. Come by any time."

"I will," I say.

We chat like that until her fifteen minutes is up and then I leave. I keep chewing on what she'd told me about an older man connected to a movie studio. No matter how I roll those dice, they keep coming up Leo Blaustein.

CHAPTER THREE

It is almost quarter past eleven when I amble over to Stage 5 to poke my nose in where it doesn't belong. I'd been scheduled to cover the monthly meeting of the Greater Los Angeles Women's Decency League, something that would normally be off my beat but the guest speaker was to be Persimmon Amanda DeSalle, wife of our esteemed employer and, it is said, a powerful figure in the executive suite given the amount of time she spends on the lot. She is wise enough to shun the spotlight and let her husband bask in the few accolades the studio receives but there are those who truly believe she is the brains of the outfit.

Given the situation at the studio, her appearance at the Decency League has been postponed to a later date which is kind of too bad. I like the lady a lot. She is a genteel Southern belle from old money but possessed of a wicked sense of humor that seldom fails to hit its mark. Quite a contrast to her husband who is mostly pompous and self righteous, a former preacher who had risen from an impoverished background and somehow used his gift of gab to make a fortune repackaging the Lord's work for radio listeners who couldn't get enough of the hosannas and hallejulahs, and were more than happy to divest themselves of their nickels and dimes to participate in Buford's skin game. The patrician Persimmon and the dirt poor Buford. They are, indeed, an odd couple but most people who know them are certain they are deeply in love. Me? I don't care one way or another. I have other things to worry about.

There is a squad car parked outside the entrance alongside an unmarked black Ford coupe. I suspect that Sgt. Kleinschmidt is on the premises, hot on the trail of possible suspects. The red warning light is off which means they are between shots so I go inside and sure enough, my favorite cop is off in the corner with Brick Baxter whom he has backed up against the wall. Only he isn't giving Brick the third degree and he doesn't have a rubber hose in his hand. What he has is apparently an eight by ten glossy which Brick has just signed for him. They are laughing it up except when Kleinschmidt turns and looks in my direction, the grin turns to a disgusted scowl. Why do I think that this cop is not about to look very far past me for his perpetrator? I sort of half wave in Kleinschmidt's direction. The scowl remains frozen on his face.

I look around. Kingman Krug, the director who claims to be Viennese but was actually born in Sioux Falls, Iowa, is conferring with the cameraman about the next setup. They are filming in the night club set which is large and lavish and cost a few bucks but since the heroine of the film, the Jezebel in blue satin, is a nightclub singer, it was pretty much necessary. There's a large bandstand under a seashell motif, a sizeable dance floor, dozens of small tables with chairs, a monstrous bar in the background, and expensive hanging chandeliers. A lot of money to waste on this crummy B movie but DeSalle must know what he's doing. For two years he hasn't made many mistakes. "Joe!" It is a female voice and when I turn May Britton hurries toward me, arms outstretched. She encircles me, holding me close, and

I think I detect a sob or two as she speaks. "Oh, Joe," she says. "It's so awful. Vivienne of all people. Sweet kid like that. I can't believe it." She chokes a little. I can't believe it either. I've been on the set seven days and May hasn't even looked at me. Not once. Not even to sneer. And as for Vivienne---Maggie--- May treated her like an upstairs maid she'd caught stealing the silverware. I look past May to her gofer. Chauffeur. Bodyguard. Frequent lay, maybe. Call him what you like. I call him Vinnie the Muscle and he is always around making sure May gets what she wants when she wants it. Russ has told me his full name is Vincent DellaFerragio, a one time soldier with the Genovese family back east. He was a made man but never served a day in prison which is how he ended up getting drafted and forced to fight the Japs in the Pacific which he apparently kind of liked. When he got discharged he started working for Bugsy Seigel who he knew from the old days in New York. Then a few months ago he got sideways of Bugsy. Instead of killing him, Bugsy told Vinnie to get lost which he was doing when he hooked up with May.

I manage to pat May on the back a couple of times. Gently. Vinnie is still watching me. "I know, I know," I say, as if I know, which I don't.

May steps back. Her eyes are dry. Whatever those sobs were they hadn't reached her tear ducts. She looks at me imploringly. "Who would do such a thing? I mean, for God's sakes, Joe. It wasn't like she was somebody, she was just this nice kid trying to get along."

I shake my head. I am trying to empathize with May's pain while trying to decide if she is actually feeling any.

"The police want to question me," she says. "I can't imagine why. I don't know anything. I mean, how could I? They questioned you, didn't they, Joe? Last night? What kind of questions did they ask? I want to be prepared." She bites her lower lip. "I don't like this, not one bit. I've got my big scene this afternoon and I can hardly concentrate. Is my makeup all right? Did I smudge it on your jacket?"

I shake my head. "You look just fine, Miss Britton," I say.

She nods vacantly. "I suppose I'll have to stand in for myself today. Maybe I can get one of the hair girls to do it." She is talking to herself as she wanders off. Weird. She'd asked me a question and then didn't wait around for the answer. I wonder what kind of world she lives in.

I don't know much about May Britton but what I do know is kind of sad. This third rate movie is a half baked comeback for her. The script says she is playing a 25 year old but she is pushing 40, maybe even a tad more. Sixteen years ago she'd been nominated for an Oscar in her first picture for Paramount but she'd lost to Marie Dressler. Her next three pictures were dreary affairs and when Paramount shucked her, Warner's took a chance. She got one starring part opposite Bogart before he was Bogart and both of them were pretty bad. After that the parts got smaller and smaller. She got married so she could say that she walked out on Hollywood and not the other way around but the marriage lasted less than a year before her husband was indicted on fraud charges and blew his brains rather than have to endure the cuisine at San Quentin. Her last part had been in '45, an eight-line day part that no one noticed. And then suddenly she was offered "Jezebel in Blue Satin". Seems the studio's new owner, Buford DeSalle had developed a crush on May thanks to that first movie of hers and when he'd bought Continental last year, making a movie with May became his first priority.

So, no, I don't know much about May Britton but I know that she is scared and that she knows this is her last chance to climb back on board the Hollywood bandwagon. And I know that she is very much an actress, self-involved and oblivious to most of the world around her. She seems bright enough, at least I've never caught her reading Louella with her lips moving, but deep down, who is she? I have no idea.

Not being a total dunce myself, when I have had time to think about it, I have considered the possibility that Maggie had not really been the intended victim. It isn't far fetched to believe that someone might have mistakenly plunked Maggie thinking it was May. I know that May has antagonized a lot of people with her diva-like airs. It was her sound stage, it was dark, and in the dark there was probably a palpable resemblance between Maggie and May. Probable? Maybe not. Possible. Maybe so.

I'd come to the set looking for Myrtle Figg, the wardrobe mistress. I'd found Maggie dead in her street clothes, not the blue satin dress she (and May as well) had been wearing all day. I figure Myrtle might have been the last one to see Maggie alive when she changed back to her civvies. Besides Myrtle is gossip central at Continental. What she doesn't know didn't happen. If somebody had it in for Maggie, Myrtle might have a line on it. The Assistant Director, a studio fixture named Al Kaplan, tells me Myrtle is back at Wardrobe which is a couple of studio blocks away from the sound stage. Next to Myrtle and maybe Scotty, the gate guard, Al is the third best source of information on the lot. His resume says he'd been here since the early days of the talkies, first in props, then construction. He'd even worked on May Britton's first picture sixteen years earlier. I am about to leave when Kingman Krug blocks my way. He is in a rage.

"What did you say to her?" he demands to know. He says "vat" instead of "what" as if I'll fall for his cheesy imitation of Walter Slezak.

"Say what to who?" I say.

"Don't play mister dumb rabbit with me, writer man. My so-called leading lady. All of a sudden the princess has a headache. She's in her trailer and she wants to see her doctor. I ask her, which one? The one that feeds her pills or the one that shrinks her head? She throws a soda bottle at me. So what did you say to this woman?"

"Nothing. She was upset. I patted her on the back. She started talking to herself and walked off. Look, a girl was killed here yesterday---'

"You think I don't know that? Everything is screwed up. I didn't get my stage until nine-thirty. I'm six hours behind schedule and now that no talent harridan who thinks she's Joan Crawford is going to cost me another couple of hours. Gott in himmel, at least Joan Crawford can act."

"And Miss Britton can't? That's funny. I heard she was going to be in your next picture," I say.

"You heard wrong, sonny. Over my dead body do I work with that woman again. This piece of dreck, I live with the bitch but next month I start prepping a real movie, a movie with soul and heart and I don't care what Mr. Buford - Holier than Thou- DeSalle thinks. I make it with who I want. I have a contract and better than that, I got a lawyer who eats gonefs like Buford DeSalle for breakfast." With that he turns on his heel and stalks off. I watch him go, then sneak a look toward the back of the stage. Sgt. Kleinschmidt has gone and Brick Baxter is sitting alone at a makeup table, checking out his wavy locks for grey hairs. I beat it before the cops came looking for me.

I catch up with Martha Brodsky, swaggering out of her office and apparently heading for the commissary for lunch. She is wearing her usual wardrobe. Cardigan sweater over a white blouse and khaki pants that are custom made to disguise her ample backside. She is only five-two or three but she is built like a sack of sugar and I have heard that people mess with her at their own peril. I jog up to her.

"Martha, you get my message?" I ask, a little out of breath.

"I got it."

"We need to talk."

"Not in public, Bernardi. Right now you're poison. I've got my reputation to consider."

I force myself to contain a laugh. Martha Brodsky is the most infamous bull dyke in Hollywood. Guys looking for work have nothing to fear from her but nubile young lasses from the boondocks, that is another story. When it comes to prey, Maggie Baumann would have been a prime target for Brodsky's affections.

"I'll buy you lunch," I offer.

"You're not hearing me. Besides I've got a lunch date. You remember Janet Gaynor? We've been seeing a lot of each other lately. I'm trying to get her into Curt Bernhardt's new picture."

"Janet Gaynor? She's married."

Brodsky smiles. "There's married and there's married, sonny. Her husband's a costume designer. What does that tell you?"

"Look, I really don't want to delve into your sex life, Martha. I just need a little information. Margaret Baumann. I'd like to look at her resume."

Brodsky stops short, a few yards from the commissary entrance. "What for?" she asks.

"Like you said, I'm in trouble with the cops. I'm trying to dig myself out."

"Can't help you."

"Can't or won't?"

"Even if I had a resume for the kid, which I don't, I wouldn't show it to you. Matter of personal privacy."

"She's dead, for Christ's sakes," I growl.

"So I hear. See you later, Joe."

She starts off. I grab her by the arm and she whirls back at me, her bicep hard as steel, her eyes flashing fire. "Get your hands off me," she snarls.

I back off, raising my hands defensively. "Okay, okay. No resume. So where did you see her? Some little theater group here in town?"

"Mind your own business and get out of my way," She starts to push past me. Risking life and limb, I block her.

"Okay, how about this? You took orders. From who? Who told you to put Maggie on the payroll?"

"Move!"

"Leo Blaustein? Was that who it was?"

Her eyes flicker for just a second and then she pushes past me, jamming an elbow into my side. As she disappears through the entrance I shout after her.

"My best to Janet! Tell her I loved her in 'A Star is Born'!"

I lie. I hated that movie.

Suddenly, I am hungry but I have no stomach for going into the commissary to watch Brodsky play footsies with Janet Gaynor. I opt for a trip home and a bowl of leftover soup while I consider where I am which I already know is nowhere.

On my car radio, I flip to a news station and manage to catch the tail end of Jimmie Fidler's Hollywood gossip show. For weeks the Black Dahlia murder case has been dominating the news. Morning news, evening news, it was all the same. The cops are no closer to solving poor Elizabeth Short's brutal death than Harry Truman is of getting re-elected. There is even talk that the cops don't want it solved, that just maybe someone in the department is involved. But that is yesterday's headline and suddenly Maggie's death is the hot story of the week. The cops aren't saying much. Yes, the coroner is performing an autopsy. Yes, several leads are being explored but they can't talk about them. What about studio press agent Joe Bernardi? Is he a suspect? No more than anyone else. Brick Baxter expresses sadness over the death of what he calls a rising star in the Hollywood firm. (He probably means firmament.) A representative for the film's star May Britton says she is too upset to talk to the press but she might have a statement later in the day. I assume that the representative is that smooth talking flunky, Vinnie the Muscle.

As I turn onto the street that fronts my apartment house I spot a familiar figure hurriedly heading toward one of those black unmarked Fords. It is Detective Johansson and I am pretty sure he has been nosing around my apartment. I know he isn't looking to move into this building. Even cops have some sense of dignity as opposed to press agents whose pay scale ranks right down there with coolie labor.

If Johansson has been in my apartment, I don't notice it. Not at first. My stomach is growling louder than ever and I reach in the icebox for the unfinished bowl of soup my neighbor, Mrs. Crimmins, had made for me the day before. Mrs. C. is a sweet old biddy pushing 60 and I still am not sure whether she is looking for a little action or if I am the surrogate son for the one she'd never had. Either way she is sweet and helpful and keeps a sharp eye on my place whenever I have to leave town for a few days of location work.

After I heat the soup on my aging pre-war gas range I sit down and start to slurp it up. It is very good but I'm not thinking about that. I am thinking about that radio broadcast and the coroner's autopsy and it comes to me that I have no idea what is going to become of Maggie's body once the cops are through with it. I don't know where she had lived here in L.A. or if she had lived alone or how many friends she might have had, if any. And it also bothers me that it is unlikely that the Baumanns of South Dakota would connect the death of starlet Vivienne Devereau to their daughter Margaret.

I get up and rummage through the middle drawer of my desk until I find my notes on Maggie's biography. I'd remembered right. Their names are Paul and Dorothy and they live in the small town of White River. I call long distance to information and get the number. A few minutes later I am connected..

"Hello." The voice is young. Very young.

"Hello," I respond. "Who's this?"

"Penny," she says. "Who's this?"

"Joe," I say.

"Hi, Joe," she replies. She has a smile in her voice.

"Penny, is your mother home?"

"No, my momma has gone away but my Nana is here."

"Could I speak to her?"

"Okay." I hear her shout. "Nana!"

In a few moments, a woman comes to the phone. She has a soft, mellow voice.

"Yes?"

"Mrs. Baumann?"

"Yes."

"Mrs. Dorothy Baumann?"

"Yes. Who am I speaking to?"

"You don't know me. My name is Joe Bernardi. I work for Continental Studios in Hollywood."

"Yes?" There is a curious hesitation.

"Have you been following the news about the death of the young actress at our studio last evening?"

"No, I haven't," she says. "Mr.--uh----"

"Bernardi. Joe Bernardi. The news broadcasts have been giving her name as Vivienne Devereau but that was just a stage name." I hesitate. This is the tough part. "Vivienne was your daughter Margaret's stage name. I'm afraid she's dead, Mrs. Baumann. I'm very very sorry."

There is a long silence, then: "Margaret? Oh, but we hadn't seen or heard from her in so very long. Dead. Oh, my."

Bingo! I start to scribble notes but as I press down, my pencil point breaks. I quickly dig out my trusty bone-handled jackknife which I've had since I was a kid and quickly fashion a new point, talking all the time, trying to get her to open up.

"I thought you'd want to know."

"Yes, I suppose so," she says haltingly.

I hear a man's voice in the background. "What is it, Mother? Who is that on the phone?"

She half covers the mouthpiece but I can still hear her. "It's about Margaret," she says. There is a long, long silence and then a man's voice reverberates in my ear. It is deep and it isn't mellow.

"Who is this?" he demands.

I give him my name and repeat what I had told his wife. "The reason I'm calling, sir, is to let you know what happened and to see if you wanted to make any arrangements about your daughter's body."

"I have no daughter," Paul Baumann says icily. "Please do not call this number again." There is a click as he disconnects. Somehow I'd always felt that family, like love of country, ran deep in the heart of middle America. In this instance, it seems not.

As I hang up, my eyes fall on my half-read copy of "The

Hucksters" by Frederic Wakeman. There is talk the studio is bidding on it though I am pretty sure MGM has the inside track. Also the money. Buford DeSalle likes to talk big but he can squeeze a penny hard enough to make Lincoln cry. My paycheck proves it. I suspect Louis B. Mayer is looking for a hot property to showcase the newly returned Clark Gable though surprisingly people I knew who always seem to have it right are certain it is going to be a breakout picture for John Hodiak. Maybe so. I've also heard that Mayer has offered a bundle of coin to borrow Sydney Greenstreet from Warners to play the tyrannical client. Perfect casting. Jack Warner would be an idiot to turn it down. The role will elevate Greenstreet at least two big notches in the Hollywood hierarchy.

But at the moment, it isn't the movie that concerns me, it is the book. Call me anal compulsive but whenever I put a book down on my desk or a table, I always line it up with the edge. Somehow the book is now sitting there at an angle and I didn't put it there like that. Slowly my eyes start to scan the room and I get up slowly. I pull open the side drawer of the desk. Someone has been rummaging through my papers and then tried to return everything to its original position. They almost succeeded. Almost.

I start checking out the apartment. My closets, my dresser in the bedroom. Telltale signs give it away. As Dash Hammett would have said, my place has been meticulously tossed. Obviously it had been Detective Johansson, and I wonder what he could have been looking for. I am not much worried because there is nothing to find. At least that's what I think until I lift the cover of my toilet tank.

It is wrapped tightly and protectively in sealskin and when I unwrap it I find a pistol. It is an odd looking thing, sort of like a German Luger, except it is Japanese. An 8mm Nambu Model 14, standard issue for the Nipponese army. I know this because the previous year I'd worked on a Franchot Tone war movie set in Burma. I don't have to think twice to realize who had put it there. Johansson has been a busy little bee. Somebody wants very much to make sure my picture is on page one of the Times the next morning. I start wondering, are the cops under that kind of pressure, the kind that says 'stick the label on somebody, anybody' with me obviously not being the sticker but the most handy stickee. And the answer I come up with is, maybe so. Four months after Elizabeth Short was cut in half and left to rot in the weeds, the cops are nowhere. And suddenly another beautiful young woman is murdered. Are they going to screw up again or are they going to nail the killer within days, maybe even hours? Unlikely? You might think so. I don't

I sit there for the longest time staring at that gun and wondering what I should do about it. Finally I get up and rummage around the kitchen area and find a covered baking dish that Mrs. Crimmins had used to send over some lasagna the week before. When I knock on her door, she responds immediately and throws me a big smile which, as I said, I am having trouble trying to decipher. I hand her the covered dish which she finds surprisingly heavy. I tell her to leave the lid on, stick it high up in one of her cabinets and not plan on using it in the forseeable future. Of course, I know she'll look but she won't care. Anything for her Joey. I give her a peck on the cheek and head out for my appointment with Detective Sergeant Kleinschmidt and his partner, the ubiquitous Detective Johansson.

CHAPTER FOUR

I am sitting at a bare wooden table, legs crossed, trying to appear nonchalant. Kleinschmidt is sitting opposite me, staring at some papers in a file folder and tapping out some sort of weird rhythm with his pencil. I am nursing a Dr, Pepper I'd brought in with me, figuring these guys weren't about to display either courtesy or good manners. I hadn't been wrong. The room is small with a good sized mirror along one wall. You don't have to be a brain surgeon to know that voyeurs are on the other side, taking in my discomfort. I fight the urge to blurt out something compromising like "Okay, I did it! Throw the cuffs on me!" I wonder if anybody ever did something like that.

The walls are cinderblock painted the color of pea soup. A big fluorescent light fixture hangs over our heads. There is one door and I am pretty sure an armed guard is posted on the other side. I'd expected Kelinschmidt to have a wire recorder on hand but if he does, he is keeping it well out of sight.

We've been silent for several minutes, Kleinschmidt tapping with the pencil and me sipping on my soda. Finally he looks up and fixes me with his patented icy stare.

"We found her landlord," he says.

"Good for you," I reply.

"Matter of fact, we found three of them. They saw the dame's picture in the paper. Two she stayed with last year. Ran out on both of them, stiffing 'em for the rent. She'd been staying with number three for the past twelve weeks. One bedroom apartment. Nice place. Fancy neighborhood. But I guess you knew that."

"No, I didn't."

"And I guess you didn't know her address either."

"That's right," I say.

"The lab guys are over there now dusting for fingerprints. Guess we won't find yours, is that right?"

"That's right," I smile.

He thinks about that for a moment. "Then I guess you two got together at your place."

I shake my head. "Sorry."

"I thought you two were--uh--pals," Kleinschmidt says, half leering.

"We were. We saw each other at the studio mostly. Twice we went out for supper at the beanwagon up the street. We talked a lot. That's mostly what we did, Sergeant. We talked."

He nods, thinking it over. "You talked. Do you like girls, Mr. Bernardi?"

"Yes, I like girls," I snap. "What the hell kind of a question is that?"

He shrugs. "Just asking."

"Let me ask you something. Did she live alone or have a roommate?"

"I ask the questions here. You get to answer."

"The reason I ask, she didn't make much money at the studio. A fancy apartment. How does she pay for it?"

"She's got a sugar daddy. That would be you."

"That would not be me. Are you saying somebody fingered me?"

"Not yet."

"Keep hoping, Sergeant. Who paid? Anonymous check in the mail?"

"She paid. Cash. Cash you slipped her along other things."

"Like I said, not me."

He starts to tap his pencil again. Then abruptly he stops and gets up from his chair, stretching.

"Okay. Answer me this," I say. "After you get through with her, what happens to her body?"

"We notify next of kin if we can find them."

"I found them and they're not interested," I say.

He looks at me thoughtfully, trying to figure out what in hell my relationship to the victim really was. "That being the case," he says finally, "the city keeps her on ice for a few days and then she gets buried at city expense." He's on the move now, coming around the table. He's not in any great hurry. In a few seconds he's directly behind me. I can feel his hot breath on the nape of my neck. It smells like peppermint Life Savers, mixed with Old Grandad.

"Any kind of a service or a memorial?" I ask, already knowing what the answer is.

Suddenly I feel the flat of his hand slam into the back of my head. My face arcs forward onto the hard surface of the table. My nose barely escapes breakage.

"She gets a plain pine box stenciled with a number. Anything else you want to know?"

I start to shake my head just as he grabs me around the throat. His grip is pure steel. I fight for breath and can't find any. "You killed her, Bernardi, we both know it. You want a shot at a jury, then start talking now. Otherwise I break your fucking neck!" He squeezes harder. "What are you trying to do, resist arrest? Dumb, Bernardi. Very dumb. Come on, asshole, you're turning blue." I'm clutching at his arm which is across my throat like an iron bar. I shake and squirm. He hardly seems to notice. "I swear to God, you murdering faggot prick, I'll kill you right here and now. Now stop fucking with me! Talk!"

The guy's an idiot. He's crushing my windpipe, I can't breathe and he wants me to talk.

"Aaron! Leave him alone!"

A man's voice. The grip on my neck eases, then falls away. I cough violently. I think I am about to hurl Mrs. Crimmins' soup. I look up. Johansson has put himself between me and Mad Aaron Kleinschmidt. "What, are you crazy?" Johansson is saying. "You wanna go on suspension? You wanna lose your shield? Snap out of it!'

"Fucking guy, I'm going to shove my piece right up his ass, faggot cocksucker!"

"No, you're going to get the hell out of here and cool off!" With that, Johansson, who is bigger by far than Kleinschmidt, shoves him toward the open doorway and into the corridor. Angrily, he pulls the door shut and turns to me.

"He's not usually like that," says Johansson."He's got a bug up his ass about this case and he's pissed at everybody, including me."

"Nice to know I'm not the only one on his hit list?"

He leans in close, checking out my neck. "You okay? That's gonna be one nasty bruise."

"I'll live."

"Can I get you something? Maybe another soda." Mine has been knocked over in the struggle. I shake my head. Tough and stoic, that's me.

Johansson sits on the table staring down at me. He puts on

his kindest, most sympathetic look. "I know this is hard on you," he says, "but police work is like this. You found the body, that puts you near the top of the list. What you gotta do is get off the list altogether. If it was up to me, I don't think you did it and I'm a pretty good judge of people. But my partner-------" He shakes his head, looking away. "I don't have to tell you Aaron has problems, you can see that for yourself. Last month, he put a guy in the hospital. The guy nearly lost an eye. Jesus, what a mess, but when Aaron gets like that, there's no way to control him."

I nod. Johansson is good. For that matter, so is Kleinschmidt. The Angel of Mercy and the Marquis deSade. Good cop. Bad cop. It's a well oiled routine and they know how to deliver it. I would guess they've been partners for quite a while.

"You get what I'm saying, don't you, Joe? If you want this off your back you're going to have to play along, give a little. Can you do that, Joe?"

"Sure," I say. "What do you want, a confession? How about the Black Dahlia case? You want me to confess to that, too. Maybe make your life a little easier."

His eyes harden for just a moment, then he slips back into his easygoing persona. "You know what I've been thinking, Joe?" I can hardly wait to find out. "I've been thinking maybe it would be a good idea if we all went over to your apartment and just sort of looked around." And there it was. The moment I'd been waiting for. "The print guys could tag along, do some dusting. If they can't find the girl's prints it'll go a long way to getting you off that list." I smile inwardly as my face displays great fear and worry. "So whatdaya say, Joe? Can we do that? Can we hop over to your place for a few minutes?"

I look up at him with a smile. My God, this guy is as smooth as oleomargarine. "Sure, why not?" I say.

"Great." He hops down from the table. "Let's do it." He starts for the door, expecting me to follow which I do. When we get to the door, he stops. "Technically, we're supposed to get a warrant, but the way I see it, it's a big waste of time and frankly, a real pain in the ass. I think as long as you're with us, I don't see the need, do you?"

"Hell, no," I smile. "I have nothing to hide."

He smiles back. "Of course you don't."

The ride over is uneventful. Kleinschmidt, now cooled off to a mere slow boil, assures me that this won't take long, they will be careful and not disruptive. They should be out of my hair in 30 minutes at the most.

As soon as we enter my apartment, the fingerprint guys start to unpack their cases. Johansson edges over to a far wall where he pretends to admire an excellent painting of the Grand Canyon which had previousy hung in a motel room a few blocks away. Two uniforms linger in the doorway, awaiting instructions. Kleinschmidt makes a beeline for my bathroom as I thought he might. He emerges ten seconds later and gives Johansson a dirty look as well as a very unsubtle shake of the head. He looks over at me. So does Johansson. I am polishing one of my candlesticks with the sleeve of my shirt, oblivious to their dirty looks

Kleinschmidt is now on "high boil" and he shouts to the two uniforms. "Toss it!" Instantly, the two guys in blue start to tear everything to pieces. Sofa, chairs, desk drawers, breakfront, kitchen cabinets. My possessions are flying around the room like bats streaming out of a cave at nightfall. I am trying to equate all of this with "careful" and "not disruptive". It's a stretch. Fifteen minutes later my place looks like the rumpus room at a two year old's birthday party after the little monsters have put in an hour or so of rumpusing. Kleinschmidt has already braced Johansson up against a wall twice to no avail. The phone rings. One of the lab guys answers it and then hands it to Kleinschmidt. The cop listens intently, glancing in my direction. He makes a note in his little pad and then sidles over to me.

"Find anything you like, Sergeant?" I ask him.

The usual glower has been replaced by a crooked smile. There is no humor in it, but it is a smile nonetheless.

"I'm gonna get you, pencil pusher. I know who you are and what you are and when I get through with you, you'll be sitting in an eight by eight in Folsom. You'll be lookin' at thirty, maybe forty years or if you're lucky, you'll get to take the gas and save the tax payers a wad of dough. Either way, I don't care just as long as you're out of my sight." He turns to the others and says in a loud voice. "Okay, fellas. That's it. Wrap it up."

As he walks off toward the door I call after him. "What about all this mess?" I say to him.

He turns with a smile. "Hire a maid," he says.

He starts again for the door and when he gets there he turns. "Oh, and uh, Mr. Bernardi. That phone call. It was from the county coroner. They finished up the girl's autopsy. Guess what they found, lover boy. Your girlfriend was almost three months pregnant." His grin gets wider. "See you, Daddy," he says as he walks out.

The next two days are uneventful except that I don't sleep very well. I try sleeping pills, hot milk, even booze and none of it works. No matter how I fight it my brain keeps focusing in on poor pathetic Maggie Baumann, pregnant with a hole in her head. She came from nowhere and went nowhere. In a way we were lot alike except that she had real parents such as they were. Maybe there'd been a time when they'd cared about Maggie, before she asserted herself and became her own person. My so-called parents were mercenaries hired by the state of Texas. The Schillings, Theo and Magda. We all lived in a two story frame house just outside of Lockhart, me and my five 'brothers' and six 'sisters', all wards of the state, all worth hard cash to Theo and Magda who parted with as little of it as possible and still be able to maintain their racket. When I was fifteen I walked out the door and never looked back. Maggie and I had that in common. I worked the oil fields, picked cotton, laid track for the railroads and read everything I could get my hands on because I knew I was never going to amount to anything more than white trash labor if I didn't start using my brain. When Pearl Harbor hit, the Army grabbed me but instead of a rifle, they handed me a typewriter. All that reading had paid off and I ploughed through WWII as a war correspondent. Met and married Lydia and immediately got shipped off to the ETO to chronicle the exploits of Ike and Patton and Bradley. When I got busted out of the service in early '46, I had no job and within weeks, no wife. Yeah, Maggie and I had a lot in common, a couple of losers on a carousel to nowhere. Kindred spirits. Maybe that's why I couldn't get her out of my mind and why it meant so damned much to me to get to the truth about her death.

As for the studio, no one has told me I am fired, no one has told me to stay away, so I don't. And as fate would have it, suddenly I am getting busy. Nothing like a corpse on a soundstage to add a little mystery to a movie. We are getting a ton of publicity. You could argue it is all the wrong kind but there's an axiom in Hollywood that says any publicity is good publicity. (Tell that to Ingrid Bergman who was getting ready to film a movie on Stromboli with that notorious roue Roberto Rossellini. Hubby Peter Lindstrom was staying home and the gossip pages were already flapping and fluttering as they crucified Ingrid without cause. Me, I think it's probably a lot of noise about nothing, but then again, Hollywood she is a crazy place.) I chat with a couple of crime beat guys and a stringer from Muncie, Indiana, who wants to write a hometown human interest story which he could sell to McCall's or Redbook. He confesses he is having a tough time tracking Maggie's antecedents in Muncie and I am not about to set him straight. Rest in peace, Maggie. Let the ghouls feast elsewhere.

It is Thursday after lunch. I am in my office trying to dream up some plausible lies about a project that Blaustein has on the drawing board. There are these two comics from back east. One's a singer reportedly well connected to the "boys" in Philadelphia. The other is a goony kid who'll do any thing for a laugh. Leo'd shown me some 8mm film someone had pirated from their act at an Atlantic City hotel and no doubt they are good. I just wonder why they'd ever want to get mixed up with Continental.

I am interrupted when some babe right out of Pomona College suddenly shows up wanting a photo/interview with May Britton. She'd snuck past Phyliss, which wasn't hard since Phyliss is still out to lunch (and it's only twenty after two). The kid wears thick glasses that match her head. She has on knee socks and her hair is in braids. I keep thinking Corliss Archer. The kid tells me she is on assignment for "Modern Screen". (Later I check and she is strictly on spec. On this I do not enlighten May. For half a day they are thick as thieves. One thing a fading actress can't get enough of is attention.)

As I watch the kid prance happily down the street toward May's dressing room, a highly polished Rolls Royce Silver Cloud pulls to a stop outside my office. The chauffeur hustles around to the rear door which he opens for none other than Persimmon Amanda DeSalle, wife of our owner and chief benefactor. I leap from my chair and race to meet her at my front door.

"Mrs. DeSalle, this is a most unexpected pleasure," I say. "Please come in."

She smiles. "Most gracious of you, Mr. Bernardi."

She enters and goes straight into my inner office. The chauffeur remains outside at parade rest next to the rear passenger door.

She has already taken a seat as I enter. "May I offer you something, Mrs. DeSalle. The selection is a little thin but---"

"Nothing, thank you. I won't take up much of your time."

"My time is your time," I smile as I sit down behind my desk. There is a half-pint of Southern Comfort in my upper right hand drawer and at the moment, I need it badly. Persimmon DeSalle, as busy as she is with studio business, rarely drops in on working proles like me. Something is afoot. She reaches into her purse and starts to take out an envelope. I pray it doesn't contain a pink slip with my name on it.

"It has been rumored around the lot that you are very concerned about the arrangements, or rather the lack of them, for the poor child killed here three nights ago," she says.

"Yes, I----"

"A selfless Christian attitude, Mr. Bernardi. You are to be commended. Am I to understand that she has no family?"

"None that will be bothered to take responsibility for her final resting place."

"I had heard that. My heart grieves for those people, to behave so callously when compassion is so desperately needed." She shakes her head sadly.

"I agree, ma'am," I say.

She hands me the envelope. I can tell it contains several sheets of paper. "My husband and I have taken it upon ourselves to give this child a proper Christian burial. A service will be held this coming Saturday at 10 a.m. at Forest Lawn Memorial Cemetary. My husband, Buford, will officiate. You do know that at one time he was an ordained minister."

"Yes, I knew that," I say.

"Following the service, she will be interred in the Sweet Dreams section of the cemetery. We will be referring to her by her Christian name, Margaret Baumann."

"Of course."

"The envelope contains detailed instructions. Contact the press, emphasize the innate goodness of the young woman, despite her transgression. Yes, I know about that, Mr. Bernardi, and we are all trying to keep it as hush-hush as possible. The Mayor has agreed to attend as has Chief Horrall and several members of the City Council. Also Miss Parsons and Miss Hopper. I would also like as many members of the profession on hand as possible, the more notable the better."

"I understand, Mrs. DeSalle. Even though she was not famous or powerful, she was one of God's children. And you and your husband have generously volunteered to guide her on her way to her final reward."

"Excellent, Mr. Bernardi."

"As well as taking some of the heat off the studio for perhaps not taking sufficient precautions to protect her while on studio property?" It just slips out. Me and my big mouth. I had to say it.

Mrs. DeSalle fixes me with a curious stare for a moment and then stands, putting out her gloved hand. A gentle smile curls her lips.

"Also excellent, Mr. Bernardi. I think perhaps you will go far in this business. Very far indeed. No need to show me out." She turns on her heel and goes out into the anteroom just as Phyliss is returning from lunch.

Phyliss, often clueless but in rare form at this moment, looks at her and says, "Excuse me, ma'am. Can I help you?"

Persimmon Amanda DeSalle just smiles and says, "No, dear, but thank you so much for asking."

Like I say, I am getting treated pretty well at the studio. Nobody is giving me the cold shoulder but the lady's visit is like a shot in the arm. I feel my future is secure and I dive into the funeral arrangements with fanaticism, managing to get commitments from Vera-Ellen, Mark Stevens, Dorothy Lamour, Edmund Gwenn, Jane Greer, and Vincent Price. Reluctant at first they are delighted to learn of the extensive press coverage Buford DeSalle has arranged for including newsreel cameras at the gravesite. In between I return a lot of phone calls and talk up "Jezebel in Blue Satin" like it was the best thing to come down the road since "Forever Amber".

The one real moment of excitement comes on Friday, three days after I found Maggie dead. May Britton is struggling with a scene in a nightclub where she has to play slightly drunk. May doesn't know how to play "slightly" anything and she isn't coming close. She has the director, Kingman Krug, on the verge of hysteria. Real hysteria. Not his usual bullshit ranting and raving in ersatz Austrian for effect. The man is genuinely apoplectic.

"No, no. In the name of God Almighty, what is the matter with you, woman? You've had two drinks. You are tipsy. You are not falling down drunk like some back alley wino!"

She spits it our coldly. "I am doing what you told me. Mr. Krug. I am taking direction."

"Direction? I waste my time talking at you and you, with your ears stuffed up and your brain in a deep freeze, you open your mouth and you give me NOTHING!"

"Sir, I have been plying my profession for many more years than you and---"

"Many more? Many more? A lifetime more? Did you perform with Wilkes Booth? Maybe that is where you picked up this ability to pop your eyes and bare your teeth like a 16 year old child which I find absolutely ludicrous, madam, since it has been decades since you have seen 16."

She glares at him. "If my performance is so unsatisfactory, Mr. Krug, perhaps one of us should withdraw from the film."

"I would, Miss Britton, but I have a contract."

"As do I, Mr. Krug."

"And I am the director."

"And I am on close personal terms with the owner of the studio. Now I'll drop my dress and show you mine if you'll drop your drawers and show me yours!"

The silence on the set is now deafening. Brick Baxter is staring in disbelief. Al Kaplan, the Assistant Director, has walked off into a corner to light up a cigarette. If I smoked I would join him but all I can do is stare in wonderment. Krug hesitates for moment and then moves toward her. Instinctively she raises her hands defensively and backs up. Vinnie the Muscle has been lurking in the shadows. Now he steps into the light and edges toward Krug but the director makes no move to strike her. I look to my left. Al Kaplan has taken a couple of steps forward. There is fury in the old man's eyes.

"You are under the impression, I believe," Krug says, "that you will be starring in my next picture, an epic film about the brave souls who endured the Alaskan wilderness in search of gold. It will rival "Call of the Wild". If I am lucky, I will get Gable. If not, maybe Tracy. In either case, my leading lady will not be you."

"You are wrong, sir," she replies. "Mr. Buford DeSalle---"

"Mr. DeSalle cannot save you this time, Miss Britton. My

contract is iron clad and gives me absolute control over casting." He has now backed her right up to her folding camp chair into which she plops unceremoniously. "Do you want to know another reason why that poor girl Vivienne Devereau's death was so tragic? Because I was secretly coaching her to play the leading part in the film. That's right, Miss Britton, your stand in who had more acting talent in her little finger than you have in your ample rear end was going play the leading role in one of the major motion pictures of 1947."

May stares at him in disbelief. So do I. Maggie had never said a word to me or, apparently, anybody else for that matter. Maybe she was afraid it was just a pipe dream, that it would all blow up at the last minute. Who knows? It is a bittersweet moment. Maggie is dead but she died knowing that maybe she really did have the talent to succeed. Part of me wants to cry, the rest of me wants to cheer.

May stands up and starts to walk away.

"Yes, Miss Britton, you go plead your case to Mr. DeSalle. Have him remove me if he dares. In fact I would welcome it. Anything to be free of this Godawful picture!"

May stops and turns back to him. "I am going to freshen my make up. I shall be back on set in fifteen minutes. I will do my very best to meet your expectations." Then drawing herself up with dignity, she snaps her fingers at Vinnie and exits the sound stage. Vinnie follows faithfully behind.

Krug throws up his hands in frustration and shares a look with Al Kaplan who can only shrug helplessly.

"Actresses!" Krug growls. "Can't live with them, can't live without them." With that he marches off to his dressing room, no doubt to console himself with a couple of belts of slivovitz.

That evening, I come home, too tired to eat, and fall on

the bed, praying that sleep will overcome my insomnia. I am exhausted mentally and physically. I am pretty sure Kleinschmidt can put together a pretty good frame and I don't know how to stop him. I can't afford to leave town and suicide seems a little drastic. I am starting to hate the movie business,

The phone rings. I have a number nobody knows. Probably some son of a bitch real estate agent.

"Joe?"

I know her voice immediately. I've heard it a thousand times curled up in some foxhole in the Ardenne or while trying to listen to some potbellied Colonel telling us what a great job we were doing getting out those stories to the folks back home. Keep finding us those heroes, he had said. We can't get enough of 'em. And pictures. Don't forget the damned pictures. Folks back home, they love the damned pictures.

"Lydia?"

"Did I catch you at a bad time?"

"No, no, I was just sitting here. Thinking."

"Don't think too much, Joe. That was always your trouble. Too much thinking, not enough doing."

"You're right," I say, not sure that she is.

"Papers say you're in a lot of trouble," she says.

"Mmm. That's how they sell papers."

'I know you didn't kill that girl, Joe. I know you couldn't have done it."

"Thanks, Lydia. Feels good, that coming from you."

A long silence. Then: "What was she like, Joe? The girl."

"Nice. A lot of fun. Young."

"Young like I was when you met me, Joe?"

"Oh, hell, Lydia, You're still young. What? 26?"

"25," she says quickly. "Were you sleeping with her, Joe?

Kinda sounds like you were but, well, I guess it's none of my business. Not any more. But were you, Joe?"

"No, Lydia, I wasn't sleeping with her." I want to say I hadn't slept with anyone, or not anyone who counted, since the divorce. But I don't tell her that. I am too ashamed.

"I want you know, Joe. I feel bad about everything. The dumb marriage. The even dumber divorce. Neither one of us was thinking very straight."

"Guess not."

"Just so you know, you're my friend, Joe. You always will be. We'll always have that much."

I'm thinking, hey, can't we just be pals even though my heart is breaking and I'm aching to put my arms around you close and never let you go.

But what I say is: "We sure will, Lydia. Let's remember the good times."

"Right," she says. And then: "And that's why I'm going to ask you, Joe. Don't keep spying on me. Don't sit outside my place til all hours. You are pretty easy to spot and frankly it doesn't bother me as much as it does Tyler."

"Tyler?" I feign stupidity.

"Tyler Banks. I've been seeing him for a couple of months now. But then you know that."

"I'm sorry, I uh---"

"The big blue Cadillac. I like this guy, Joe. Don't screw it up for me. He's solid. A business manager for a lot of big stars and some that are going to be. I'll be honest, Joe. We're talking marriage. You see what this means to me, Joe."

"Look, Lydia, I'm sorry. I-uh---"

"Joe, when I said I knew you didn't kill that girl, that's what I meant. The papers put her time of death around eight o'clock.

At eight o'clock you were parked across the street watching my house."

"Oh, Jesus, Lydia----"

"If it ever comes to that, I'll tell the cops just as long as it doesn't jeopardize what I have going with Tyler. Fair enough?"

"More than fair. Thanks, Lydia, I---"

"I love you, Joe. Always will. Let's just keep going our separate ways. That way we can keep that love alive."

"Sure, baby. You're right."

I hear a click. She's hung up. The good news is, Kleinschmidt isn't going to railroad me for murder. The bad news is, if it gets out where I was that night, I'll probably lose my job.

CHAPTER FIVE

I can't leave it alone.

It is five past seven when I call Bunny Lesher. She is a staff writer for The Hollywood Reporter and a pal. I've given her a few exclusives now and then, making her look good with Bud Wilkerson, the publisher. She is in solid, thanks in part to me, and she knows it.

"'Lo." A groggy voice.

"Bunny, wake up, it's me."

"Who?"

"Joe. Joe Bernardi."

"Oh, hi, Joe, are you in jail or something? You need me to bail you out?"

"No, no. I'm fine."

Her voice is still fuzzy and disoriented. "What time is it?"

"Seven o'clock---"

"Jesus-----"

"I need a favor."

Silence.

"Bunny, are you there?"

"Yeah, yeah, I'm here." Then more quietly, to herself. "Where the fuck are my glasses?"

"Bunny, I need a favor."

"You said that."

"Guy named Tyler Banks. You know him?"

"Yeah, I know him. You planning to sell your story to Universal?"

"Nothing like that," I say. "What do you know about him?"

"He's a hot shot personal manager. Flavor of the month. Left MCA to go out on his own maybe a year ago. That's about it."

"Can you get me a rundown on him? All the gory details. You know the drill."

"Sure. I guess. What can you give me on the Devereau killing?"

"I didn't do it," I say proudly.

"Thanks for the bulletin. What else?"

"Nothing printable. When I get something you get it first."

She thinks about that. "Tyler Banks?"

"Tyler Banks."

"I'll get back to you," she says and hangs up.

A quick shave and a shower and I am in my Studie V6 heading for the lot. The company'd shot late last night and the call sheet for this morning shows a ten o'clock start. Brick and the crooked lawyer played by Barry Kelley who always plays a crooked somebody or other will be going at it. Two goons are on the sheet as well as a couple of stunt guys so it looks like a fight sequence. May isn't due to show up until nearly five. That is fine with me. The one I want to see is the director, Kingman Krug.

He has an office in C Building next door to Stage 3. I park nearby, grab a container of coffee from craft services on 3 where they are shooting a test for a guy named David Wayne, fresh off a big hit musical called "Finian's Rainbow". Only other thing I know about him is that he's short, maybe even shorter than Alan Ladd. Just what the town needs, I say to myself. Another midget.

I climb the stairs to Krug's office, a little out of breath. The door is open and I knock. It swings open. Krug is sitting at his desk on the phone, a script open on the desk in front of him. When he sees me, he waves me in and motions to the chair across from his desk. He is not in the best of moods and whoever he is talking to doesn't have to listen to his phony Austrian accent.

"Look, I understand about Gable. Okay, okay, I get it. Even if I get him, which I can't, all of a sudden my picture is Son of Call of the Wild. This is aggravation I don't need. But Tracy? What the fuck is his problem?" He listens intently. His complexion is slowly taking on the color of a boiling lobster. "Sea of Grass?" he shouts. "Sea of Grass? He's signed to do Sea of Grass? It's a fucking soap opera! Is he crazy? And what's with him and the Hepburn dame? What, do they come together in a package like Smith and Wesson? Is the man afraid to make a movie on his own without that skinny dyke to lean on?"

He reaches for a cigarette and lights it with a flick of his zippo. "Are you kidding? I've got more dresses in my closet than she does." Then, in disbelief: "They're what? You're crazy. Whatdayamean she keeps him sober? All right, all right, forget it. The guy wants to kill his career, that's his problem? Who else you got?" Silence. "Robert Preston? Are you out of your mind? Call me when you sober up!" With that he slams the receiver down on the cradle. He looks up at me. "My brother in law. He's helping me cast the picture."

I nod. "Working with family, it'll kill you."

"Amen to that, my friend. So, Joe, what can I do for you? I liked that piece you slipped into Variety. Had no idea I was such a great fucking director. Nice work. What are you after? Another story?"

I shake my head. "Vivienne Devereau."

"Nice kid."

"Were you really going to use her in your next picture or were you just trying to bust May's balls?"

He shrugs. "I was ninety percent sure the kid could do it. That's why I kept working with her. Most days after we wrapped. A couple of Sundays. She was good, Joe, and she was fresh. There was a buoyancy about her, a love of life. She couldn't hide it even if she wanted to."

"How about the day she died? Did you work with her that day?"

"No, she said she had something she had to take care of."

"She didn't say what?"

"No, she didn't."

I hesitate.

"What about May?"

"What about her?"

"What about her contract?"

"She didn't have a contract, not with me and on "Treasure of the Klondike", I had final say on all casting. It's in writing. DeSalle wanted the picture and he gave me what I wanted. The whole schmeer, my friend. Big name casting, technicolor, exterior location shots in Alaska and Canada. And for his support for this major motion picture, I agreed to direct Miss Britton in this so-called comeback picture. Can't think why they keep calling it that, Joe. Coming back from where? To me, she's a never-was."

I nod thoughtfully as I take a sip of my coffee which has already turned tepid. "Guess you knew Maggie--Vivienne---was pregnant."

"I'd heard."

"Probably would have raised hell with your shooting schedule."

He shrugs. "We had ways to deal with that."

"You say, we? Does that mean she told you?"

"As soon as she knew. She promised me it wouldn't be a problem."

"Abortion?"

"She said it wouldn't be a problem," he repeats.

I slowly finish off the coffee and look Krug straight in the eye. He gets the message.

"It wasn't me, Joe." I say nothing, continuing to stare and waiting for him to elaborate. He smiles. "You don't know everything about me, Joe. And that's good. Some things are best kept under wraps. Brick Baxter came to me two months ago and asked me for a shot on this picture. We went out to dinner. I liked him. He seemed to like me. We've been liking each other pretty steadily for the past six weeks, the ungrateful son of a bitch. Does that answer the question you didn't ask me?"

I stand and toss my empty coffee cntainer into his waste basket. "It does, Mr. Krug. Thank you."

"Call me Kingman, Joe. And don't look so nervous. You're not my type."

I laugh self-conciously and go to the door. As I reach it I turn back. "I'm curious, Kingman. Just what makes Brick Baxter an ungrateful son of a bitch?"

He smiles. "He's starting to suffer from delusions of talent. Three weeks ago he met with DeMille about the part of Samson in DeMille's new picture. He heard they were having callbacks this coming Saturday and he wanted the day off. I told him no way. He got really pissy as only a queer can get pissy and swore he was going to get to those callbacks no matter what. He walked out, slammed the door and didn't talk to me for a whole two hours."

I nod, trying to picture it. Brick Baxter as Samson. The image eludes me.

As I clamber down the steps to the street, Russ Parmalee wheels up in his studio golf cart. "I've been looking all over for you", he shouts.

"You found me," I say.

"Hop in."

"Where to?"

"The holy of holies, my friend. Third floor of the Palace. Mr. DeSalle wants to see you."

"Oh, shit."

"My thoughts exactly," Russ grins as he swerves to avoid an elephant being led by a Sabu-wannabe.

"Any idea what it's about?"

Russ shrugs. "Probably not going to fire you. He always leaves that to Leo. On the other hand, Leo's going to be there, too."

"Great," I mutter.

"If it helps any, the cops are up against a brick wall. They've got nada."

I frown. "The papers say they're running down several leads. At least according to Chief Horrall."

"If you were Chief Horrall and every paper and radio station in town was screaming for results, especially in light of the way they've been bungling the Black Dahlia case, what would you say?"

"Gotcha," I nod as we pull up to the Palace.

Buford DeSalle's office is everything they say it is only more so. As soon as Russ and I are ushered in, the first thing I notice is a quartet of stags' heads staring down at us. They look as if they wished they were elsewhere. Joining them are a mountain lion, a moose and a wolf. A stuffed grizzly bear is planted in a far corner, standing on two legs, front legs pawing the air. (Or they would have been if the creature hadn't been so dead). There are photos everywhere including one of a teenage boy in shorts and sneakers holding up what looks to be a live five foot long water moccasin. The kid has a goofy grin on his face and I take him to be Buford DeSalle as a lad.

I marvel at this man, this latter day Billy Sunday who has parlayed his Come-to-Jesus scam into a more or less thriving Hollywood motion picture studio. No MGM or Paramount, to be sure, but constantly busy and modestly profitable. He and his wife, Persimmon, came west in 1945 and bought Continental and all its assets from its founder Sam Harvey who at 71 was still running it with his son. At first Sam was adamant. He wouldn't sell under any conditions even as his son Will was trying to get him to retire. And then a gruesome mugging on the street near his home settled the matter. With Sam tragically dead, Will sold out and retired to the Hawaiian islands. Buford immediately created several series of low cost movies with recurring characters: private eye Rick Landers, singing cowboy Hale Brownell, noble defense lawyer Dan Winfield. The money started rolling in and Buford started expanding the studio output with a wide range of cheapie B-pictures.

The great man himself, now considerably older than the goofy kid with the snake, is seated behind his desk. Leo Blaustein is seated to his left. Neither makes any attempt to rise as we approach the desk. Out of the corner of my eye I spot Martha Brodsky, the casting director, sitting on a sofa against the wall. She seems to be inspecting the laces on her sensible shoes.

We stop in front of the desk. DeSalle looks at me, then gestures to Russ. "Chief Parmalee, you may take a seat on the sofa next to Miss Brodsky." As Russ does so, DeSalle turns his attention back to me. He is a big man, heavy set, you might even call him fat. He reminds me a lot of Laird Cregar, the villain of "This Gun for Hire" and "The Lodger". Weighing in at 300 pounds, Cregar had dieted himself to death in 1945 while filming "Hangover Square" on a regimen of prescription pills. He'd wanted to become a leading man. He failed.

"Mr. Bernardi," DeSalle says in a booming stentorian voice. "Did you or did you not kill the young woman known as Vivienne Devereau?"

I swallow hard. "I did not, sir."

"The Lord despiseth a liar, Mr. Bernardi."

"As well he should, sir," I reply.

"The police believe you are guilty, sir. I have great faith in the police."

"So do I, sir, but in this case, they are wrong."

DeSalle nods. "You have been asking a lot of questons, Mr. Bernardi. You have come close to making accusations. I find this unseemly."

"With all due respect, sir, finding myself in a prison cell for forty years for a crime I did not commit, that would be unseemly as well."

He glares at me coldly. I shuffle my feet nervously, dying for a chair to sit in.

"You knew this girl well?" he asks.

"Yes."

"Intimately?"

I shuffle again. "I don't know what you mean by----"

"Of course you do!" he explodes. He gets up from behind the desk and stalks toward me. "I am speaking here of carnal knowledge, Mr. Bernardi. Did you have carnal knowledge of this child?"

Suddenly, in three days, Maggie had morphed from a professional stand-in into a helpless nubile child. I can feel them strapping my arms down and putting the little metal yarmulka on my head. Nonetheless I fight back. "I did not, Mr. DeSalle, and any person who says I did is a damned liar!"

His eyes widen, blazing with anger. "Do not blaspheme in my presence."

In for a dime, in for a dollar. I am not about to back down. "Then do not stand here and accuse me of defiling a young woman, or worse, taking her life. I am innocent on both counts and I will not be slandered, not even by you, Mr. DeSalle!" My voice level has risen to match his.

"Bernardi!" Leo yells, starting to rise from his chair but slumps back down when DeSalle raises his hand and waves him to be silent. He continues to stare at me for the longest time, then the slightest hint of a smile curls his lips.

"Forgive my rude behavior, Mr. Bernardi. I do not know you well and it was important to find out what kind of man you are. Leo! Bring Mr. Bernardi a chair."

Leo looks around, confused. "There is no chair, sir."

"Bring him your chair, you fool," DeSalle growls, "and then go sit on the sofa."

Leo quickly does as he is told as DeSalle goes back around his desk.

"You wish to know under what circumstances Miss Devereau, or more accurately, Miss Baumann, came to be hired by this studio." He looks sharply toward the sofa. "Miss Brodsky?"

Martha sits up straighter. "It was at the request of Mr. Blaustein, sir," she says.

DeSalle looks toward Blaustein.

"Leo?"

Leo squirms awkwardly.

"On your feet!" DeSalle barks.

Leo jumps to his feet, takes a deep breath and manages to gasp quietly, "Yes, it was my idea. I persuaded Miss Brodsky to put her on the picture."

"Continue," DeSalle says, leaning back in his leather covered swivel chair, lacing his hands behind his neck.

Leo continues, shifting his weight nervously from one foot to the other. "I met her at a diner in Van Nuys. She was the cashier. She was so beautiful, I just assumed she was a struggling actress. I said something to that effect and she assured me she wasn't. I could hardly believe it. She seemed to have all the qualities so I gave her my card and told her to call me. She did and one thing led to another. We became---good friends. At some point, I learned that she was, indeed, an aspiring actress and that she had recognized me and decided to let me "discover" her. Eventually, after a lot of pressuring on her part, I asked Miss Brodsky to put her on 'Jezebel in Blue Satin' as a standin. I told Margaret that it was an opportunity that would lead to other things."

DeSalle nods. "I see. And when you say you were good friends, may I assume that you were intimate?"

Leo is sweating now. His eyes are red with fear as he faces his employer. "Sir, I--uh---"

"Were you?" DeSalle roars. "Did you defile this young woman, you a married man of seventeen years?"

Leo can only nod, eyes staring at the plush carpet by his feet.

"And you not only had carnal knowledge of this child, you impregnated her as well," DeSalle says, half shouting.

"No, no. I took precautions!" Leo whines.

DeSalle stares at him in disbelief. "Good Lord Almighty, now you would have us believe that this young woman whom you had cruelly deflowered was sleeping with other men?"

"No!" Leo says. "I mean, I don't know. She might have been. But it wasn't me."

"Even with precautions, accidents happen, do they not?" DeSalle leans forward in his chair, eyes seemingly piercing into Blaustein's soul.

"Yes, I suppose."

"You suppose," DeSalle sneers. "I have seen enough of you this morning, Mr. Blaustein. You are dismissed. Miss Brodsky, you may also leave. Mr. Bernardi and Chief Parmalee, please remain."

When the others have left, he gestures us to the sofa and comes around his desk and takes a chair sitting opposite us. For a moment, he is silent, rubbing his hands together, much as Pilate must have done when he sentenced Jesus to the cross.

"So," he says, "now we have the answer to two of our mysteries. One, how the young lady gained employment at this studio and two, how she found herself in a family way. I must say my heart grieves. Even though Leo is of the Hebrew persuasion, I have always felt him to be a moral man. He is, in many ways, like a brother to me,"

I am not sure where DeSalle is going with all this, but I feel like piping up: "When do we call the cops and have his bony ass dragged down to headquarters?" De Salle saves me the trouble.

"Yes, Leo's behavior was reprehensible and at the Day of Judgement he will have much to answer for, but Mr. Bernardi and, you, too, Chief Parmalee, Leo did not kill Miss Baumann or whatever her real name was."

"Yes, Baumann," I volunteer. "Margaret Baumann."

DeSalle looks at me and nods. "On the night the young woman was so cruelly murdered, Leo was at my home, along with his wife. The four of us had dinner followed by several hours of contract bridge. It is one of the few vices my wife Persimmon and I allow ourselves. So you see, even though Leo appears to be a very likely suspect, he could not possibly have been responsible."

Russ clears his throat. "Excuse me, sir, but have you passed this information on to the police?"

"I have not, nor do I intend to," DeSalle says.

"Excuse me, sir," I say, "I'm no lawyer but it seems to me that you are withholding evidence in a murder investgation."

"I am not, Mr. Bernardi, since I know for a fact that Leo cannot be guilty. Yes, it would probably be helpful for them to know that Leo was the father of the unborn child but frankly, I am loath to let the police get involved any more than needs be. They have completely fouled up the Black Dahlia investigation, No doubt they would do the same here. Despite what I said earlier about police proficiency, Chief Horrall is a dunderhead at best and a thief at worst. I wouldn't trust him to wash my car. I am aware, Mr. Bernardi, that you are already a target in their rush to judgement completely without motive or proof."

"Yes, sir, but you needn't worry about me. I have a solid alibi and can produce it if I have to."

"I'm glad to hear it," he smiles. "So, let's permit the police to bumble around the studio, but let us help them as little as possible. We still have eleven days to go before we finish 'Jezebel in Blue Satin'. We have $180,000 invested in this film and I will permit no interruption in the shooting schedule. Do I make myself clear? Mr. Bernardi. Chief Parmalee. No more poking around. As far as this case is concerned, it is closed."

"Yes, sir," I say.

Russ chimes in, agreeing, and I can see the look of relief on his face. With DeSalle's blessing his job is secure.

Russ wheels me back to my office where my car is parked and I'd just about made up my mind to play hookey the rest of the day. It is bright and warm, Hollywood Park is open, and a great weight has been lifted from my back. I know that Buford DeSalle is on my side and I know that Lydia could thwart whatever nefarious plans Detective Kleinschmidt has in store for me. I don't need to go to the set. The backbiting and the doubledealing will survive very nicely without my participation. I decide, however, to check for messages. Maybe something really important has popped up. Maybe Twentieth Century Fox is offering me a job.

Phyliss is sitting at her desk, daintily polishing her nails. Without looking up, she nods toward my office. "You've got company," she says.

Sure enough. Mousy little Myrtle Figg, the wardrobe lady, is sitting primly on my guest chair. She smiles up at me as I enter. She is barely five feet one and thin as the ham slices at Charlie's Deli down the street. She is smart and she knows her job but she isn't a self promoter. That's why, after twenty two years and a parade of Costumer Designers have come and gone, she is still the head wardrober outfitting casts with other people's designs.

I lean down and kiss her on the cheek. "How's my little Edith Head this morning?"

She glares at me in mock anger. "Don't you start with me, Joe Bernardi. I came in peace. Don't make me walk out in anger."

"Okay, okay. Truce. You know I love you, Myrt."

"You damn well better. Now what is it you want to know because whenever you come sniffing around wardrobe, you need information that only yours truly can supply."

"True enough."

"Leo Blaustein," she says.

"What?"

"It was Leo got the girl pregnant."

"Jesus, Myrt. Now I don't even get to ask the questions."

She shrugs. "Keep up or fall behind, up to you."

"Well, I know about Leo. He just made a huge mea culpa in DeSalle's office. He's also got an alibi for the time of the killing."

"Bullshit."

"DeSalle himself provided it. Ironclad."

Her face falls. "Oh."

"Anything else?"

"One other thing, but the timing's all wrong."

"What do you mean?"

"Dodobrain. Brick Baxter. At least twice last week, he slipped her the salami."

I shake my head in disbelief. "Oh, come, everybody knows Brick's a powder puff".

"Yeah, he likes people to think it, even though he makes a show of trying to hide it. I call him Dodobrain but Brick figured out a long time ago that with all the homo producers and directors flitting around town, being a vision in pink is a sure way to pick up work."

"I don't believe it."

She shrugs. "Don't take my word for it. Ask Herr Krug. Our director caught the two of them in a ferocious clinch sans wardrobe a week ago Wednesday. May I say there were words. Loud words."

"Funny. I talked to Krug earlier. He never said anything about it."

"Why would he? I'm told he was mad enough to kill. Of course, he'd never kill Brick. He had a picture to finish. The girl, that's something else again. Her he didn't need." She gets up and goes to the door, then smiles back at me. "Anything else you need to know, Joey dear, just holler." She leaves.

I plop down at my desk. What the hell is going on? Brick Baxter a hetero? Has the world gone mad? And if true how does all that figure in Maggie's death? Brick would have no reason to kill her. Krug? I couldn't see him risking everything to satisfy his ego or take revenge. And then I remember that I am no longer investigating this case. I am home free and under orders from my boss to mind my own business. Maggie Baumann's murder is someone else's problem.

My phone rings. I wait for Phyliss to pick up. It rings again and I realize Phyliss has no intention of picking up, not with all that red glop she is putting on her fingernails. I lift the receiver.

"Bernardi."

"It's me."

"Who's me?"

"Brenda Starr, Reporter. Idiot! It's Bunny."

"Bunny!" I reply heartily.

"You wanted to know about Tyler Banks?"

"I sure do," I say.

"Buy me lunch."

CHAPTER SIX

ot wanting to appear cheap I had suggested The Brown Derby at Rodeo and Wilshire. I have a little cash in my wallet and even after filling the gas tank for three bucks, I still have enough to cover the lunch tab, even if she orders the $2.25 Kansas City steak. If she opts for champagne on the side I will be in trouble.

On the way over I get caught in traffic and flip on the radio to see if there have been developments. Buddy Clark is singing "I'll Dance At Your Wedding". This I don't need. I turn him off. Developments will have to wait.

The parking valet gives my Studebaker the once over but takes it anyway. I head inside, trying to give the impression that I am a welcome regular. As I approach the maitre'd's desk, I hear the woman just walking off call him Armand so I take my cue.

"Excuse me, Armand," I say with a jovial smile. He smiles back, pretending he knows me. "Reservation for two. Bernardi. Continental Studios. I'm meeting Miss——" Just then I see her sitting in a booth along the wall. She is waving to me. "Never mind. I see her. Oh, and Armand, Selznick's been hounding me all day. I'm not here, n'est pas?" I wink. "Merci."

I scoot off, leaving Armand staring after me, and slip into the leather covered booth next to Bunny who looks ravishing, as usual. If it weren't for the torch I am carrying for Lydia, I would jump her bones in a New York minute. As it is I peck her cheek and say, "You look great. Smell great, too. What is that stuff?" I ask.

"Lifebuoy," she replies. "But thanks for noticing, Joe."

I grin. "By God, if you weren't spoken for---"

"But I'm not," she smiles sweetly.

I frown. "What happened to what's-his-name, the pineapple mogul from Hawaii?"

She laughs. "He went back to his little grass shack. Not quite the mogul I thought he was. His Daddy got fed up and yanked his allowance."

"Sorry."

"Come day, go day. Such is the life of a middle aged working girl."

I look at her in mock horror. "What? Not scribbling for Bud any more? Plying your talents at the corner of Hollywood and Vine?"

She jams me with her elbow. "If I did I'd be making a hell of a lot more than I am now."

"No argument here," I say.

"Thank you, sweetie. I love you, too."

It goes on like that for several minutes until the waiter has the temerity to interrupt by asking us to order. Bunny opts for the Cobb salad which goes for a buck and I join her. I am suddenly feeling so flush I suggest wine but she declines and orders an iced tea. Something about calorie count. As far as I am concerned she needn't have bothered. Her count is just fine by me.

At last we get around to the subject of Tyler Banks. She takes a sheet of paper from her purse and scans it. "Tyler Banks, president of the personal management firm of Tyler Banks and Associates, except there are no associates, just a secretary, receptionist and file clerk all rolled into one. Her name is Vera and by all accounts she is a looker and also pretty bright. Whether there is any hanky-panky, no one knows."

"Be nice if there was," I mutter to myself.

Bunny looks at me funny but I don't elaborate. "He left MCA a year ago taking a couple of clients with him. Tom Helmore and Julia Dean. If MCA noticed, they gave no sign of it. Since then he has picked up a few over the hill stars like Conrad Nagel, Gale Sondergaard, and Nancy Kelly and a couple of up and comers, or so he thinks. A kid named Douglas Dick---" She glances up at me. "You'd think he'd change it. Another one named Farley Granger. He got his first film right out of high school. Hasn't done much since. And--uh-- a cheesecake babe named Shelley Winters whose one piece of film is as a silent seat filler in the last two minutes of an Arturo deCordoba turkey called 'New Orleans'. Oh, hell, Joe, you know the routine. The new Gable. The new Cooper. The new Bette Davis. Blah, blah, blah. I called a couple of people who should know and they say that Banks can barely pay the rent." She shakes her head. "If it weren't for his wife's money, he'd be out on the street."

I straighten up. "Wife?"

"The former Amanda Ann Flaherty of the real estate Flahertys. Her old man owns most of the Simi Valley." She smiles. "You wouldn't know where that is. Mostly it's inhabited by bears and coyotes but in ten years it'll be worth tens of millions."

"And they've been married how long?" I ask.

"Six, maybe seven years."

"Kids?"

"Two. One of each."

I slump back on the bench staring straight ahead. This is great news for me. It's terrible news for Lydia.

"Joe, what's wrong?" Bunny is shaking my arm.

I look at her. "Nothing. I'm fine. I just uh---" I see the waiter coming with our salads. "To hell with it. Let's eat."

For the rest of the meal I try to keep it light but I fail miserably. Bunny knows she's struck a nerve but doesn't know what and I can tell she feels for me. My frustration turns to anger. I seriously think about giving her Leo Blaustein as the father of Maggie's baby. Only cowardice and a deeply ingrained sense of self preservation stop me.

When we say goodbye at the front entrance, I take her in my arms and hold her tight. I can feel her respond.

"Call me?" she says.

"I will," I say, knowing I won't. Everything that I am is invested in Lydia and right now I haven't a clue as to what to do about it.

It isn't until I turn onto Olympic, cruising past Fox Studios, that I notice him for the first time. I've been listening to H.V. Kalternborn excoriating the President for threatening to draft every coal miner in the country into the U.S. Army if John L Lewis, the head of the UMW, takes them out on strike. Suddenly I am beginning to feel a little respect for the haberdasher from Missouri. Apparently there is considerable steel in his backbone.

But now my attention is on the silver-colored '40 Lincoln Zephyr that is tooling along about four car lengths back, trying to remain inconspicuous and doing a lousy job of it. I know it isn't a cop unless the LAPD has suddenly won the Irish Sweepstakes. Flatfoots like Kleinschmidt wear cheap suits and drive Fords. Just to be sure I take a left on LaCienega and then a quick right onto Wilshire. He stays right with me. I'm intrigued. Who the hell is this clumsy dolt and why is he tailing me?

A couple of blocks later I pull to the curb and duck into a Rexall to buy box of chiclets. While I'm in there, I call Russ at the studio and tell him what's going on. Russ tells me to kill another few minutes, then go to an address he gives me.

"There's an alley next door. Turn in, go about halfway down. Make sure this guy follows you in. Then stop. I'll take care of the rest."

I do what I am told. I order an egg cream from the fountain, nurse it for a couple of minutes, and then nonchalantly walk outside to my car. I slip behind the wheel and take off. Sure enough, there is the Zephyr, hot on my tail. I don't speed up but keep a nice steady pace, like I was out for a Sunday drive. Three obvious turns don't lose him and then I am at the address. I turn into the adjoining alley. No sign of Russ but somehow I know he's around. Behind me the Zephyr pulls into the alley. I stop. Suddenly, in front of me, a big studio equipment trailer pulls into the alley and halts, blocking the way. I turn and look back through my rear window. The Zephyr has stopped and then behind him, I see a studio cruiser turn in and speed right up to the guy's rear bumper. Russ jumps out of the cruiser and makes for the Zephyr. In front of me, a burly guy hops down from the cab of the trailer carrying a huge monkey wrench. He races past me to help Russ. I recognize him right away. Dutch Magyar, the head of studio transportation, is a guy you really don't want to fuck with. Not if you like living.

I get out of my car and head back toward Russ who already has the guy out of his Zephyr and backed up against a wall. Dutch is next to him, awaiting orders. He looks anxious to pitch in. Very anxious. He keeps slapping that big wrench into his open palm while his eyes remain fixed on my unwelcome shadow.

"Look, I don't know what you think you're doing---," the guy protests.

"Shut up!" Russ says to him as he grabs the guy's wallet from his jacket pocket. As I rush up to them, he flips the wallet open and checks his identification. "You're a long way from Chicago, Mr. Clancy," Russ says as he hands me the wallet. "You know this guy, Joe?" he asks me.

I look at the ID, look at the guy whose name is Dave Clancy and shake my head. "No idea," I say. Then to Clancy: "Why were you following me?"

"I wasn't. I---"

Dutch slams the huge wrench against the wall, only an inch from the guy's ear.

"Okay, okay!" the guy whines. I thought he was going to piss his pants. "I'm a reporter---"

"Oh, fuck," Russ mutters, turning away in disgust and then looking at me. "I thought these guys only came out at night when the moon was full."

"I'm working on a story," Clancy says. "I mean, I'm trying to work on a story. The murder, you know. At the studio. My paper sent me here. The Chicago Sun-Times. Go ahead. Check me out. I swear to God, I'm legit."

The guy looks from Russ to Dutch and then to me. I hand him back his wallet and shrug at Russ as if to say let him be.

"You sure?" Russ asks.

"I'll handle it," I say.

"Okay, Dutch, back to work."

Dutch looks disappointed. He throws one more dirty look in Dave Clancy's direction and then starts to trudge back to his truck.

Russ heads back to his cruiser. "I'll check out Chicago for

you," he says. "See you back at the factory." I nod. When Clancy and I are alone, I can see him visibly sigh in relief.

'Thanks," he says.

I just nod. "Either you're who you say you are or you're not. That wrench in Dutch's hand. It's not a rental. He owns it and he knows how to use it."

"Right," Clancy says.

I give him the once over. There's a neediness about him and he gives off a faint smell of fear. What he's doing here, tailing me, playing private eye, I think he's in over his head and he knows it. He's not a big guy. Average height but scrawny. His hair is overly long and he wears horn-rimmed glasses with an obvious thick prescription. He wears a cardigan sweater with leather patches at the elbows and because it's a size too big for him, he seems to shrivel into it. It's my bet he was 4F during the war. He doesn't seem like much of a threat but still, something doesn't seem right.

"So how does tailing me get you a story, Mr. Clancy?"

"I think you know a lot. I think to protect your own ass you're going to try to get to know a lot more. Besides your name was all over the papers and I don't know anyone else who's involved." He tries a sheepish smile on for size.

I smile back. "Honesty in a newspaperman. What next? Virgin starlets?"

"Maybe we could talk a little," he says.

"Maybe we could. Follow me back to the studio."

When we arrive, I take Clancy straight to the commissary. I've eaten. He hasn't. In fact he said he'd arrived early that morning having driven straight through from Chicago. Except for a four hour nap outside of Las Vegas he hadn't slept in 48 hours and he looks it. He knew I worked for Continental and he knew my picture from the newspapers. He'd waited across the street from the studio until I'd left for my lunch date with Bunny Lesher at the Brown Derby.

"What can I getcha?" Chickie, the waitress asks, pad in hand, pencil poised.

"Burger, I guess," Clancy says.

"The works?"

"Sure, why not?"

She turns to me. "Joe?"

"Just coffee, Chickie. I already ate. Brown Derby."

She smirks. "And ain't we hotsy-totsy?" she says as she ambles off.

For the next fifteen minutes I unsubtly pump Clancy about who he is and where he comes from. His answers sound okay, maybe a little too okay. Like they'd been rehearsed. What I got mostly was that he had a Masters Degree in English Literature and like I figured, he'd been 4F in the war. At one point the phone rings and Chickie waves me over. It's Russ. Clancy checks out. He's been with the Sun-Times for almost two years. Only one thing doesn't fit. He works for the financial editor. Stocks and bonds. Dollars and cents. I ask him about that.

"How'd you like to spend the rest of your life going blind looking at ticker tape? I wanted to be a real reporter. They kept telling me to wait my turn. I'd get my chance."

"And this is it?" I ask "The big break they're gonna gjve you?"

"Not exactly," Clancy replies. "They think I'm on vacation."

I smile. "Gutsy move."

He shrugs. "Had to do it. I was going nuts."

"So there's nothing personal going on here," I say.

"Personal? What do you mean?"

"Like maybe you knew this girl. Something like that."

He shakes his head. "It's a story. And a big one. That's it."

He fumbles in his pocket for a near empty cigarette pack and extracts one, lighting it with a brushed chrome Zippo. 'Come on, Joe. To you all this---" He waves his arm around---- "all this is ho-hum but to me, I mean, this is like a fairyland. The movie stars, the parties, it's a different world. I sit in my crummy office back in Chicago and check stock prices and commodities and futures. I mean, could it be any more boring? And then what? Suddenly a murder right on top of the Black Dahlia case and I'm saying to myself, Dave, what the hell are you doing in this cold, windy, snowy iceberg of a city. I'm through. Swear to God. I'm gonna make something of myself or die trying."

I smile at him. I think I see a lot of me in him. He reads me wrong and glowers.

"Go ahead and laugh but I feel it. This is my ticket to the city desk, maybe the crime beat. Hell, maybe there's a book in it." He furrows his brow. "Unless maybe that's your idea, Joe. I didn't think---I mean, I don't want to get in your way."

I shake my head. "No problem, Dave. These days, books and I don't exactly get along."

"Okay," he says, "as long as I'm not stepping on your toes."

"You're not."

Just then Chickie sidles up to the table and leans in, whispering. "Better get over to Stage 5. Big trouble."

I nod and get up. "Give my friend a big piece of apple pie while I'm gone."

Clancy starts to rise. "I'll go with you."

I wave him back down. "You stay here. This is studio business. I'll be back."

I hurry off, leaving Clancy behind with his half eaten burger. He doesn't look happy.

As I jog toward Stage 5, I can see the studio ambulance parked by the stage entrance. Russ's cruiser is parked next to it. Inside, Brick Baxter is lying on the floor, his head propped up with a pillow. He is writhing in pain. The expressions on the faces of the onlookers vary from genuine sympathy to total indifference. May Britton, seated on her camp chair, falls into the latter category. I move to Russ who is watching the ambulance driver and his assistant try to make Brick comfortable.

"What happened?" I ask.

"Fight sequence gone wrong," Russ says. "Brick took a wild swing at one of the stunt guys, slipped and slammed up against the bar. He says it's his back. Doc Verone is on his way."

Brick did, indeed, look like a man in agonizing pain. Whether an aspirin dispenser like Fred Verone could help, that was a whole other matter. Career wise, Verone was only one step up from an elementary school nurse.

"Look, are we wrapped or what?"

May Britton's dulcet tones break the near silence.

"We'll let you know, Miss Britton," says Al Kaplan, the assistant director.

"Well, let me know quick, Al. We've been sitting here like this for twenty minutes and my ass is getting sore."

Kaplan laughs and moves to Krug's side. They whisper to each other. Then Kaplan announces: "Everybody take an hour! Back on the set at three o'clock!" He looks over at May and winks. She winks back.

The crew scatters like autumn leaves in a windstorm, all except May who crooks her finger in my direction, beckoning. I move to her.

"Yes, Miss Britton?"

"My dressing room. Six o'clock."

"What's up?"

"Story conference. Bring champagne. I'll supply the glasses." Then she and Vinnie the Muscle depart.

Now what the hell was that all about? I'd heard stories about May, the same kind of stories you heard about Joan Crawford and Loretta Young. So, sure, I'd be there at six, I had to if I wanted to keep my job. When stars summon, even at Consolidated Studios, the hired hands fall into line. But was she really hot for my body? Somehow I didn't think so.

I turn and look at Russ who is grinning. He's heard the whole thing. "Who knows, Joe? You might get lucky."

He leaves which is what I want to do but feeling it my duty to show a modicum of sympathy I approach Brick and kneel down.

"How're you doing, Brick?"

"Crappy," he winces.

"Back?"

He nods. "Can't figure how it happened. I know how to throw a punch. Owww. Shit." He looks at the ambulance guy. "Come on, man. Gimee a pill. The pain's killing me."

"No can do, boss. Gotta wait for the doctor," he says.

Brick groans again. "If that asshole director thinks he's gonna shoot me any time soon, he's got another think coming." Then he frowns. "Joe, don't let Hedda and the others know about this. Kinda makes me look bad, don't you think?"

"Mum's the word," I say and stand up as Dr. Verone and his little black bag full of pharmaceuticals enters.

I cross over to Al Kaplan. "What do you think?"

The old timer has seen it all. He shrugs. "I think Baxter won't be shooting for a couple of days."

"That's what I think," I echo. And then I suddenly remember that tomorrow is Saturday, the day DeMille has scheduled the call backs for the part of Samson. I take a closer look at Brick as Verone feeds him a couple of pills. Either Brick is in excruciating pain or he's a better actor that any of us ever gave him credit for. As expected the doctor orders Brick off his feet for the next 24 hours and plenty of bed rest at home alone. I am now convinced more than ever that Verone does not make his living by the dispensing of pills alone.

Dave Clancy has finished his pie and is working on a steamy mug of coffee when I get back to the commissary. He's writing on a lined pad of legal sized yellow paper.

"The great American novel?" I ask as I sit.

He shakes his head. "Notes for the story. Color. What the studio looks like. The commissary. Your friend Chickie. Good detail makes for a good story."

"Who told you that? Some English professor?"

He nods. "As a matter of fact, yes. So what happened?"

The devil in me pops to the surface. I tell him about Brick's predicament. "A present from me to you. Call it in to your entertainment editor. Hedda and Louella don't have this one. I'd like to see their faces when they find out they've been scooped in Chicago."

Clancy smiles. It's a nice smile. I'm beginning to like this guy. "You got a place for the night?" I ask him. He shakes his head. "I have a reservation at the Biltmore but I haven't checked in yet."

"I've got a sofa with less than a dozen lumps and it's a lot cheaper than the Biltmore."

He shakes his head. "Oh, no. That's very nice but----"

"Not nice, Practical. Like you said, I'm not through with this story, not by a long shot and I may need some help. A little leg-work. Questions to be asked of people who know me but not you. It's not charity, Mr. Clancy, it's business."

"In that case," he grins, "call me Dave."

CHAPTER SEVEN

It has now been four days since I discovered Maggie Baumann's body and the cops are no closer to solving her murder than I am. And I know more than they do. Like Leo's role in Maggie's pregnancy and Brick's bedding of Maggie (twice) not to mention the fact that he had all the motive in the world for shutting down the picture. Hedy Lamarr, for example. Now there was a motive. And May. What about dear sweet May who had clawed her way to the top when talkies first came on the scene and was perfectly capable of using her claws to stay on top? Would she really stand quietly by and watch a rank amateur steal the part of a lifetime from underneath her nose? I should think not. Of course May wouldn't have had to do the dirty deed herself. There was always Vinnie, ready and willing to pitch in. Or maybe it was someone else altogether. An old boyfriend with a jealous fixation. Perhaps even a deranged celebrity stalker though Maggie was hardly a celebrity. And that brings me full circle to one of my earliest theories. A darkened stage. Two women in the same blue satin dress. Murder by mistake.

I take Dave Clancy over to my place, show him around. A one bedroom apartment. The grand tour doesn't take long. The news on my car radio was more of the same. Police stupidity.

Graft. Incompetence. One idiot newsman suggested that the Black Dahlia and Maggie had been iced by the same person though how that follows, I cannot figure.

At 5:30 I leave Dave to fend for himself. I tell him I have an appointment on the lot. I don't elaborate. I'll be back when I get back. If he gets bored there is a movie theater two blocks away, around the corner. They are showing "The Bishop's Wife" with Cary Grant as an angel (who knew?) and "The Brasher Dubloon" with George Montgomery playing Philip Marlowe. I've heard Raymond Chandler is so displeased he's given up drinking.

Dave says he'll be just fine. He has reading to catch up on. He doesn't press me about my rendezvous, which I find strange. Newspapermen are nosy about everything. Maybe all those stocks and bonds have dulled his brain.

May Britton's dressing room is not part of any building but is one of four tiny bungalows sitting side by side next to hair and makeup. It used to be known as The Adele Mara bungalow but that was before Miss Mara walked out on her contract to star in a Republic Picture called "The Catman of Paris". When the Catman failed to do any business, even in Paris, she tried to come back but her 8x10 glossy had already been turned to the wall. One does not defy the moguls of Hollywood without suffering retribution.

May opens the door wearing a lacy pegnoir that is so sheer I can see through it all the way to Anaheim. Her hair is down, all full and free and her makeup is in perfect position for an assignation. It is hard to believe she is on the nether side of 40. I produce the champagne bottle from behind my back with a big smile. She glances at the label and forces a smile in return. Okay, so it isn't Taitinger's. Three bucks a bottle is my absolute limit, even for movie stars.

She moves to me, gives me one of those patented movie star air kisses and bids me enter. I do so. I watch her as she snatches the bottle from my hand and takes it to a nearby ice bucket to chill. It is pretty obvious she's started without me and when I smell her breath for the first time, it isn't anything close to Tattinger's, it's Gilbey's gin.

"Make yourself comfortable," she says, grabbing a couple of flutes from the sideboard and putting them on the coffee table.

"I'm fine," I say, drawing my houndstooth sport jacket a little tighter to my body and wondering how hard I am going to have to fight to protect my manhood.

"I'm looking forward to a pleasant evening," she says. "Just the two of us."

"Speaking of that," I say, "where's Vinnie?"

'Seeing family,' she says. I decide not to probe for her definition of the word 'family'. "I told him to take the night off."

"No worries?"

She smiles. "No offense, Joe, but you've always seemed mostly harmless. Am I wrong? Is there a seething he-man hiding beneath that button down shirt?"

"Probably not," I grin sheepishly.

She nods in agreeement. "Probably not."

She goes to the bucket, grabs the champagne bottle and with a proficiency born of years of experience, unscrews the plastic cap and pours herself a healthy swig. It isn't even cold yet but she doesn't seem to care.

"Okay, Joe, here's how it's going to be. We have a few drinks, we tear each other's clothes off and tumble into the sack and then when we are good and sated and only half-sober, we can talk business. Or we can forget all that other crap and just talk business."

"Well,-----" I start to say.

"By the way, Joe, do you like girls? I ask only because I've never seen you with one."

"I'm not a homo, May, but I am sort of committed."

"Engaged?"

"Not exactly."

"Going steady?"

"Not exactly."

May hesitates, swaying ever so slightly. "Have you ever met this woman?"

"She's my ex. I haven't gotten over it."

May shakes her head in disgust. "Oh God, one of those." She takes another swig of champagne. The bottle is already half-gone.

Just then the door chime rings.

"Get it," May says heading toward the sideboard. "I need a refill."

I open the door. There is a kid standing there carrying a huge basket of flowers. "Britton?" he queries.

"I'm Britton," May says, hauling herself into view. Her face lights up. "Ooh. Flowers! I love flowers!"

"Where shall I put them, ma'am?" the kid asks.

She points to a small table near her fireplace. "Over there. Joe, give the nice young man five dollars. I have to go potty." She weaves her way into her bedroom and closes the door. I turn to the kid, give him the change in my pocket which totals seventy six cents. "Here's your five bucks. Have a nice night." I edge him toward the open doorway and close it behind him. I cast a glance toward the flower basket. They are pretty, they smell good and they are expensive. The other thing I notice is, there is no card. I almost chase after the kid to find out where they'd come from but decide against it. He'd probably think I was trying to give him a bigger tip.

A few minutes later, May emerges from the bedroom. She's turned in the pegnoir for a terry cloth bathrobe and that sweet glow of femininity is gone from her eyes.

"Okay, Joe. Let's talk turkey. Better yet, let's talk about little May's career."

"What about it?"

"I'd like to have one. I mean, that's what this picture is all about or didn't they tell you that? I haven't worked in two years. I've still got the talent but gravity is butchering the rest of me. If I don't make a splash in this picture, I'm going to have to work the streets to make a living, or worse, marry some dull clod of a hardware mogul."

"I understand that," I say.

"Then why don't you get me some fucking press? My brain dead director gets this overblown puff piece in Variety. Brick Bonehead, minus his shirt, has his picture in every movie mag in town. The next thing you know they'll be writing nice things about the screenwriter. But about me? Not a fucking word. Why is that, Joe?"

"I'm doing my best for you, May. Didn't I get you that Q&A in 'Screen Stories'? And what about that supermarket opening in Azusa? You got plenty of press out of that one."

"Joe, you're not hearing me. I am a big star. I am an Academy Award nominee. If Dressler's pals at MGM hadn't rigged the vote I'd have my little gold man right there on the mantlepiece. I wouldn't be having to do this dreck to prove I'm an actress. For Christ's sakes, Joe, treat me with a little respect."

She moves to me suddenly, wrapping her arms around me and searching for my mouth with her own. I struggle to free myself. As I do she lashes out at me with her fingernails, raking the side of my neck and drawing blood. She stares in horror and backs away slowly. "My God. I'm sorry," she says softly. "I'm sorry. I'm so sorry."

I shake my head sadly. I feel bad for her. Really bad. I've been plugging away for her for the past three weeks, contacting everyone I have pull with and even some I don't speak to any more. I couldn't break through. She is last century's news. The picture is rumored to be garbage and she is garbage in it. Everywhere I had turned it was the same story.

She sinks down onto the sofa. There are tears in her eyes. Not glycerin tears. The real kind that I didn't think she was capable of.

I grab a tissue and dab at my wound, then sit beside her. "I'm trying as hard as I can, May. I'll keep pitching, I promise."

"I know, I know," she says softly. "It's not your fault, Joe." She hesitates for a moment. "I think they're going to shut the picture down."

"No," I shake my head.

"There's a murder hanging over us. The longer it goes on, the worse it gets. They'll pull the plug, wait and see."

"You're wrong, May. They're very close to an arrest. Believe me."

She looks me in the eye and snorts. "You mean, Leo Blaustein? Just because they think he was the father of the baby. Or should I say, DID think?"

"What do you mean?"

"I mean, they did a blood test on the fetus. No way Leo could have been the Daddy. Sure, maybe he killed her, but somebody else knocked her up."

I am confused. "I hadn't heard----"

"You haven't heard because they haven't let it out. But I

know because I got it straight from Vinnie who got it from people on the inside who know. Do I have to draw you a picture?"

I shake my head.

"Maybe you'd better go," she says quietly.

"I think that's a good idea."

We get up and go to the door. I toss the blood-stained tissue into a wastepaper basket and then take both her hands in mine.

"Think good thoughts, May. We'll get through this and the picture's going to be good. I've seen some rushes. You're wonderful. Everything you're hoping for is going to happen."

"You think so, Joe?" She squeezes my hands back and smiles.

"I know so. Now go to bed, get some sleep and deal with tomorrow tomorrow."

She leans forward and kisses my cheek and I leave.

The air outside her dressing room is fresh but chilly and I need it. I'd lied about the film and about the rushes and about her performance. The picture is a dud and everyone knows it and maybe DeSalle will shut it down though I doubt it. He is on the hook for a couple of hundred thousand bucks. A finished picture might get a lot of that back. An abandoned film gets him nothing.

As I start to climb into my car, my eyes fall on a car at the end of the street, just pulling out and turning the corner. I am sure it is the Zephyr. Is it possible Dave has followed me here? But why? A newsman's curiosity? I'd found it strange he hadn't asked me where I was going. Maybe there is a lot more newshound in him than I figure.

I find a very convenient parkng spot a couple of spaces away from the walkway that leads to my apartment house entrance. The Zephyr is parked across the street about a half block down. I jog over to it and place my hand on the hood. It is very warm to the touch.

Dave is curled up on the sofa reading when I come through the door. He looks up.

"That was fast," he says.

"Quick date," I say. "No movie?"

"No, I thought I'd just hang around here and read."

I nod. "Did you go out and pick up something to eat?"

He shakes his head. "I fixed myself a peanut butter and jelly sandwich. Hope you don't mind."

"No problem," I say. I grab one of the dinette set chairs and bring it over, turn it around and straddle it. "Maybe you could tell me why you followed me to the studio tonight."

His eyes flash apprehension as he sits up straighter. "No, I didn't----"

"The hood of your car is still warm. You didn't beat me back here by more than five minutes."

"Look, Joe----"

"No, you look. I give you the hospitality of my home and you lie to me. I don't know what you're up to ---"

"Nothing. A story, that's all. I told you that."

"Quit the bullshit. What's going on?"

His eyes narrow and his expression hardens All of a sudden, I'm looking at a different David Clancy. "I'm trying to get some straight answers, Joe, speaking of bullshit."

"What's that supposed to mean?"

"It means I think you had more to do with that girl than you're willing to talk about. I read the newspapers, Joe. Are you saying they were lying? About you and Maggie Baumann?"

"That's exactly what I'm saying," I tell him.

"Yeah, well, I might say the same thing if I'd gotten a girl pregnant and suddenly she ends up murdered."

"You're crazy."

"I don't think so," Clancy says. "She was at the studio a little over three months. She was two, two and a half months pregnant. That says somebody at the studio. I say maybe you, Joe."

"She was a friend. Jesus, man, does everythinghave to be about sex? I was at the studio about three days when she first got hired, just long enough to say hello, and then I was in Arizona for seven weeks trying to drum up some enthusiasm for a crappy sci-fi bug movie we were slapping together with John Agar and Hillary Brooke. 'The Tarantula That Ate Tombstone'. Hell, it was so bad, I couldn't even get the local papers interested. Maybe if Shirley Temple had visited the set to see her husband, I could have gotten some ink but she didn't and all I got out of that shoot was sunburn and chigger bites. When I got back to the studio I started work on 'Jezebel'. That was about a week before they started shooting. I only knew Maggie for three weeks at the most. That answer your fucking sleazy question?"

Clancy raises his hands apologetically. "I'm sorry, Joe. I'm new at this stuff. I just want to get it right."

"Well, get it right someplace else. I want you out of here."

"Joe, I said I'm sorry."

I stand up, balling my fists. "Apology accepted. Now grab your stuff and get the fuck out. Now."

He gets up slowly from the sofa and for a second I think he is going to swing at me, he looks that mad. But then he goes to get his suitcase which he hadn't even opened. "If that's the way you want it----"

"That's the way I want it. Maybe that reservation at the Biltmore is still available."

He heads for the door. "I thought we were going to work together on this case. I was looking forward to it."

"I don't work with people I can't trust. And Dave, don't let me catch you following me again. Next time I'll call the cops and you can explain to them just who the hell you are what the hell you're doing in this town because, honestly, I haven't a clue."

Dave hesitates for a moment, then leaves, closing the door softly behind him. I go to the window and pull back the curtain. I watch as he gets into the Zephyr and drives off. Despite what I had said to him, I have a feeling I'll be seeing him again soon.

CHAPTER EIGHT

aturday. I wake up groggy. Still not enough sleep. The clock by my bed reads 8:17. Just enough time to shave, shower and dress. Breakfast will have to wait. Woolworth's opens at 9:00 and I want to get that suitcase from Natalie Bloom before anyone else finds out about it. Then I'll have to turn around and head out on the 34 to Forest Lawn in Glendale for Maggie's service. I want to be there but even if I didn't I'd have to show. Something tells me Persimmon DeSalle is taking attendance.

Normally Saturday would be a full workday for the company but out of respect for Maggie, first call has been delayed until 1:00.

I throw up the shades to gauge the weather. Cloudy, grim, intermittent drizzle, maybe a cloudburst later in the afternoon. Nice day for sticking a loved one into the ground.

I finish my ablutions and slip into my dark gray suit, the one I never wear except for occasions like this. Ditto my black knit tie. I grab a handful of toilet paper and rub my shoes vigorously. It isn't a spit shine but it will have to do. For the briefest of moments I think about slipping on a black arm band but veto the idea. Too much is too much. I am presenting exactly the right appearance.

As I drive to Woolworth's I wonder about Brick Baxter. Would he show or would he be over at Paramount flexing his muscles for Mr. DeMille? I certainly have no illusions that Brick will be home in bed, recovering from his devastating "back injury".

The doors open at nine sharp and Natalie is right there behind the perfume counter, looking as fresh as a newly picked carnation. As I approach her, she reaches down behind the counter and brings up the suitcase. Not a suitcase really. Just an overnight bag.

"I read about the funeral in the paper so I thought you might be in a hurry," she says.

I smile, taking the bag. "You really are too smart for this place."

"Thanks. After I went through everything I closed up the bag and accidentally locked it. Don't have the key."

"Not a problem. Look, Natalie, about the bag. Nobody needs to know about it except you and me."

"Okay," she says.

"But I don't want you in trouble with the cops. If they don't ask, don't tell. If they know about the bag, tell the truth. Anybody else, it's none of their business."

"Gotcha," she says

I reach in my pocket and hand her a couple of ducats.

"Here's a couple of tickets for Grauman's. They're showing a pretty good picture with Mitchum and Kirk Douglas. They're good any time."

Natalie's face lights up. "Thanks, Mr, Bernardi, my Aunt Brenda just loves Robert Mitchum."

I smile at her. Poor kid. I feel sorry for her, Sharing a bag of popcorn with your aunt. I feel like screaming, "Natalie, get a life!" But I don't. I just turn and leave the store, tossing the overnight bag into the back seat of my car.

Forest Lawn is a sprawling complex of marked graves, crosses, mausoleums and ten foot high walls that contain private niches where the cremated remains of the loved one can be interred forever. And Maggie, the unfortunate never-was from White River, South Dakota, will spend eternity alongside the greats of Hollywood like Jean Harlow, Irving Thalberg, Marie Dressler, Lon Chaney, Carole Lombard, and Tom Mix as well as thousands of lesser knowns. Not exactly what she had in mind when she arrived about a year ago, full of hope and determination.

There are two studio buses parked in the lot next to the chapel. The DeSalles had apparently arranged transportation for those who wished to pay their final respects. The DeSalle's Silver Cloud is parked next to the entrance. In the lot itself, besides the buses, are several dozen private cars ranging from rickety Model A's to the latest models to come off Detroit's assembly lines. Clustered nearby are a dozen reporters, a couple of photographers with their Speed Graphics at the ready and even a newsreel cameraman from Fox Movietone News. A couple of the reporters try to brace me for news on the police investigation but I play dumb. I see nothing, I hear nothing and I know nothing. I brush past them as politely as I can.

Low volume organ music is filling the chapel as I step through the door. The smell of gardenias is overwhelming and baskets of flowers are stacked everywhere. It is a setting befitting the passing of a double Oscar winner.

Contrary to what I had surmised, no one is taking attendance but there is a large open 'guest book' immediately inside the doorway and those who choose not to sign it probaby do so at their own peril. The chapel itself is not large but neat and tidy and designed to give comfort. I scan the room and spot some of the celebrities who had committed to coming. There are also a couple of surprises. Joe Cotten and his wife, Pat. Anne Revere. Sue and Alan Ladd. Herbert Marshall. Danny Kaye and his latest "friend". Al Kaplan is here along with some of the cast members like Barry Kelley and Leonore Aubert but two faces are conspicuously absent: Brick Baxter and May Britton. Brick I can understand but May is too Hollywood savvy to skip a thing like this.

Russ is sitting in one of the back rows and I slip in next to him. "Just in time," Russ says. "The old man's planning to do about 40 minutes which is short for him. After that three verses of 'Amazing Grace', we put her in the ground, and then it's back to work."

"We've got a couple of no-shows," I say.

"I noticed," Russ says, "and I'm not the only one." He nods in the direction of Persimmon DeSalle who is standing by the lectern, eyes scanning the crowd.

"Brick I can figure," I say. "He wants that DeMille movie pretty bad. But May? I don't know. Maybe she slept through her alarm. She was pretty pie-eyed when I left her last night."

Russ looks at me with a schoolboy grin on his face. "Oh, ho. You took the bait. How'd that work out for you, old sport?"

"Not the way you think," I say.

"You're kidding. I heard she was the easiest jump in town."

I shake my head. "Not from where I was standing."

Just then there's a rustling in the room as Buford DeSalle appears and takes his place at the lectern.

At first he is quiet. You have to strain to hear him.

"My friends, I come here today with a heavy heart to bid farewell to a fine and decent woman. I did not know her except in passing but those who were close to her tell me she was a gracious human being, imbued with an abiding love for our Lord and Savior, Jesus Christ. Was she without sin? She was not but who among us is?"

Slowly the whisper turns to a drone, louder but matter of fact. Then he starts hitting his t's and his d's, spitting them out and before you knew it, he is in full preacher mode, spewing the terrors of hellfire and damnation to those who fail to follow the path of the Lord. No wonder the little ladies of Ashtabula showered him with money week after week after week.

As his voice gets louder and his fist starts pounding the lectern more regularly, I look out the window and see a studio security cruiser pull up and skid to a stop. I nudge Russ. "You've got company," I say..

Russ gets up quickly and hurries to the back of the chapel. I go with him. His deputy, a stringbean of a kid named Andy, whispers frantically into Russ's ear. He isn't giving him the weather report. Russ signals me to follow and the three of us go outside.

Andy is a mass of frazzled nerves. "The maid found her this morning around nine o'clock," he says. "Her throat had been cut from ear to ear. The place was soaked with blood, I mean, Jesus, Russ, everywhere you looked. I called the cops and left Lou in charge. I know, I know. He's just a kid but I thought you ought to know."

Russ nods. "You did right, Andy. Any idea when she died?"

"Doc Verone heard what happened. He came over just in case there was something he could do. I mean, he couldn't. What the hell, all that blood. He said she was cold as ice and rigor was settng in. She'd probably been dead nine or ten hours. Just a guess, he said,"

"I'd better get back to the studio," Russ says.

"I'll go back too," I say. "The papers get a hold of this all hell's going to break loose. First Maggie, now May."

"Andy, you stay here. Soon as the funeral's over, you take Mr. DeSalle and Mr. Blaustein aside and tell them what happened. In private, Andy. Reporters are crawling all over the place. We want this under wraps as long as possible."

"Yes, sir," Andy says, but even as he says it, out of the corner of my eye, I can see Harry Frakes of the Herald-Express watching the three of us and wondering what the hell is going on. If Harry gets a whiff of the story, we'll be dead. Once he gets a grip on something he never lets go.

On the way back to the studio I check my radio just in case. They're talking about food prices. The raptors haven't got the story yet. And what the hell is the story? May Britton is dead and it sure wasn't suicide. She loved herself too much and besides, who slits their own throat from ear to ear? Certainly not a narcissist like May. She'd be thinking ahead to the open casket. And so as I drive my mind bounces back to that first night when I discovered Maggie dead and I wondered if maybe she hadn't been killed by mistake. Two women sheathed in blue satin and in the dimness of a poorly lit sound stage the wrong one gets plunked in the head with an 8 mm caliber bullet from a Japanese pistol. This time the killer makes good.

Another thought occurs to me and it isn't pleasant. Aside from the killer I may have been the last person to see May alive. Maybe. If Doc Verone is right she was killed around midnight and I was home in bed communing with Orpheus. Could I prove that? Probably not. What if Sergeant Kleinschmidt and his buddy, the Swedish bulldozer, find out I'd been with her last evening? How will that go down? Not well, I'm thinking. Suddenly I'm feeling a tightness around my throat and it isn't the collar of my brand new dress shirt. It feels more like the thick grip of a noose. I chalk it up to a writer's vivid imagination but the feeling stays with me. As I turn my car into the front gate at the studio, good vibrations do not attend me.

I park my car and start to walk quickly down the street toward May's dressing room. As expected the cops are all over the place. Two unmarkeds, one of which I know belongs to Kleinschmidt and Johansson, as well as three black and whites and the coroner's van. Before I get halfway there, Russ intercepts me, grabbing my arm and pulling me into an alley between the Prop Department and Stage 4.

Russ's face is grim. "I need answers, Joe. You gotta give it to me straight. Did you kill her?"

I shake my head. "Aw, come on, Russ----"

He grabs my shirt and bunches it in his massive fist yanking me toward him. "No bullshit, Joe! Yes or no?"

"No, I didn't kill her!" I protest. "Jesus, Russ----"

"They're in there dusting for prints. They're going to find a lot of yours," he says, letting go.

"Sure, I was there. You know that."

"What time did you leave?"

"I don't know. Six thirty. Seven. No later than that,"

"Anybody see you there?"

"No," I say. Then I remember. "No. Wait. A kid delivering flowers. He saw me."

"Kleinschmidt's already found him. The kid's on the way to the studio. You say you left at seven. Anybody see you leave?"

"No". Then again I remember. Dave Clancy. But how reliable is he? I don't even know the game he's playing and the wrong answer and he could put me behind bars. I keep my mouth shut.

"After you left, where'd you go?"

"Home."

"Can anybody vouch for that?"

"No." I lie again.

"And you were home all evening?"

"That's right," I say. "I read until about ten, then went to sleep." I don't like the look on his face. "What is it, Russ? What's going on? What are you not telling me?"

"Where's your knife?"

"What?"

"Your knife. The bone handled jackknife. The one you always carry around with you?"

"In my pocket."

"Let me see it," he demands.

I hesitate for a moment, then reach in my pocket and show it to him. He looks at it carefully.

"Is this the only one you have?" he asks.

"Yeah. Why?"

"Because there's one just like it, covered with blood, sitting on the rug next to May's dead body."

"Oh, shit," I say quietly.

Russ nods. "Right."

Just then a car horn beeps impatiently out on the street. It's another cruiser. Sitting in the passenger seat, eyes straight ahead, is the flower delivery kid from the night before. The cruiser passes by.

"It's a frame, Russ. They're after me. I don't know why."

"Who's after you?"

"The cops," I say. "They missed me the first time. Now they're finishing the job."

Russ is confused. "What the hell are you talking about?"

I tell him about the third degree, how they were on my case

the minute they walked onto the soundstage."You remember, Russ. When I told you I said they liked me, what did you say?"

Russ nods. "I said they think you did it."

"Then Tuesday afternoon, I'm going home. Just as I get to the apartment building I see Johansson hurrying out the door. He gets in his car and drives off. I go inside my apartment. Johansson was good but not that good. I know the place has been searched, but why? What for? I get nervous. I keep checking. Then in the tank of my toilet I find the gun. I mean, I assume it's the gun. A Jap model 8mm wrapped in oilskin."

Russ shakes his head. "They wouldn't----"

"They did!" I override him. "They're so fucking anxious to pin this on somebody and I mean quick. Or maybe somebody with a lot of clout is ordering them to serve me up on a turkey platter. Either way I'm the guy they saddle with the brass ring."

"Blaustein," Russ theorizes.

"I don't know," I say. "I hear he's not the daddy."

Russ nods. "Not only that, I have a hard time believing he was having a fling with the girl. According to his wife, and the bitch couldn't wait to tell me, the guy hasn't been able to get it up for years."

I frown. "Then why that stupid confession?"

"Orders maybe," Russ says.

"From who?"

"Who do you think?"

"DeSalle? The holy of holies?"

Russ throws up his hands in frustration. "Joe, I haven't a clue. I can't make sense of any of this." He hesitates and then exhales. "Okay, so where's the gun now?" he asks. Then quickly, "No, don't tell me. The less I know the better. So then what? With the cops?"

"They bully me for a while at headquarters, then Johansson suggests maybe in the interest of clearing myself, we should go to my apartment and look around. Since I have nothing to hide, I can't very well object but of course, I know what they're up to. As soon as he enters my place, Kleinschmidt makes a bee line for my bathroom and when he comes out he looks like a parboiled lobster. Now they toss my place for good. They open up my salt shaker like maybe I have a gun hidden there. A very small gun. Finally they go away but I know they haven't given up."

Russ shakes his head as if he can't believe it. "And so here you are."

"Here I am," I say.

"Fucking cops. I always knew they were a corrupt bunch of bastards but this. This is way past the limit." Russ is really fuming.

"So what now," I ask.

Russ thinks for a minute. "Look, I'm not you but if I were----" He hesitates.

"If you were," I say, urging him.

"I'd start by turning around and getting the hell away from this studio. I'd put my head down and keep it there and pray that some kind of evidence'll pop up to clear me."

"Just makes me look more guilty," I say.

"Can't look any worse than it does now. She scratches your neck. Everybody's seen the bandage. They'll be looking under her fingernails. They found the tissue with your blood all over it. Then there's the flower boy, the bone-handled knife, your prints everywhere you look." He shrugs as if to say I rest my case.

"And how do I prove my innocence hiding out somewhere with my tail between my legs?"

"First of all, Joe, you probably don't. You're not a cop. I am. In a way. I can nose around, find out what's up. Keep you informed. All I know is if they get you into a cell, you're finished."

I think about it. In a lot of ways he's right, mostly that last part. I nod. "Okay. I'll call you later."

"Right," he says. Then, "Joe, I'll be in over my head but I'll do my best for you. By the way, since I assume you're not going home, how do I reach you?"

'I'll call you," I say. And then I turn and making sure I'm not seen I stroll back to my car and get the hell out of there.

At first I just drive aimlessly. I don't know where I am or what I'm doing and I have nothing that even vaguely resembles a plan. And then it comes to me that there's a piece of this puzzle that I can deal with and that's Dave Clancy. He almost certainly saw me leave May's bungalow around seven. Maybe if I were really lucky he hung around outside my apartment the rest of the night and can provide me with an alibi. On reflection, I'm pretty sure I'm not going to be that lucky. There are only two things I know about Clancy for sure. He's driving a 1940 Lincoln Zephyr with Illinois plates and before I so stupidly invited him to bunk in with me, he'd made a reservation at The Biltmore. It is a long shot but The Biltmore it is because I have no other place to go.

Los Angeles has been described as fifty towns in search of a city. It sprawls forever in every direction. If it had a midtown, and that is debatable, that's where you would find The Biltmore Hotel, an overpowering edifice in the style of the Spanish Italian Renaissance, public rooms decorated with myriad murals and frescos, several restaurants and over a thousand guestrooms. Built in 1923 it was the largest hotel west of Chicago and in fact, may still be. I am impressed but I am not intimidated because I know that regardless of a hotel's cachet, a desk clerk is a desk clerk.

I sidle up to the desk and the brightly eager uniformed young man whose name plate reads "Gregory" smiles at me in greeting.

"Good morning, sir," he says. I glance at the clock on the wall behind him. It reads 12:41 but I am not inclined to split hairs.

"Good morning, Gregory," I say. "I hope you can help me. My friend and I were partying very late last night and we were, shall I say, not totally in control of our faculties. Well, Dave gets out of the cab because he wants to try one more nightclub and I just want to go to bed and after we have driven off, maybe twenty minutes later, I find his wallet on the floor of the cab."

"Oh, dear," says Gregory for want of something more intelligent to say.

"Oh, dear, indeed," I say. "So we drive back to the club where we left him off and there's no sign of him. Worse yet, I have no idea what hotel he is staying at but Dave is a man who treats himself to the very best of everything so here I am, hoping I've come to the right place."

"Let us hope you are right," says Gregory. "Full name?"

"Clancy. David Clancy".

Gregory opens the huge registration ledger and starts to scan the names of recent arrivals. He clucks his tongue a couple of times and then shakes his head as he closes the ledger.

"Sorry, sir. He's not staying with us."

I smile. "Did I mention that he is well connected to the government in a clandestine way? He could be using an alias." I do a good job of describing Dave but Gregory seems unimpressed.

"Again, sir, I'm terribly sorry but---"

"Did I also mention that he's driving a 1940 Lincoln Zephyr with Illinois plates?" As I tell him this, I am surreptitiously sliding a sawbuck in his direction. He looks at it as if it were the carcass of a diseased vermin. He steps back.

"Please, sir. I cannot help you," he says, greatly annoyed.

I reach for my wallet to sweeten the ante just as he is trying to catch the eye of a burly guy standing by a potted palm who I take to be the house detective. I take back my tenner, put away my wallet, turn on my heel and make for the door before the situation turns ugly.

Since I have little chance of stumbling across Dave in this huge sea of humanity they call The City of Angels I decide to start at the other end. I drive to Schwab's Drug Store where, years ago, a size 38 Lana Turner was discovered wearing a size 32 sweater and the rest was history. But today I am not interested in Lana Turner or any reasonable facsimile. I collect a huge handful of dimes and quarters and settle down in the phone booth where I place a call to the financial editor of the Chicago Sun-Times. I don't get the head guy because he has left for the day but I do get through to his assistant whose name is Prudence. I identify myself and my Hollywood studio connection which seems to impress her.

"Dave Clancy? Oh, yes, he's a wonderful journalist. Very good with stock analysis. I think he's been with us at least three years."

"Just to be sure we're talking about the same man---"I describe him in detail.

"Oh, yes, that's Dave."

"Do you have any idea how I could get in touch with him?"

"Well, I suppose you could try the hospital," she says.

"Hospital?"

"Good Samaritan. That's where they took his grandmother. She suffered a awesome heart attack. Dave was terribly worried when they called, poor boy. She was over 90, you know, but I understand they are very good with heart patients."

"And when was this call?" I ask.

"Oh, let me see. At least ten days ago. Maybe more."

I nod to myself. Ten days. That would put it at four days before Maggie was killed For whatever reason Dave Clancy had come to Los Angeles, it wasn't to investigate a sensational murder story. Prudence and I chat for a few minutes more and she doesn't have much else to give me except that Dave's leave of absence is open-ended.

As soon as I hung up from Pru, I call Good Samaritan and ask whether they have admitted any 90+ cardiac patients in the past couple of weeks. Why am I not surprised when they said they haven't?

My third call is to Russ at the studio. He picks up immediately.

"Can you talk?" I ask.

"Yes,"

"What's going on?"

"Nothing good, Joe. The flower guy identified you right away from your picture. A half dozen people identified your jackknife---"

"No, A jackknife, not my jackknife", I insist.

"You and I know that. Sergeant Kleinschmidt doesn't."

"Russ, I'm going to need your help. There's a wild card running around the city and we've got to find him. You remember that guy you and Dutch helped me with in the alley?"

"Clancy."

"That's him. He knows a lot more than he's let on."

"I can talk to Kleinschmidt. Maybe they can issue an APB but on what pretext? He's gonna want to know why."

"Because Clancy's been lying through his teeth since Day One," I say.

"Not a crime. But speaking of Clancy, he was at the funeral."

"I didn't see him."

"He never came into the chapel. Dutch saw him outside. When they were laying the girl to rest, Clancy was standing on a knoll maybe a hundred yards away. By himself. Just watching. When he saw that Dutch had spotted him, he just turned and walked away."

"Proves my point," I say. "He's involved."

"Okay, I'll see what I can do. Meanwhile, don't go home. Cops are crawling all over your place. Every squad car's got your picture and in about an hour, the five o'clock news is going to be spreading your name all over L.A. County. Oh, and that new TV station, KTLA, they're going to be putting up your picture on a news break every thirty minutes".

"Great," I say, totally depressed.

"And one other thing," my friend says to me, just to cheer me up even further, "they're offering a $5000 reward."

"I'll be in touch," I say, hanging up and scooping up what is left of my small change. I exit the phone booth, take a quick look around for either a Lana Turner lookalike or a cop holding a gun. Seeing neither I head for my car.

CHAPTER NINE

ith Kleinschmidt and his bloodhounds hot on my trail, two things become painfully obvious. I am going to have to hide myself and also hide my car. And given Russ' description of the zeal with which the authorities are pursuing me, I'd better do it quickly.

Barely eight years old, Union Station is already something of a landmark in the L.A. area along with Wrigley Field, the Venice Beach Boardwalk and of course, the HOLLYWOOD sign. Designed to service the Union Pacific, Southern Pacific and the Atchison Topeka and the Santa Fe railroads, it is a beehive of activity around the clock. Saturday afternoon is particularly busy as the Super Chief readies itself for the semi-weekly trip to Chicago.

I park the Studebaker in a spot close to the entrance and then take up a position where I can see most of the parking lot as well as the entrance. I didn't have to wait long. Wearing a seersucker suit, he is driving a ten year old Chevy and he is in such a hurry he leaps out of his car without locking it and half-runs, half-stumbles toward the entrance carrying a substantial suitcase. Lugging Maggie's overnight bag which I'd gotten from Natalie Bloom, I follow him in as he hurries to the ticket counter and buys a round trip ticket to Chicago on The Chief. Seersucker leaves the return reservation open but it is obvious from the size of his bag that he plans to be there quite a few days.

Ticket in hand, he runs to Gate 14 where The Chief is preparing to leave. I follow and watch as he gets through the gate and climbs aboard. Five minutes later The Chief pulls out of the station and I am confident that the rumpled gentleman with the overstuffed bag won't be returning to L.A. any time soon.

Assuming the guise of a slightly inebriated and churlishly rude passenger, I approach the ticket counter.

"One way to Chicago on The Chief," I slur.

"I'm sorry, sir," the ticket agent says. "The Super Chief has left the station."

"Whatdayamean, left the station? I wanna go to Chicago. That toddlin' town, you know what I mean?" I force a garish grin and start to fumble for my wallet.

"I'm sorry, sir----"

"How much for Chicago? Just one way. Not coming back. No, sir."

The agent is getting a little annoyed. Good. I want him to remember me. "Sir, the train is gone. It has left."

"Left? Can't have left. I'm supposed to be on it. How much?"

I "accidentally" drop my wallet on the floor and when I bend down to pick it up, I fall over. I struggle to my feet. "Okay, okay. I'm okay."

By this time a security guard has come to my aid. "Just want to go to Chicago, that's all," I tell him.

"I'm afraid you're too late, sir," the guard says.

I look at him indignantly but bleary-eyed. "Well, where can I go?"

The guard exchanges a look with the agent. The agent says, "The train for Seattle leaves in thirty minutes."

I brighten perceptibly. "Seattle. I've always wanted to go to Seattle," I say. "Any place but here."

I buy my ticket and wander off toward the departure gates. When I am sure they are no longer watching me, I duck out a side door and hurry into the parking lot. The Chevy is not the most sophisticated machine to roll off the assembly line and I am able to hot wire it within seconds. I toss Maggie's overnight case in the back seat and take off. Soon I am tooling along North Alameda heading toward civilization. Two cop cruisers pass me by going the other way, another comes up on my rear and whizzes past, determined to pull over a baby blue convertible with a knockout blonde behind the wheel. I'm not sure what he's going to charge her with but chances are, he'll think of something. In this nondescript ten year old Chevy I have become invisible. I start to relax.

As Russ had warned, the radio news is grim. My name is mentioned often. I am described as a highly placed executive at Continental Studios which certainly must come as a surprise to Leo Blaustein. Now they are broadcasting my physical description. I am waiting to hear the phrase 'armed and dangerous'. Suddenly I am no longer relaxed and I know that I have to find cover immediately.

Forty minutes have passed. I pull to the curb and park four doors away. The street is starting to come alive with men coming home from work and neighborhood kids playing stickball in the streets. The smells of roast chicken and spaghetti sauce fill the air. I cross the street to the opposite sidewalk, ever watchful as I approach her house. In the daylight it seems smaller but it is well kept up. The paint job is new and the lawn is well cared for. A flower bed fronts the house, alive with petunias, pansies, azaleas, and a couple of rose bushes. It's a dazzling array of colors. She might be home but I doubt it. Her job at the real estate office keeps her busy until at least seven o'clock most nights, sometimes even later. I turn into her driveway which leads to the rear of the house. I don't rush, I amble, and when I reach the back door, I press the buzzer just to be on the safe side. Silence. I take out my jackknife and jimmy the lock. I let myself in and close the door behind me. The sun has been going down for the past half hour and the interior of the kitchen is dim but I don't turn on a light. The last thing I need is a curious neighbor sticking his nose where it doesn't belong.

I walk through into the tiny living room. Everything is neat. Magazines are in a rack, ashtrays are empty and clean, the pillows on the sofa are plumped and arranged symmetrically. I put down the overnight case and plop down into an easy chair by the front window. The lace curtains provide cover as I look out onto the street. Darkness is falling fast now. The street lights come on. I settle back in the chair and wait.

An hour goes by. It seems more like ten. I'm itching to open the overnight bag and check out the contents but by now it's pitch dark and I don't dare turn on a light. My watch reads ten past nine. She should have been home long ago and then it occurs to me that she may be with Banks. Dinner for two in some dimly lit cafe. The thought grates on me. Maybe she's going to bring the son of a bitch home with her. God, no. For a fleeting moment I consider getting the hell out of there but the moment passes. Where could I go? I decide to take my chances and stay. I check my watch again. It's twelve minutes past nine.

Slivers of moonlight shine into the room through the half-drawn shades. Across the room is the phone. The darkness and the oppressive silence are getting to me. I decide to call Russ if only to hear a human voice. My nerve endings are raw. I want to scream.

"Parmalee," he says as he answers.

"It's me," I say.

"Are you okay?"

"For now. What's going on?"

"The same only more so," Russ says.

"Nothing new?"

"Not much. The coroner's narrowed down the time of death to somewhere between nine and ten o'clock, but you know he's mostly guessing."

"I thought these guys were supposed to know what they're doing."

"You'd think so. We pay him enough. Oh, and the cops are checking alibis."

"Haven't got one, thanks," I say wryly.

"I figured that. You're not the only one."

"Tell me."

"Brick Baxter says he was home alone, wearing a back brace, incapacitated, unable to drive. I could almost believe him except that he was seen at Paramount around four o'clock walking briskly toward the DeMille building without the back brace so he's full of crap".

"Nice to know I have company," I say.

"Leo was home with his wife and she backs him up but you know what that's worth."

"Not much."

"Our boss is the only one so far that looks solid. He was meeting with a bunch of people from the Hollywood Press Association trying to drum up some enthusiasm for that Teddy Roosevelt biography the studio put out in February. These people give out awards like the Oscars. They don't mean much but I think DeSalle thinks any award is better than none at all. Anyway the cops say he checks out."

"How about Vinnie the Muscle?"

"I don't think they've caught up with him yet," Russ replies.

"And Dave Clancy?"

"No sign of him."

"Are they even looking?" I ask.

"I don't know. I doubt it. Look, Joe, I talked to Kleinschmidt. I told him everything you told me. He doesn't care. He knows who killed the Baumann kid and who killed May Britton and that guy is you. He's going through the motions just to cover his ass but it's you he wants. He's not going to raise a finger to go after anyone else."

"I get it."

"Sorry. It's just the way it is. I don't know. Maybe you should just turn yourself in, get yourself a good lawyer----"

"No. The frame's too good, Russ. Clarence Darrow couldn't save my ass."

"Especially since he's dead."

"Mmm. That doesn't help either."

I'm staring at the front window when car headlights suddenly appear and turn into the driveway.

"Russ, I gotta go," I say quickly. "Call you tomorrow." I hang up and move to the window as Lydia douses the lights and gets out of the car. As she starts toward her front walkway, a second car races up to the curb and skids to a stop. It's that fucking Cadillac and sure enough, the oily Mr. Banks leaps from behind the wheel and tries to intercept her before she can reach the front door. He grabs her by the arm but she shrugs him off and keeps walking. He tries to block her way. She yells something at him. I don't get all of it but it isn't complimentary. He yells back. She yells again and struggles past him. I'm tempted to go outside and kick the bastard in the nuts. I know I can't. I can only hope that she fights him off hard enough to enter the house alone. If not----I don't want to think about it.

She opens the front door. I'm standing behind it. I hear Banks' voice. "I'll call you!"

Lydia turns back toward him. "Don't call me, Tyler. Not tomorrow. Not next week. Just get out of my life!" With that, she comes in and slams the door shut and as she does, she finds herself staring into my face. Her eyes widen, she opens her mouth as if to scream but thinks better of it. I say nothing. She says nothing. Outside Tyler calls out, "I'll call you tomorrow!" He seems to have a hearing problem.

Lydia and I stand there like statues, both listening. We hear his car start up and he peels away from the curb, burning rubber. Only then does she speak.

"Jesus Christ, Joe, you scared the hell out of me."

I mumble an apology.

"I didn't kill her, Lyd. I swear to God," I say.

She nods. "You came all the way over here to tell me that? I believe you, Joe. I know you that well."

"If you want me to leave I will, but I have no place else to go. If the cops catch up with me, I'm as good as dead."

"No, no. It's okay," she says, turning on the lights. I get a good look at her. Her make up is messed, she's been crying and she's still the most beautiful girl I've ever known. She's not tall. A shade over five-four with hazel eyes and auburn hair and and a mouth that begs you to kiss her. She is full where she is supposed to be but her hips are slim and when she walks she has a quirky gait that borders on the obscene. I loved her the first moment I saw her and I still do.

"I could be putting you in danger, Lyd. I mean, nobody knows about you and me. No way they can track me here but still and all----"

"I said, it's okay, Joe." She moves to the two windows that front the house and makes sure the shades are drawn all the way. "I must look like hell," she says.

"No," I say.

"I'm sorry you had to see that. The son of a bitch. What kind of a jerk am I, Joe? Tell me. Am I stupid? Am I some sort of brain dead fool?"

"Of course not. He's the jerk, not you."

"Thanks for saying it."

"I mean it."

"Then thanks for meaning it." She manages a smile. She has a great smile.

"How long have you been here?" she asks.

"I don't know. Three hours maybe."

"Have you eaten?"

I shake my head. "I'm not hungry."

"Come in the kitchen. I'll fix you something." She starts off. "Wait a second. Let me lower the shades". She goes into the kitchen and pulls down the shades and closes the curtains. I'm momentarily safe from prying eyes. Before I know it she's got bread in the toaster, is percolating some coffee and cooking up a bowl of Wheatena. Only then do I realize I am starving.

Finally she says, "I'm sorry you had to see that."

I shrug. "Your business, not mine."

"Sometimes I wonder what I see in him. There are times he seems like the nicest guy in the world. A real charmer and he sure can make me laugh. Other times-----". She leaves it hanging as she puts my toast on the table along with butter and jam. "We never did get a chance to fight much, did we, Joe?"

"We never got a chance to do much of anything except love each other, Lyd." Our eyes meet. She looks away. I want to scream at her. Don't you know what this guy is? Can't you see it? But I keep quiet. Centuries ago messengers bearing bad tidings got themselves killed. I can't bring myself to tell her.

I dig into my food. Lydia pours herself a cup of coffee and sits down. We chat idly about this and that. She asks about my novel, the one I've been writing for the past four years.

"How's it coming?" she asks.

I shrug. "So-so." It's a sore subject. I don't want to talk about it.

"I loved the first two chapters. How far have you gotten?" she asks.

"Chapter Two," I say. Then I shake my head. "I've got nothing to say, Lyd. Whatever it is, I'm dry. There's nobody home."

"I don't believe that," she says.

"Maybe it's the job. Maybe the war that grudgingly allowed me to live. I think about it now and then and once in a while I take out the pages but the guy who wrote them, I don't know him. Maybe I never will again."

"No, Joe, I think you're wrong, I think---"

I look up at her sharply. "Drop it, Lyd. Just drop it." The tone of my voice surprises even me and we both fall silent.

Then she says, "So what happened, Joe? How'd you get yourself into this mess?"

I take a deep breath and tell her everything I know. Finding Maggie's body. The cops planting the gun, trying to railroad me to take the heat off the department. Being hounded by Dave Clancy who certainly is not here looking for a story but I know he's involved, right up to his bellybutton. I tell her about my confrontation with May in her dressing room and the bloody knife left next to the body to incriminate me. I wonder if someone has it in for me for personal reasons or if I am just a handy patsy. I can see it from Kleinschmidt's point of view. He has good reason to believe I'm guilty and sooner or later he's going to catch up with me. I can't hide forever and every minute I spend with Lydia puts her at risk. The law calls it "accessory after the fact".

"Don't worry about me," she says.

"But I do worry, Lyd. This is just temporary until I can come up with some way out from under this mess."

She reaches across the table and takes my hand and squeezes it. She smiles. "I think you need some sleep," she says. "I've got a couple of blankets in the closet. The sofa's actually not bad." She gets up and goes to the linen closet. I put my dishes in the sink and then follow her into the living room. She's brought two blankets and a pillow and she starts to fashion a bed for me.

"I can do that," I say.

"I've got it," she replies and straightens up. As she turns she brushes up against me. We are close. Very close. Every nerve in my body is tingllng. I want her so bad I could cry. Our eyes lock and neither of us speaks and then she turns away and heads toward the kitchen.

"I'd better straighten up the kitchen," she says.

"I'll get it," I say.

"No, it'll only take a couple of minutes."

"I said I'll get it," I tell her firmly. "Go to bed. Try to sleep."

She hesitates, then nods and goes to her bedroom door. She turns back to me and throws me that gorgeous smile. "Good night, Joe," she says and then she goes into her bedroom and closes the door.

After I clean up the kitchen I come back into the living room and douse all the lights except for the table lamp next to the sofa. I pick up the overnighter and test the latches. They're locked. I take out my jackknife, spring the latches and look inside. There isn't much there. A couple of blouses, two pairs of nylons, some toilet articles, and a copy of "The King's General" by Daphne DuMaurier. Tied up with a rubber band are some unpaid bills, several personal letters and a postcard from someone named Jennie mailed from Rome with a 'wish you were here' sentiment. I flip through the pages of the book and as I do, a photograph falls out onto the floor. I lean down to pick it up. And that's when it grabs me.

It is a photo of two people. A man and a woman. Both young. Both leaning on the fender of an old Model T. Both smiling. One of them is Maggie and she looks to be stlll in her teens. The man is young, too, but more likely nearer twenty. He has his arm around Maggie's shoulder and I recognize his face immediately.

I turn the photo over. Maggie has written something. The blue ink has faded badly but the inscription is legible.

"Me and Dave. 1936. Happier times".

CHAPTER TEN

'm aware of her smell before I actually open my eyes and see her. She's wearing Chanel No. 5. It's all she's ever worn and my mind is awash with memories of days gone by. She's leaning down to me, gently shaking my shoulder and whispering my name. The living room is still very dim because of the closed curtains and the pulled shades but I see that she is dressed for work. On her the pale yellow jacket and skirt with the lime green silk blouse look like a million bucks.

"Hi," I say groggily, struggling to sit.

"Don't get up," she says. "Try to get some more sleep."

"I don't think so," I say.

"I'd stay home today, Joe, but you know real estate. It's a weekend business and we're busy as hell at the office. It might look funny if I didn't show."

"No, no. You're right."

"I'll try to get off early. How about I bring home some Chinese?"

"Sounds great."

"Mongolian beef for you, moo goo guy pan for me, just like the old days."

I shake my head, smiling. "Good memory, Lyd." Before I

shipped out for England, I think that's all we ever ate. "What was the name of that place? Ling's Dragon Palace? I wonder if he's still around."

"Where do you think I'm going to get the takeout?"

"You're kidding."

"Still there. Still crowded. The old man and his wife haven't changed a bit."

A moment of stillness passes between us. "We really screwed things up, didn't we, Lyd?"

"Not you. Me, Joe. I jumped too fast. I should have given us a chance."

"Not too late," I say hopefully.

She just smiles as she stands up. "There's hot coffee on the stove. Eggs in the fridge. Just help yourself. I'll try to be back by six."

She goes to the front door and opens it.

"Lyd," I say, "I need to use your phone today."

"Fine."

"I may have to rack up a lot of long distance."

"The phone's yours, Joe." She blows me a kiss and goes out. The room is suddenly very quiet, like a tomb. I hope that isn't an omen. I pick up my watch from the coffee table. It reads 8:13. I have calls to make but not this early. I get to my feet and trudge off in search of a bathroom.

Breakfast isn't much. Toast and coffee. I wash the dishes and clean up the kitchen. I take a hot shower and try to shave with a safety razor Lydia probably uses on her legs. With soap for lather I make a bad job of it and nick myself twice. By the time I've redressed it's past nine o'clock and I place a call to Russ at the studio. One of his deputies answers the phone and I hang up.

I go to the suitcase and take out one of the letters I found in the bundle of correspondence. I read it again for the fifth time.

Dear Maggie,

I guess I'm happy that you've caught on at one of the movie studios though I think you are made of better stuff. What happened to all those dreams of Broadway? I really don't like hearing about you and Brick Baxter. Honestly, honey, he's a third rate actor and he's just using you, that's all. Or are you using him? I hope not. Whatever you decide to do with your life, don't sleep your way to the top. It would break my heart. So, do you think there might be a chance you could sneak off for a few days? I miss you a lot. As ever, I love you. Always have. Always will.

Dave

I find notepaper and a couple of pencils in a drawer in the kitchen. I need them because I'm going to be taking lots of notes. My first call is to telephone information in White River, South Dakota. I tell the operator I am looking for a distant cousin, Phoebe Clancy, but I've lost her phone number and can she help me. She tells me there is no Phoebe Clancy in White River or any of the tiny nearby hamlets. I am, of course, not surprised by this. I ask if there are any other Clancys in the area. She gives me three phone numbers. All are dead ends. They know of no David Clancy living anywhere in the area. They are all remarkably friendly and disappointed that they cannot be more helpful. Mrs. Grace Clancy in particular feels very badly. Eighty-three years old, she knows just about everyone in Mellette County and has perfect recall of every birth or funeral over the past sixty years.

I reconnect with telephone information and get the number of the local high school. Within minutes I am talking to the principal, a Miss Agatha Gates who is new to the area and has been

with the school district for less than two years. She is sure, however, that Elmer Corcoran will be able to help me. He has been
teaching biology for the past twelve or thirteen years. If a young
man named David Clancy attended White River High, Elmer
will know about it. I leave Lydia's number as well as my apartment number for him to call and hope for the best.

I try Russ again. Again the phone is answered by a deputy
and again I hang up. I'm getting an uneasy feeling about what
may be happening outside the walls of my self imposed jail. I
had looked for a radio the previous evening, but didn't see one.
I realize now that I hadn't checked Lydia's bedroom. Sitting on
the nightstand next to the bed is an old pre-war Philco table
model. I turn it on and start searching for news.

Not much has changed. My name is prominently mentioned
but so far 'armed and dangerous' is not part of the equation. A
press conference held by a Deputy Chief of Police has proved
worthless except for one interesting tidbit of information. Harry
Cohn has just announced that Columbia Pictures will be devel-
oping a film based on the Black Dahlia murder. The Deputy
Chief is not pleased by this. He cites the ongoing investigation
and says the department will not cooperate with Columbia on
the making of the film. What he does not say is that he is afraid
this movie will make the Los Angeles Police Department look
like an asylum for incompetent dolts. He is right to be worried.

Lydia's bedroom is at the side of the house and the curtains
of the one window that look out on her neighbor's yard have
not been pulled. As I turn off the radio I spot a man lurking near
the neighbor's driveway. He is wearing a cheap suit, unpolished
brown shoes and a fedora. Only if he had his badge pinned to
his jacket pocket could I be more certain that he is a cop.

I move quickly into the living room and cautiously push aside an inch or two of shade. I peer out. Across the street are two black Ford sedans. Two guys are sitting in one of them. Another guy in a fedora is standing on the sidewalk staring at Lydia's house. A fourth guy is at the front door of the house across the street, talking to a middle aged woman in a housedress and gesturing in my direction. These gentlemen are only slightly more obvious than the cop lurking outside Lydia's bedroom window.

Panic grabs me in the gut. How could they have found me? Maybe a neighbor who spotted me the night before as I approached Lydia's house? But then why didn't the cops show up immediately. I refuse to believe that Lydia has given me up. If she has I don't care what happens. Let them shoot me. Nice and clean. No trial. No complications. Case closed.

This moment of self-destructive insanity goes as fast as it came. I hurry through to the kitchen and peer out the window into the backyard. I see no one. They may be lurking in the bushes but I have no choice. I must move now or I won't be able to move at all. I open the door, take one more look around and then run toward the other neighbor's backyard. A half dozen orange trees provide a bit of cover and I'm pretty sure I haven't been spotted. I race to the next yard and duck down behind a brick barbecue grill. No shouts. No whistles. No gunshots. I believe I am now very close to where I parked the Chevy but I have no idea how to cross the street without being seen. I decide to keep racing through the backyards until I reach the corner house. When I get there I move toward the front and look up the street. The cops are now moving toward Lydia's, two dead on and the other two angling in from the sides.

It's then that I notice the flower bed. Someone has been planting bushes and has left behind a shovel and a hoe, some work gloves and a floppy sun hat, all neatly piled by the garden. I move quickly, tossing away my suit jacket and peeling off my shirt. I put on the hat and sling the hoe over my shoulder and walk out to the street, then cross to the sidewalk where I start to amble in the direction of the Chevy. As disguises go, it isn't much but the cops are now pounding on Lydia's door and paying no attention to anything else.

When I reach the car, I toss the hoe onto the back seat and slip behind the wheel. Again, it takes little skill to hot wire the ignition but when the car starts up, I see that one of the cops has turned and looked in my direction. I meet his gaze innocently and he turns back to Lydia's front door which he and his partner are in the process of kicking in. I am just pulling into the street when the cop turns and gives me a second look. That second look was one look too many. He shouts at his partner and points in my direction. They start to run toward me as I floor the accelerator. I speed past them but they are already at their car and in a matter of seconds are peeling out after me. The other cops have now been galvanized. They hurry to the second car. The race is on and I'm pretty sure my chances of winning it are somewhere between zero and nil.

I turn at the corner, desperately trying to get my bearings. I need a main thoroughfare to have any chance at all but without a map, I'm only guessing. A kid starts to chase a ball that has rolled into the street. I yank the wheel and barely miss him. The car slams into the curb, tips, almost rolls. An oncoming car blares its horn at me. Behind me I can picture the cops radioing the entire LAPD squad car fleet. A cross street looms up. I've got a STOP sign but I ignore it. Ahead I can see cars. I'm pretty sure it's Vermont Avenue. I glance at the speedometer. I'm doing nearly seventy in a thirty mile zone. A black and white appears out of nowhere. He's on my tail and his lights are flashing and his siren screaming for me to pull over. I can't believe what I'm doing. I've got to stop before somebody gets killed. Like me. But something won't let me quit.

I reach Vermont. Another STOP which I ignore as I take a right and try to meld into the rushing traffic. This time I am not so lucky. A fully loaded beer truck tries to cram itself into the space I am occupying. He clips my rear end and suddenly I am whirling out of control, tires screaming in agony. I bounce off a panel truck and skid across two lanes of traffic before I jump the curb and plow into a telephone pole. My body jerks forward and I can feel my head hit the windshield. In a moment blood is pouring into my eyes. I fumble for the door handle but can't find it. Then rough hands are grabbing me and pulling me from the car. I feel myself being tossed to the ground, then flipped onto my stomach as my arms are yanked behind my back and manacles jammed onto my wrists. A heavy shoe kicks me in the ribs twice just for the hell of it.

The race is done with. As expected I have finished second. I no longer have the will to struggle. I decide to pass out.

CHAPTER ELEVEN

Twenty four hours have passed since the Chevy and I did our dance of death on Vermont Avenue. I am sitting in a cell for one in the L.A. County Jail. Obviously someone thinks I'm too dangerous to be allowed to mingle with the general population of thieves, muggers and murderers. I am wearing a loose fitting grey outfit made of something resembling burlap. The ensemble consists of a hair shirt and string tied pants. They itch and they smell but I'm getting used to it. There is a bandage on my forehead and I'm pretty sure I got a few stitches to stop the bleeding. I've also got a tight bandage around my rib cage which hurts like hell. So much for medical attention. I guess I'm lucky they didn't let me bleed to death.

I am sitting on a cot fitted with a mattress at least one inch thick. Last night I tried sleeping on it without much success. The place is a morass of noise and confusion. Voices are constantly raised, cell doors being opened and then slammed shut. I can hear grown men crying. I can hear guards threatening miscreants with bodily harm. Curses and insults fill the air constantly. Only the stone deaf could sleep in conditions like these.

Except for officialdom and that fool lawyer the studio sent over, I have seen no one and talked to no one. If I am entitled to one phone call, they have yet to offer it and I have yet to ask. Sergeant Kleinschmidt pulled me out of my cell early this morning for an interrogation. I'd expected the worst but he laid off the rough stuff. I guess he could have used a confession but I had the feeling he was sure he didn't need it. All the pieces fit together nicely and he seemed very pleased with himself. I suspect he saw a lieutenant's badge somewhere in his near future.

When I was returned to my cell a tray with cold oatmeal and even colder coffee was waiting for me. Since I hadn't eaten since breakfast the day before, I forced them down. A few minutes later Russ showed up in full studio uniform. They'd relieved him of his pistol, probably a wise idea, but he somehow looked naked without it.

"You look like hell," he said by way of greeting.

"I actually don't feel that good," I said. "How'd you manage to get in here?"

"It sure wasn't easy. I guess I'm technically a part of the investigative team. Anyway, Kleinschmidt okayed it."

"The man has a heart of gold," I say.

"Without question."

"So what's going on out there or do I not want to know?"

"Well, your picture is on the front page of the local papers. Your arrest has been likened to the capture of Bruno Hauptmann. Chief Horrall has been preening for the reporters since seven o'clock this morning. He promises a speedy trial and an even speedier execution. Have I missed anything?"

I hesitate. "What's happened with Lydia?"

"They picked her up at the real estate office and brought her in for questioning. After an hour, they let her go. I think that's the end of it. They're assuming you forced her into cooperating."

I am confused and afraid to ask the question which I ask

anyway. "How'd they find me, Russ? Nobody knew about us. They couldn't have."

"Are you asking did she turn you in? No, I don't think so. Kleinschmidt says they got a call early this morning. Muffled voice. Almost certainly a man. Kleinschmidt thinks it was probably one of her neighbors. When they asked for his name he hung up on them."

I nod. God, I hope that's the way it was.

"Anything on Clancy?" I ask.

"Joe, there's nothing on anybody and there won't be. As far as the LAPD is concerned, this case is closed. Now, have you got a lawyer?"

I shook my head. "A guy from the studio showed up last night wearing a three piece suit and carrying a fifty dollar briefcase. He said DeSalle had sent him. He as much as admitted that DeSalle thought I was guilty but that a good Christian did not fail his brother in time of need."

"Yeah, that's the boss, all right," Russ said.

"The guy was useless. A contract lawyer. No clue as to what to do or how to get me out of here."

"That's not going to happen, Joe. Capital case. No bail."

"Yeah, I know. Anyway, I sent the guy and his briefcase packing."

"I'd have done the same," Russ said. He pauses for a moment. "Joe, I did a little digging. For what it's worth it might answer a few questions."

"Like?"

"The Black Dahlia murder. The lead detectives when it first broke were Kleinschmidt and Johansson. They had the case for about five weeks and were getting no place while the papers were reaming the department day and night for incompetence or worse. Apparently the Chief couldn't stand the heat so he threw the two detectives to the wolves. Johansson got demoted and Kleinschmidt got a reprimand in his jacket. The two guys who replaced them haven't done any better but I've been told that Kleinschmidt and Johansson are two very pissed off cops."

I nodded. "Now it's starting to make sense."

"You were the first one in their crosshairs. Wrong time. Wrong place."

"But they couldn't make an arrest stick without a frame," I say.

"Exactly."

"Not a lot I can do about it," I say.

"You could go to the papers but I doubt it would help. Good or bad, right or wrong, cops stick together."

I nod again because I know he's right.

"Which brings us back to the subject of a lawyer. Like it or not, you're going to need one."

"I know."

"Do you know anyone?"

I shake my head.

"Do you want me to find somebody for you?"

"No, not yet, Russ. I'm too tired to think straight. I think maybe I need some sleep."

He took the hint and stood up. He shook my hand, squeezing it. "Hang in there," he said.

After he left I laid down. I tried but sleep wouldn't come. I surmise that the time is now well past two o'clock. I can't say for sure because they have taken my watch, my wallet and my jack-knife. Yes, and even my shoelaces in case I try to hang myself. I am more exhausted than ever but still I cannot sleep. My brain is buzzing with unanswered questions. I've been singled out to take the fall for two murders and I have no idea why or who is behind it.

I hear a key in the lock of my cell door and look up as one of the guards is opening it. "Let's go," he says. I start to ask 'go where' but decide not to. I am quickly learning that in the County Jail silence is golden. Keep your mouth shut. Don't make trouble. Do what you're told.

The guard leads me into a small room adjacent to the booking area. As I enter I see Vinnie the Muscle standing against the wall. A distinguished looking man with snow white hair is sitting at a table. He gets up as I enter and approaches me, hand extended.

"Mr. Bernardi, my name is Arthur Baxendale and I have been retained to represent you."

I am immediately wary. "Retained by who?"

Vinnie moves away from the wall. "You don't need to know that," he says sharply. He has been carrying a large paper bag which he tosses in my direction. "Here's some clothes," he says. "As soon as you change we can get the hell out of here."

"And how do we do that, Vinnie?"

Baxendale smiles. "I've arranged bail, Mr. Bernardi."

"Bail? But I thought----"

"Judge Farraday is a close personal friend. I convinced him that you were not a flight risk nor were you a danger to the community."

"Yes, but---"

"Put on the clothes, Bernardi," Vinnie says. "This place is giving me the creeps."

I can see that Vinnie is in no mood for further conversation on the matter and anything has got to be better than the bedlam I just left. I change clothes and after signing some papers and retrieving my personal belongings, we are out on the street where a shiny new Packard Clipper is parked at curbside. Vinnie opens the rear door. I hesitate, then climb in. Baxendale gets in and sits beside me. Vinnie sits up front next to the driver whose face I can't see but he is big and beefy and balding. The car pulls out into the street and merges into the traffic. I have questions but I keep them to myself. We ride in silence, north on Sepulveda and then a right onto Sunset Boulevard. A few minutes later the car turns into the entrance to the Bel Air Estates. A uniformed guard waves as we approach and the gates open wide. As we pass through them, we enter another world.

Bel Air is a sea of diamonds in the midst of the rocky shoals of Los Angeles. Those who live here are beyond rich. Residents of Beverly Hills window shop here anytime a home goes on the market. They do not buy. They cannot afford the down payment and those who need a mortgage are laughed out of the bank. My fears of ending up dead in some back alley are momentarily assuaged. There are no back alleys in Bel Air.

Baldy makes a right turn. Daylight is slowly disappearing but I see that several foursomes are still hacking their way around the luxurious Bel Air golf course. I may be crazy but it seems to me that each golfer has two caddies. Baldy makes another turn and we pass a mansion that could double for Tara in "Gone With The Wind". Two doors down is another mansion which makes the Tara wannabe look like housing for the servants. Baldy pulls into the driveway and we are confronted with another set of gates. A swarthy looking man steps out of the guard shack and looks us over. His jacket is open. He is carrying a pistol which looks like a small buffalo gun. Baldy nods. The guy nods back and reaches for a switch inside the shack. The gates open wide. As we drive through them I notice another man standing off to the side of the driveway. He is carrying a Thompson submachine gun. For the briefest of moments it occurs to me that I may be about to meet the Governor of the state of California.

The Packard pulls to a stop in the circular driveway. We pile out of the car. Another man with a Tommy gun is standing by the entrance. He raps twice on the front door and someone inside opens it for us. This man is wearing a butler's regalia. The .45 in his shoulder holster tells me he is not Arthur Treacher. He leads the three of us down a corridor and ushers us through an archway into a magnificently designed room into which my apartment would fit three times. Vinnie looks at me and points to an overstuffed easy chair near the fireplace. I get the hint and sit down, almost sliding off since this chair, like the rest of the chairs and sofas in the room, is covered with protective vinyl.

The butler leaves the room. Vinnie takes up a position leaning against a wall. He seems to have an aversion to sitting. Baxendale crosses over to twelve foot long bar and fixes himself a drink. He doesn't offer me one and I don't ask. I twiddle my thumbs. No one speaks. Baxendale sits down opposite me and stares at me as if I were some as yet undiscovered species of a bottom dwelling ocean fish. I would like to ask him a couple of questions but Vinnie has already expressed his opposition to that idea. So I sit. And I wait.

I am about to nod off when I notice that Baxendale has quickly arisen from his chair. I glance to my left. Vinnie has pushed himself away from the wall and is looking past me to the archway. I turn as a man enters the room. I don't need to be introduced. The only guy who has had his picture in the paper more often than this man is Earl Scheib who will paint any car for $14.95.

Salvatore Maggio is short and squat with a jowly face and

dark bushy eyebrows. His lips are full beneath a very narrow mustache. His steel-blue eyes are piercing. He still sports a full head of hair which is turning grey. He looks from Baxendale to Vinnie and then stops, fixing his gaze on me. I look around not quite sure what I should be doing. I decide to stand. A smile crosses Maggio's lips. He waves his hand for me to sit back down now that I have shown him proper respect. He looks at Baxendale and points to the bar. The lawyer hustles over to fix his employer a drink. Maggio sits in the chair vacated by Baxendale and Vinnie resumes his favorite resting place against the wall.

Maggio is an independent businessman although no one knows exactly what business he's in. He is closely allied with the heirarchy of Teamsters Local 399 which bargains for a large chunk of Hollywood's studio employees. Often, when the union is beginning negotiations for a new contract, Maggio will sit in on the talks as an honest broker for both sides. His neutrality is a subject of much hilarity among studio executives on the cocktail party circuit except that nobody's laughing.

Baxendale hands Maggio a wine glass fllled with what looks like a robust Cabernet. He sips it, never taking his eyes off mine. Finally he says. "I would offer you a glass, Mr. Bernardi, but I am particular who I drink with, at least until I get to know them."

I nod, not knowing what to say to that.

He continues. "I have just spent a million dollars on you, Mr. Bernardi. Well, perhaps not spent. I expect to get it back when I return you to the police. I say this so you will understand that I have gone to a great deal of trouble so that we may have this conversation in private away from prying ears."

I nod again. There is a trace of an Italian accent but he has done a good job of Americanizing his speech. But that aside, my immediate concern is, where the hell is this going?

Sensing my curiosity, Maggio gets right to the point. "Did you kill May Britton?"

"No," I croak.

"Can you prove that?"

"No, I can't."

"Then why should I believe you?" he asks.

I think carefully before answering. I sense that if I weasel or beg or show fear, he will eat me alive. So I don't do any of those things.

"Maybe you shouldn't," I say meeting his gaze without wavering.

"That is the answer of a very brave man or a fool. Which are you, Mr. Bernardi?"

"I'm a guy whose balls are in a bear trap, Mr. Maggio. I have been neatly framed for, not one, but two murders. I have no idea why and I have less idea who is behind it. Now I find myself being questioned by a man who has the power to have me killed with a snap of his fingers. Few people have ever found themselves in such a position and since I am apparently not all that bright, I don't know what to do about it. I did not kill May. I liked May. That's my story and I'm sticking by it."

Not once did I lose eye contact and now I am holding my breath, hoping that Vinnie is not sneaking up behind me with a revolver in his hand.

Maggio watches me carefully. He, too, has maintained eye contact. Now he nods slowly. "I believe you," he says.

I exhale audibly. My armpits are wet but my underwear is still dry. I consider myself very lucky.

"Do you enjoy a glass of wine, Mr. Bernardi?"

I smile. "I do. I'll have what you're having."

Now he smiles and snaps his fingers at Baxendale who quickly moves back to the bar to pour me a drink.

"Tell me how you got into this predicament. Leave nothing out. We have plenty of time."

"Sure," I say. I take my wine glass from the lawyer, sip it, and nod appreciatively. Maggio nods back. Then I tell him what I have been going through. As requested I leave out nothing. I deal only in facts. I don't speculate. I do, however, remind him that Vinnie is a possible suspect given his closeness to May as well as his unsavory background which has been common knowledge since his first day on the set.

Maggio raises his hand slightly. "I will vouch for Vincent", he says imperiously. He has no idea how relieved I am to hear that. "The woman he was with at the time of----" He hesitates momentarily. "At the time of Miss Britton's death was reluctant to verify his whereabouts the first time she was questioned by the police. She will not make that mistake again."

"As it should be," I say, thinking this is not a man to be trifled with.

"You are probably wondering why I am bothering myself with all of this?" Maggio says.

I shrug. Yes, the thought has occurred to me.

Maggio turns to Vinnie. "Vincent. The photo."

Vinnie moves quickly across the room to a table on which a dozen or so framed photos are displayed. He selects one and brings it to Maggio who looks at it quietly for a few moments.

"I did not know the young lady who was shot. I am told she was a very nice, very warm person. I am sorry for her death." Then he hands me the photo.

I guess it to be at least twenty years old. Maggio is slimmer, his hair is still dark, his body in excellent shape. He is smiling proudly. Standing next to him is a young lady wearing the cap and gown of a newly graduated high school student. She is smiling and she is beautiful and there is no doubt at all, she is May Britton.

I look up from the photo into Maggio's eyes. I sense well hidden moisture. He is no longer smiling.

"Her name then was Angelina Maria Maggio. She had had two older brothers. They both had died. In Chicago. They were young. The circumstances are not important. Her mother is also dead. The cancer. When this picture was taken she was eighteen years old and she was all I had left. I had plans for her. Big plans. She will never have to want for anything. But she, too, had plans and they didn't include me. We had a terrible fight. We screamed at each other. We said things we really didn't mean but which we could never take back. She had money of her own inherited from her mother. She left the house and moved to New York where she met and married this Jewish man who was well connected to the theater crowd. She was not yet twenty. He was at least forty. You know who I am talking about, Mr. Bernardi. The director on the movie."

I look at him in disbelief. "Kingman Krug?"

"No, no. The other one. The assistant. Albert Kaplan." He reads my bewildered expression. "I see you did not know. They weren't married long. Less than a year. Long enough for her to use him to get ahead. In any case, she did well and worked steadily. Then came Hollywood. Motion pictures made her a star. She kept busy. She didn't write. I didn't write. Years went by. We were both stubborn. She made movies until no one wanted her any more. I did what I could to help out her career but then I did not have the influence. Only when I came here to Los Angeles from Chicago two years ago to work with the union did I have enough juice to make things better for her."

The light dawns. "You got her the part in the picture."

He shrugs. A slight smile.

"I always thought she got the part because DeSalle had this schoolboy crush on her."

He shakes his head. "That was Angelina talking, making stuff up to make herself feel good. DeSalle had no idea who she was. Earlier this year I knew that there was a good possibility of a union walkout. I made a pact with the man. Cast May Britton in the movie, Continental Studios stays in business even if there's a strike."

"And DeSalle jumped at it."

"The man is not a complete fool," Maggio said.

"Did he know she was your daughter?"

"He knew."

"And what about May? Did she know that you were behind her getting the part?"

"She knew nothing. In her mind she was and always would be a star. Her talent got her the part. Nothing else. And now you know, Mr. Bernardi, why I must learn who it was that savagely murdered my little girl."

"So that you can kill him?"

"That is not your concern. Be grateful that I believe you were not involved." He looks over at Baxendale. "Arthur, please be good enough to return Mr. Bernardi to the police."

Vinnie and the lawyer start in my direction. I put up my hands.

"Whoa. Now hold it just a second. You and I are on the same side, Mr. Maggio. I want this son of a bitch as badly as you do."

"I am on no one's 'side', Mr. Bernardi. I am capable of dealing with this on my own."

"Really? I don't think so," I say sharply. Here I go getting ballsy again. It gets his attention. "There are people I can talk to that you can't. There are people who will lie to you but will tell me the truth. Are you going to go chasing after Dave Clancy? Hell, you don't even know what he looks like. Like it or not, Mr. Maggio, you need me." He gives that a little thought, looking over at Baxendale who just shrugs. "Look, you've already put up my bail. I'm not going anywhere. At least give me a chance."

Maggio looks again at Baxendale.

"Arthur?"

"Your call, Sal," the lawyer says.

Vinnie pipes up. "If he screws with us, Mr. Maggio, you can leave him to me."

I look at Vinnie and force a smile. Vinnie doesn't smile back.

Maggio says to Vinnie "Take him where he wants to go. Get an address and a phone number."

"You won't regret this, Mr. Maggio," I say.

He looks at me, deadpan. "We'll see," he says.

CHAPTER TWELVE

A week ago Maggie Baumann was a happy smiling young lady in love with life and with her job at Continental Studios. I, myself, was not that happy but I had a steady job for the first time in a year and things could have been worse. Well, things got worse in a hurry.

It is Monday morning and I wake up in my bed in my apartment. The clock reads 8:24. Before long Mrs. Crimmins will hear me stirring about and come knocking on my door. Chances are she'll arrive bearing some kind of muffins which would be good since I know there is no food in the kitchen.

At first I had asked Vinnie to take me to Lydia's but on the way I got cold feet. With all that had happened, I decided I had better call first. When I did there was no answer. The time had been 10:45 in the evening and either she was out or she was sleeping very soundly. Thus the switch to my place. I called her again at midnight from my kitchen. Same result. Now I look over at the phone and wonder if it is too early to try again. I decide it's not. I call. The phone rings a dozen times. No one answers. I hang up.

While I am getting dressed I listen to the radio. I am still a major story although it appears that the press has yet to realize that I am out on bail. They fixate on my near brush with death as I tried to outrun the police, additional proof that I must indeed be guilty. The "B" story on most of the broadcasts involves a waitress who walked into her husband's used car dealership and shot him dead along with his secretary, his chief mechanic and some poor slob who had driven onto the lot to get his brakes looked at. This story shows every sign of supplanting me as the titillating scandal of the day.

I need to talk to Russ so I call the studio. Again the phone is answered by a deputy but since I am now legally a free man, albeit on a short leash, I leave my number and ask him to have Russ call the first chance he gets. According to the papers, "Jezebel in Blue Satin" has been shut down and there is no talk of reshooting with a new female lead. Buford DeSalle is apparently going to eat the two hundred thousand he's already laid out. I suspect that a good tax accountant will probably whittle that down to pocket change because that's the way things are done in the movie business.

But with the picture abandoned some of the people I am most interested in, like Krug and Brick Baxter and Al Kaplan---especially Al Kaplan---will be moving on to other projects and I don't want to lose sight of them. And while it is true that any one of them could have killed both Maggie and May, deep down I know that the key to getting myself cleared of the charges against me is to find Dave Clancy.

I pick up the photo which I had left on the nightstand when I turned in. The picture is eleven years old. Clancy is eleven years younger but it is the only thing I have to go on. An idea starts to form in my otherwise infertile, coffee-starved brain.

There is a knock on my door. I have a pretty good idea who it is. I open the door and sure enough, there is Mrs. Crimmins carrying a plateful of sliced banana bread. I welcome her in, grabbing a slice of the bread as she goes by. It tastes every bit as good as it smells.

"I thought I heard you come in last night, Joseph. I am so happy the police decided to let you go," she says with that shy little smile of hers. I do not disillusion her with talk of a million dollar bail bond.

"Mmm, good," I say, finishing the first slice and reaching for another.

"If you like I can fix you a proper breakfast," she says hopefully, planning to wheedle me into her apartment for more than just eggs and bacon.

"A lovely offer, Paula," I say, "but I have a full day ahead of me." I always call her Paula when I need something from her and what I need this morning is critical. She has a lumbering old Hudson sedan in the parking garage beneath the building. Since her husband died five years ago, she seldom uses it. I broach the subject of borrowing it just for the day. She doesn't hesitate for a moment.

"Why don't we go to my apartment so I can give you the keys?" she says and there's that smile again. I smile back and tell her it would be more helpful if she could get the keys and bring them here. She's disappointed but heads for my door which has been left open. She turns.

"Your plans for the day, Joseph. Will they be dangerous?"

"I don't think so," I reply. "Why do you ask?"

"I thought you might need the gun," she says and goes out.

The car is a 1937 Custom Eight and as I look it over it seems in very good condition. Because it hasn't been used much, it smells of must and it starts unwillingly but I manage to get it out onto the street. I check the gas gauge. It reads almost empty. At twenty-three cents a gallon, this 8 cylinder gas guzzler is going to break me but I have no choice. I fill the tank and drive to Arnie's Camera Shop a few blocks away.

Arnie is a good guy and I have used him several times when the studio's photographic facilities broke down. I show him the photo of Maggie and Clancy and tell him I need a hundred copies yesterday. He starts to explain that he will have to take a photo of the photo to get a new negative and...I interrupt him. I don't care how it gets done but I will be back after lunch to pick them up. And, oh, yes, bill the studio as usual.

Before I get back in the car, I duck into the local Bob's Big Boy and slip into the phone booth to call Russ. This time he answers the phone.

"Where the hell have you been?" I ask.

"Visiting my lawyer," he says.

"And why in hell would you need a lawyer?"

"It's a long story, Joe, but it basically comes down to some asshole process server sneaking onto the lot trying to corner Mr. DeSalle and when I found this dirtbag, I handled him in such a way that he will be very reluctant to sneak onto the lot again."

"In other words, you beat the crap out of him."

"As much as I could without killing him. My number one job is protecting Mr. DeSalle. I like working here, Joe, so whatever it takes---" He leaves the rest unsaid.

"Well, I can't believe they let me out on bail," I say after Russ tells me that I have been suspended without pay and am persona non grata on the Continental lot.

"Believe it, Joe. This is L.A. Judge Milo T. Faraday has price tags hanging all over his judicial robes. I'd say you cost Maggio at least ten bills. Maybe more."

"But the D.A.----"

"The D.A. has to argue cases in front of Faraday. He is not about to challenge him and besides, there are rumors—only rumors, mind you—that the Mayor has a piece of Faraday's action."

"I think I missed my calling."

'I think we both did. So, now that you are flitting about, free as a bird, what can I do for you?"

"Well, for starters, I need to know what's going on with Krug and Baxter and Al Kaplan."

"Okay. Krug's on the lot starting to prep the Alaska gold rush picture. He'll probably be hanging about for the next three months minimum. Brick Baxter is reported to be up for a series of quickie westerns at Republic."

I am puzzled. "Why would they do that? I heard Bill Boyd has finally shut down the Hopalong Cassidy series. No interest, no market."

"Maybe no market for a 52 year old hero. Guess Republic thinks Baxter might draw an audience. Besides I've heard that Herb Yates thinks there might be a future for these shorties on television."

"No way."

"Yates hasn't been wrong often, Joe. Maybe he's onto something. Now what's this about Al Kaplan? Are you serious?"

I tell Russ what I learned from Sal Maggio. He is as surprised as I was. He is equally surprised to learn of May Britton's parentage.

"That explains a lot," Russ says. "The woman couldn't act. She could barely say her own name. She had to be connected somehow but Sal Maggio? I guess May took after her mother. As for Kaplan, he's not going anywhere. They found him two nights ago on the back lot, passed out and smelling like a distillery. He's in County Hospital drying out. Poor bastard. He'd been on the wagon for over thirteen years."

"Doubtful he killed her," I say.

"Very," Russ replies, "but when it comes to love, people do strange things. Love and hate are often close to one another."

I agree and then tell him my plan for finding David Clancy. I can sense he doesn't like it much but he agrees to go along because he is a friend and he knows I am innocent and he knows that, bail or no bail, I am in deep, deep trouble. I arrange to pick him up outside the studio at precisely 2:30.

By now I am more than a little concerned about Lydia's whereabouts so when I hop into the car, I make a beeline for the real estate office where she works. Most of the employees sell. Lydia files. She also answers the phone, types up contracts and correspondence, and most important of all, keeps the coffee hot and perpetually available. She is the most organized person I know and the job suits her like a size 2 silk slip.

As soon as I walk in the door I know she is not there. A frazzled fifty year old who has never worn a size 2 in her life is trying to answer the phones and type letters and update the open house listings, all at the same time. I learn later that she is the realtor's wife dragged in for the day when Lydia becomes a no show.

"She took off yesterday afternoon. Had a hot out of town date with some guy. I think they were going to spend the night at the Hotel Coronado in San Diego. She swore she'd be back this morning but as you can see, she is not and I am ready to scream at the next person who calls me on that fucking telephone." The phone rings. She stares at it coldly, then lifts the receiver and after a few moments, lowers it onto the cradle. She turns to me with a smile. "Now is there any other way I can help you?"

Stubborn fellow that I am, when I leave the real estate office I go in search of another pay phone. I spot a booth a block ahead next to a fruit and vegetable stand. I reach in my pocket and verify that I'm carrying plenty of change. Several minutes later I am connected to the operator at the Hotel Coronado in San Diego.

"Lydia Bernardi," I say. "She's a guest."

Several moments go by. The operator says, "I'm sorry, sir, we have no guest by that name."

"Is it possible she checked out earlier today?" I ask.

"No, sir. We have no Lydia Bernardi either yesterday or today."

"What about Lydia Grozny?"

A moment's hesitation. "No, sorry."

"Okay. How about a Tyler Banks?" I ask.

Again there is a pause. Then she says, "Would you like me to connect you, sir?"

I slowly replace the receiver on the hook and exit the booth. I feel a great weight pressing on my chest and I am able to breathe only with difficulty. I look up into the sky. The clear blue of the morning has been supplanted by roiling gray stratae and nimbi. They match my mood perfectly. I buy an apple from the fruit stand and eat it in lieu of lunch. By the time I get back to the camera shop, Arnie has my photos ready. I ask him to separate them into two bags which he does.

I pull up at the studio's main gate at 2:30. Russ is waiting. He eyes the car suspiciously but gets in anyway. As we pull away, he says, "It smells like a cat died in the back seat."

"Wouldn't be surprised," I say. "Are we all set?"

"I'm expected. You're not."

I shrug. "We'll deal with it."

"No, amigo, you will deal with it. This is your party, not mine."

I look over at him. He looks me in the eye, then shakes his head as he turns away. His participation in my grand plan is grudging at best.

My favorite cop, Aaron Kleinschmidt, is sitting at his typewriter, hunting and pecking with two fingers. He doesn't notice us until we are right on top of him and when he looks up, his expression is as sour as an unripe lime.

"What the hell are you doing here?" he growls.

"He's with me," Russ says.

"Then you both can take a hike." He turns back to his typewriter.

"I'm here to give you the real killer of Margaret Baumann and probably May Britton as well," I say to him.

He looks up with a smile. "Gee, how nice," he says and turns once again to the report he is typing.

Russ pipes up. "You know, Sergeant, I could never tell if you were stubborn or just plain stupid and now I think it's a little bit of both."

He smiles again. "This coming from a studio rent-a-cop." He points to the doorway. "You've got about ten seconds to disappear."

I shake my head. "No wonder you almost got your ass fired. I can't even figure how you made sergeant unless it was by kissing somebody's ass." Russ looks at me as if he thinks I might have gone just a wee bit over the top but I'm not going to let his expression stop me. I'm on a roll. "If you handled the Black Dahlia the way you're handling this one, you're lucky you're not walking a beat in Watts."

Kleinschmidt gets up with fire in his eyes and belly bumps me. "Are you threatening me?' he says.

"No, I----"

"Because if you are threatening me, I have a legitimate reason to have your bail revoked."

"I am not threatening you," I say.

"Good. Then go."

"I'll go, Sergeant, but I'll tell you where I'm going if you don't sit down and listen to me. The Times and the Herald-Examiner have been hounding me for an interview and so far I have said no. But now I am going to meet with them and tell all about your clumsy attempt to frame me including your partner's ludicrous planting of the murder weapon in my toilet-----"

His eyes narrow.

"Oh, yes, I know all about that and a lot of other things including the fact that you are doing all of this on direct orders from the Chief of Police."

"That's a lie," he shouts, his face starting to turn crimson as he belly bumps me again.

"Well, maybe so," I say, trying not to give ground, "but it'll make a great story and the Chief will be floundering around for days trying to deny it and it won't take him long to realize that this shit storm coming down on his head was caused by you and by this time, you may be praying that he sends you to Watts where at least you won't lose your job or your pension. Now do you want to listen or do I leave? Your choice."

He is glaring at me. I glare back. I would welcome a chance to destroy the smug son of a bitch and he knows it. After a moment, he points to a nearby chair. "Sit down," he says. "You, too", he says to Russ and then he settles into his own chair and leans back. "Talk," he says, "and this had better be good."

I tell him all about Dave Clancy. How he followed me and how Russ and Dutch Magyar trapped him in the alley. (Russ nods in verfication.) How he said he'd just arrived in town that very day except that he probably arrived four days earlier. How he said he had come to write a story about the murder of Maggie Baumann so he could break out of the rut he was in at the paper. How he denied knowing Maggie personally. How he followed me to May's the night she was killed and then lied about it and how he could have gone back there and killed her after I threw him out of my apartment.

"Could have? All very interesting, Bernardi, but do you have any proof he did that?" Kleinschmidt asks.

"I'm not through. Clancy is an old boyfriend of Maggie Baumann." I reach in my pocket and hand him the original photo of him and Maggie. "That's Maggie eleven years ago. The guy is Clancy. Turn the picture over." Kleinschmidt does so. He reads the fading inscription. 1936. Dave and me. Happier times. He looks at me and hands the photo back.

"Proves nothing" he says.

I hand him the letter. Warily he unfolds it and starts to read, I think maybe I've now got his attention.

"And? I'm still looking for proof here," he says. He's softened. The belligerence has disappeared.

"You'll get your proof when you pick him up and question him because I know how you question people, Sergeant. You have your technique down pat."

"So you want what? An APB? Hell, you don't even know if the guy is still in town."

"He's in town, trust me. He's holed up somewhere but I can tell you what he's driving. A silver colored 1940 Lincoln Zephyr with Illinois plates. And as for identifying him---" I reach in my jacket pocket and take out one of the envelopes containing fifty copies of the original photo. I hand it to Kleinschmidt. "Just have your squad cars keep one of these taped to the visor.

Between his picture and the description of the car, you should catch up with him inside of 24 hours."

Kleinschmidt opens the envelope, peers in. He looks back at me and I can see the wheels turning. Then he puts the photos on his desk alongside the letter. He doesn't hand them back to me. This is a good sign. He looks over at Russ. "Next time you want a meeting with me, leave the trash at home."

Russ nods.

"Anything else?" Kleinschmidt asks. When we don't answer, he turns his attention back to his typewriter. Russ and I take that as a sign we are no longer needed and we leave.

I drop Russ back at the studio and again I thank him for helping me get in to see Kleinschmidt. Russ still isn't sure this is going anywhere but I'm better off than I was two hours ago.

I find a phone booth and call Vinnie and tell him I'm going to drop by. I have something for him. I can hear the sneer in his voice as he tells me that nobody just "drops by" Mr. Maggio's home. He says he will meet me at the main gate in thirty minutes. Thirty minutes later I drive up and Vinnie is leaning on the Packard, smoking a cigarette. I walk over to him and hand him the other envelope. I give him a version of what I told Kleinschmidt. You've got people out on the street, people you do business with. Give them a photo. Maybe one of them will spot Clancy. The more eyes out there looking, the better our chances of finding the guy.

"And Vinnie, if you find the guy, do me a favor and don't kill him. He's all I've got."

Vinnie nods and starts back to his car.

"Hey, Vinnie," I call after him. "I understand you were in the Pacific during the war, killing Japs."

He turns back to me, a grin on his face."Yeah, I was there.

I had a gun in my hand, not a pencil. I really liked my war, Bernardi. How was yours?"

"Pretty quiet," I say, "except for the day I shot up three Nazi machine gun nests and took 17 prisoners all by myself." I smile, pretty sure he'll get that I'm kidding.

He smiles back, a kind of warped humorless smile. "I didn't take prisoners," he says and I am pretty sure he is not kidding.

"Did you bring back any souvenirs, Vinnie? Battle flag, sword, anything like that?"

"Watches and rings. Anything made of gold. The rest of the stuff was for chumps," he says.

I nod. "Then I don't suppose you brought back an 8mm Nambu 14 pistol."

His eyes narrow momentarily. Then he waves at the gate guard and gets back in his car. I watch him disappear into the bowels of Bel Air as the gate slowly closes.

CHAPTER THIRTEEN

I turn into the driveway and down the ramp into the underground parking area where I return the Hudson to its designated spot. I switch off the ignition and put my head back, closing my eyes. It is still bright daylight out. I keep telling myself there are things I must do, places I must go, but I can't think of any. The fate of Dave Clancy is in the hands of Sergeant Kleinschmidt and Sal Maggio. I can only wait and hope. I consider looking for Krug or Brick Baxter to ask them---what? I am out of questions and at this moment, I am totally exhausted. I know I need sleep badly.

I open the car door and start up the ramp to the street level where I notice a strange car parked halfway down the block. It does not belong to any of the neighbors and there is a man behind the wheel who is not moving. I surmise the man is either a policeman or one of Sal Maggio's gunsels. Both have a vested interest in seeing that I do not leave the country, or even the city, for that matter. A third possibility is that it might be Dave Clancy but that would mean he'd gotten rid of the Zephyr and I can't see him doing that. I throw a friendly wave toward the parked car and mount the steps that lead to the apartment house entrance.

My little apartment is just as I left it in the morning including the plate on the dinette table displaying the last two slices of banana bread. I pick one up and start eating. My red apple lunch has worn off and my stomach is now growling in rebellion.

Knock, knock. I turn and look toward my door. I have no doubt who it is and I am in no mood to be mothered. On the other hand, I'm going to need her car again so I go to the door and open it, pasting on my sincerest smile. And there is Lydia, smiling back at me.

"Hi, Joe," she says, stepping inside and giving me an affectionate hug. I notice that Mrs. Crimmins has been standing just behind her.

"I found her in the hallway when I came back from shopping. Just sitting there, Joseph. Waiting for you. Well, I couldn't let her do that so I invited her in for tea."

"She was very kind, Joe," Lydia says, moving into my miniscule living room.

"You should never have let her divorce you, Joseph. You weren't thinking. She's a dear thing, she really is," Mrs. Crimmins says.

"And I'll bet she told you our whole life history together," I say, giving Lydia a look of mock annoyance.

"Oh, not everything. Not the private moments." She smiles and heads for the door. "Well, I'm going to leave you two alone. Now, Joseph, it's suppertime and I am very sure you have nothing in the kitchen to eat so I am fixing spaghetti and meat balls and I am going to make enough for all three of us." She raises her hand before I can speak. "No thanks are necessary. I'm delighted to do it." And out she goes leaving us alone.

Lydia smiles at me knowingly. "You have a devoted disciple," she says.

I know what she's getting at. "She's old enough to be my mother".

Lydia nods. "Often the older wines are the best."

"Oh, for God's sake," I mutter, shaking my head.

"Just kidding, Joe. I think she's a dear but I'm pretty sure that mothering you is not her number one objective."

I have to laugh. "Sometimes it gets a little dicey but so far, my honor is intact."

"I admire your will power. Many men would have succumbed at the first wink of an eyelash." Her gaze falls on the last remaining slice of banana bread. "Mmm. This looks good." She takes a bite. "Tastes good, too. Let me guess where it came from."

"No guess. You win," I say. "Look, Lyd, she really is a great old girl and if you're not in the mood for spaghetti, I can tell her---"

"But I love spaghetti," she says as she flops down on the sofa.

I clear my throat. "I'd offer you something to drink but---"

"I'm not thirsty. Sit down, Joe." She pats the other half of the sofa. When I hesitate, she says more seriously, "Please. We have to talk."

I sit. And suddenly my stomach is once again knotted up. She has just gone away for two days with a man that I despise but she obviously doesn't. I am terrified of what she is about to say.

"Yesterday morning, Tyler asked me to go with him to San Diego. To talk and to clear the air between us and, uh, I agreed because I felt there were a lot of things that needed to be said and a lot of issues that needed to be resolved."

I shake my head. "Lyd, I really don't want to hear this."

"Please, Joe. Just listen. He had booked a lavish suite at the Hotel Coronado. When we arrived around suppertime we found champagne waiting for us along with a beautiful array of flowers and a huge bowl of fruit. He wanted to take a dip in the ocean. I stayed in the room to relax in a hot tub."

My expression is blank. I give nothing away. I want to kill the bastard.

"He's back by six-thirty and right away, he wants to get me in bed," she continues. "I fight him and he backs off. He says he loves me, more than the stars in the heavens."

"Didn't Jo Stafford just record that for Decca?" Now, even more, I don't want to hear this. Maybe she'll get the hint and shut up.

She throws me a dirty look but she doesn't slow down.

"I said to him, if you love me so damned much, why don't you marry me? He looks at me with this terrible expression of disbelief that I would have the nerve to start talking marriage again. He looks me dead in the eye and he says something like, 'Baby I'd marry you in a flash but the business isn't there yet. I'm working fourteen hours a day just to keep the place going. Some weeks I can't even make payroll. I can't marry you under conditions like that. You deserve the best. You deserve to be treated like a queen and until I can do that, I won't let you take the risk."

She starts to laugh and then I see that tears are forming in her eyes and she chokes, out of breath and then the tears come in earnest. I move to her, cradle her in my arms, holding her as close as I can, trying to end the sobs that are wracking her body. I keep murmuring how sorry I am.

"He's married, Joe. The son of a bitch is married," she gasps.

I freeze. No words rise to my lips.

Lydia looks up at me. Her mascara has run down her cheeks. Her eyes are red. Her nose has started to run and her lipstick is smeared. She is a mess.

"He told you that?" I finally manage to say.

"Of course not," she says. "He's been stringing me along for months. Why would he stop now? He knows a good thing when he's got it." She bites her lower lip and gets up from the sofa and moves to the window that looks out onto the street below. "He's not stupid. He didn't even tell his office girl where he was going. The only person who knew was a kid actor named Farley Granger that John Houseman wants for a movie he's prepping with RKO. His wife knew about Farley so when the office was no help, she called Farley and he gave her the number of the hotel. She called while I was in the tub. After I got dressed I checked messages. She has a nice voice," Lydia says quietly. "No doubt she's a very nice lady."

I get up from the sofa and move to the window and fold her into my arms. She nestles close to me and I can feel her heart beating against my chest. The tears have stopped. She is quiet, very quiet, as she says, "I'm such a fool, Joe."

I tell her no. Men like Tyler Banks prey on women. She wasn't the first. She won't be the last. I tell her it's better to love and be hurt than to curl up into a shell and trust no one. With Banks and others like him, it's a sickness. They're searching for something to fill an emptiness within themselves which they never will be able to do. They are half men, half boys. In many ways they are to be pitied. I almost laugh at myself. Here I am, dispensing advice to the lovelorn like Mary Worth.

There is knock on the door. Mrs. Crimmons' timing couldn't be worse but I go to answer it because if I don't she will just keep knocking. She is holding a large bowl of spaghetti and meatballs in red sauce. She is smiling, then stops as she looks at my face and past me to Lydia. The smile fades.

"I think maybe it would be better if you two ate by

yourselves," she says. "I'm sure you have a lot of catching up to do." She thrusts the bowl of spaghetti into my hands and hurries back into her apartment without a backward glance. I kick the door shut and put the bowl on my dinette table. I'm aware that Lydia has come up behind me and as I turn, I find her in my arms and her lips searching hungrily for mine. I slip my arms around her and hold her close. My hand slips down to feel the soft roundness of her buttocks and I can feel her gasp. Her hands are suddenly tearing at the back of my shirt, trying to free it from my trousers. Impulsively I scoop her up in my arms even as her lips stay locked on mine and her tongue searches through my mouth. I lay her down on the bed and start to yank at the buttons of her blouse while she tugs at my belt. She whips it through the loops and then struggles to unzip my fly. I toss her blouse to one side and yank her skirt down past her knees. She is wearing white cotton panties and my hand slips inside of them to feel her wetness. I hear her moan and then her hand is inside my trousers and I fight to contain myself. I tear off her panties and pull down my pants. She spreads wide and I just manage to enter her before I explode in spasms of passion. She is right with me, gasping and clawing at my back. Our tongues intertwine. I drink her in and then we are laying there together, half dressed and totally spent. Sleep claims us both.

An hour later we awaken. This time it is different. It is quiet and calm and the moments are long and satisfying. In the early hours of the morning we awaken again and again, we do everything we can to satisfy each other. As I look into her eyes, my heart is full. I lost her once. I will not lose her again.

CHAPTER FOURTEEN

When I awake, she is gone. She has left me a note. It is short and sweet and professes undying love. I find this encouraging. She will call me later and we will make plans for the evening. A Ronald Reagan movie is now playing down the street but I am in no mood for Reagan, especially if he is going to mangle John Van Druten's "Voice of the Turtle". A swell western with Charles Starrett is playing a few blocks away but I think if it comes to a vote, we'll be dealing with the turtle.

The clock reads 8:33 and I think about staying in bed for the entire day. I have no job. I am not needed by either the cops or Sal Maggio who may or may not be looking for Dave Clancy. I am, however, ravenously hungry since Lydia and I were too busy pursuing alternative avenues of pleasure to eat Mrs. Crimmins' sumptuous dinner.

I shave, shower and dress with the thought of ambling down to The Egg and I, a breakfast and brunch diner that serves up only omelets of all descriptions. It's always crowded, especially at this hour but Phil, the owner, can always find a table for me, even when there's a wait. In return for this hospitality, I supply Phil with autographed photos from some of Continental's "stars" which he proudly plasters all over his walls. How having a photo of Helmut Dantine hanging over the coffee maker helps business I will never know, but Phil is always delighted with each new glossy.

I glance into the bowl of spaghetti and notice that some of it has been spooned out. Then I discover a small pot on the range which holds remnants of tomato sauce and I realize that Lydia has breakfasted on last night's dinner. I stick a finger into the sauce and taste it. Mmm. Excellent. I spoon some into the pot and put the flame on low. Phil's omelet will have to wait for another day.

I am just finishing up when the phone rings. I answer it.

"Mr. Bernardi?" a man's voice says.

"Yes."

"This is Elmer Corcoran. Agatha asked me to call you."

My mind is a blank. Who is this guy?

"Agatha Gates," he says. "The principal at White River High School."

"Oh, yes," I say, the light having belatedly dawned. "About David Clancy."

"Yes," Corcoran says. "I'm very sorry, Mr Bernardi, but I have no recollection of the young man. I went back over several of the yearbooks from that time, mid to late thirties, and there's no record of him."

"Well, I was pretty sure that was the case but I had to be sure. Thanks for getting back to me, Mr. Corcoran."

"Not a problem, sir," he says.

Almost as an afterthought, I ask him, "By the way, do you remember a Maggie Baumann?"

There is a pause as I hear him muttering to himself. "Maggie Baumann. Maggie Baumann. No, I---Oh, wait. Yes. You mean Margaret Baumann. Yes, I do remember her. I had her my first year teaching at the school. Advanced Biology, I believe. I had her for most of the year."

"Most of the year?" I ask curiously.

"Yes, she dropped out shortly after second semester began."

"Do you know why?"

There is a long silence before he says, "May I ask why you wish to know that, Mr. Bernardi?"

I explain to him who I am and how I fit into the inquiry into her death. He recalls now that he had read about the studio murder but didn't realize that Maggie was the victim.

"She was a very sweet girl. I'm sorry she came to such a terrible end," Corcoran says. "I can tell you what the rumors were, Mr. Bernardi, but they were just rumors. I have no first hand knowledge."

"I understand."

"It was said that she was pregnant. She couldn't have been more than sixteen. A horrible predicament to be in. She was absent for several days in a row and when her parents were contacted, they said she had moved out of state to live with an aunt somewhere in the south."

"Nothing more specific than that?"

"I'm afraid not. I wish I could be more help. I liked her. I really did. So did most everyone else."

We chat for a minute or two more and then I hang up. I am starting to get a really sharp picture of who Maggie was and where she had come from. I think about a young girl named Penny who puts her grandmother on the phone instead of her mother. There are days when I think life is really crappy and this is one of them.

There is a knock at the door. I assume it's Mrs. Crimmins about the car but when I open up, I find a uniformed cop standing there.

"Mr. Bernardi?"

"That's right."

"Would you please come with me, sir?" he says.

"What for?"

"Sergeant Kleinschmidt wants to see you."

"Look, officer, I'm out on bail---"

"I'm just following orders, sir. Don't let's make this difficult."
I check him out. He's wearing a gun. I'm not. I decide to go
with him.

We've been in his patrol car less than five minutes when I
realize he is not headed toward police headquarters.

"Are you lost, Officer?" I say.

"No, sir," he replies.

I point off to my right. "The division station is that way."

"Yes, sir," he says. "We're going to the hospital."

I'm surprised. I try to pump him. He just keeps focusing
straight ahead. He hands me several variations on 'Sergeant
Kleinschmidt will fill you in.' I fall silent.

L.A. County General is located in the Boyle Heights District
of Los Angeles and the huge art deco style building is almost
sixty years old. It boasts 600 beds and hires a lot of doctors and
nurses. This is where people come when they have no money
and the emergency ward is busy around the clock with everything from runny noses to multiple gunshot wounds.

I find Kleinschmidt standing by the admitting desk just inside
the emergency entrance. Beyond him I can see two doctors and
a nurse working on a patient whose face I cannot see. I walk up
to him but before I can ask a question, he says to me, "Show me
your hands." He doesn't wait for a response. He grabs my wrists
and yanks them toward him. He looks my hands over carefully,
front and back. He looks up at me. "Where were you last night?
After midnight," he says.

"What? Your guy in the unmarked didn't tell you?"

He seems puzzled.

"What are you talking about?"

"Your birddog in the black sedan parked across the street. You're telling me he wasn't yours?"

"I don't know what you're talking about."

"Must have been a bill collector then," I say. "But for your information I was in all night and I can prove it if you promise not to give the press the lady's name." I look past his shoulder again. One of the doctors is approaching.

"What's going on, Sarge?" I ask.

"Brick Baxter. Early this morning somebody mistook his head for one of Joe Louis's light speed bags."

The doctor taps Kleinschmidt on the shoulder. "He's awake now, Sergeant. You can talk to him."

Kleinschmidt heads inside and I follow right behind. If he notices he doesn't say anything.

The doctor says, "Don't take long. We've given him morphine for the pain. He won't be concious long."

I can see why they've given him morphine. Brick looks as if he got into a fight with an angry cougar who hated his last movie. There are cuts on his face and two have been stitched. There is blood everywhere. One of his eyes is completely closed and his nose is unnaturally canting to the left. Through puffy lips he is trying to drink water through a straw and making a bad job of it.

"Mr. Baxter, you remember me? Sergeant Kleinschmidt?"

Brick looks up at him and nods.

"Can you talk?"

"Dunno. I can try." It comes out sounding like 'icon fry'.

"Who did this to you?"

Brick shakes his head.

"You don't know or you didn't see him?" Kleinschmidt asks.

Brick struggles to be understood. "Hit me from behind. Something hard. Rock. Piece of wood. I fell. When I look up he's coming after me. Dark glasses. Hat pulled down. Didn't recognize him."

"Would you know him if you saw him again?"

"Maybe. I don't know," Brick says.

Kleinschmidt reaches in his jacket pocket and takes out the photograph. He holds it close to Brick's face so he can see it clearly. "This guy?"

Brick stares at it hard, his face screwed up in concentration.

"Maybe. I didn't get a good look. He kept punching at me. I'm on my back. I can't fight back. He won't stop. I say 'Take my money'. He says 'I don't want your money'. Why'd he have to keep hitting me like that?"

His words are slurring badly now and his good eye is starting to glaze over. The doctor taps Kleinschmidt on the shoulder and shakes his head. Kleinschmidt nods. We move back into the waiting room.

Kleinschmidt is pensive. He looks at me. "It happened outside Baxter's duplex about six o'clock this morning. It was still dark. He was going to drive to Las Vegas to spend a couple of days at that casino Bugsy Seigel just built. Apparently the guy who jumped him came out of nowhere."

"You think maybe Dave Clancy," I say.

"The milkman drove up just then and scared the guy away. Otherwise Baxter might be dead by now. The milkman says the guy ran to his car halfway down the block. He says he doesn't know much about cars but it was a silvery color, a small two-door. Yeah, I think maybe Dave Clancy." He frowns. "But why?"

"Clancy came after me pretty hard before I booted him. As much as accused me of getting Maggie Baumann pregnant. I showed him how it couldn't have been me. So maybe Brick Baxter was next on his hit list."

"It fits," Kleinschmidt says. "Old boyfriend still carrying a torch. Comes to the city pissed out of his mind, ready to take out the son of a bitch that killed her."

"Which would mean that Clancy didn't kill her."

"I might be leaning that way."

"Does that mean I'm back on the hot seat?" I ask.

Kleinschmidt shrugs and then tosses me the faintest of smiles. "I'll let you know," he says. "You need a ride back?"

"I'll grab a cab," I say.

"Suit yourself," he says and he leaves with his entourage. I make sure he's gone and then I go in search of the drunk tank.

I find Al Kaplan sitting on the end of his bed smoking a cigarette. He's sporting a three day growth of pepper and salt beard, his hair is a tousled mess and his eyes are lifeless. He doesn't even see me approach.

"Al?"

He looks up at me and a wan smile crosses his lips.

"Hey, it's the king of the bullshit. How ya doin', Joe?"

"Hangin' in, Al," I say. Al was always amused at what I went through to get ink for my pictures. "How are they treating you?"

"Okay," he says. "Three squares a day. That's good. No booze, that's bad. An hour with some pointy-headed psychiatrist. That's even worse."

"When are they letting you go?" I ask.

He shrugs. "Maybe today. Maybe tomorrow. Who cares?" He tosses his butt on the floor and squashes it out. He taps another cigarette from his pack and lights up. "You want to sit down?"

"Let's take a walk," I say.

"Sure."

He gets up and secures the ratty bathrobe they've given him. He's wearing paper slippers and he has to shuffle to keep them on his feet. We wander down the corridor toward a sitting area that features a sofa and a couple of overstuffed chairs. It's supposed to be for visitors and since I'm a visitor we sit.

"What happened, Al?" I ask.

For a moment I'm not sure he heard the question. He's staring off into space, unfocused. "She shouldn't have died. Not like that. Who would do a thing like that?" he asks.

"You two went back a long way," I say. "Broadway. 1929." Al looks at me sharply. "Beautiful young girl, you help her out, get her a part in a show. She marries you. It doesn't last long. She becomes a star and leaves you behind. Is that about it?"

"Where'd you get all that?" he asks.

"Her father."

Al nods with a knowing smile. "The loving, all-powerful Salvatore Maggio." Al grinds out this cigarette and lights a third. "She hated the son of a bitch, you know."

"I figured that."

"He offered me twenty-five thousand bucks to divorce her. I told him where he could shove his money. I suppose he could have killed me but he didn't. Six weeks later, May decided to divorce me. I always wondered if twenty five thousand dollars was involved in her decision."

I sense that Al is getting ready to open up. I keep my mouth shut.

"Even after the divorce I stayed with her. Damned fool, that was me, but I couldn't help myself. Two more shows and I worked on both of them. Props. Stagehand. Crappy jobs just to stay close and then when she went off to Hollywood, I stayed right with her. If she resented it, she never let on. I think she kind of liked having me around. Gave her a kind of validation she never got from her old man. That's what I was, you know. A substitute father. I didn't mind. Whatever kept her close, that was okay with me."

"And all those years here in Hollywood, you never got together?"

"Almost did. Thirty-seven it was. She was doing some real garbage films. That nomination had kept her career alive for years but she was coming to the end and she knew it. She let me move in with her because by that time I was making a decent living as a director. Mostly two-reelers. You know, filler stuff. But it paid good and it was steady and I think maybe May saw a chance to use me again. You know, I get a big break, I bring her along. So we're living together in this little house in West Hollywood. She's drinking a lot because things aren't going well but I try to overlook it. Then I find out she's seeing this guy on the side. A third rate producer who's promising her the world except he's full of crap and one night I lose it and we start screaming at each other. She's really drunk and the drunker she gets the meaner she gets and all of a sudden she reaches into a drawer and takes out a pistol which I didn't know was there and she shoots me!"

I react to this.

"That's right. She shoots me. Catches me right here." He touches a part of his shoulder. "Still got the scar where the bullet went in. So I run from the house, I run and I run because I think she may be coming after me and then when I finally get back to the house a couple of hours later, she's gone. Clothes, jewelry, everything. Even the gun. It's a year before I talk to her again.

By this time she's married and divorced that bum of a producer. I see her in the street and I walk up to her and I apologize for what happened. So what does she do? She takes my face in her hands and she kisses me and says how sorry she is." He shakes his head sadly. "Unbelievable, right? I'm fifty years old and I can't get her out of my system. Pathetic."

He stares down at the floor. He is a beaten man. May Britton was the centerpiece of his existence and now she is gone and it's my feeling that Al Kaplan no longer knows who he is or why he sticks around.

"I have a question, Al. May wanted that part in Krug's new picture. Maggie was in the way. Do you think Maggio had her killed?"

Al looks at me and he ponders the question. Slowly he shakes his head. "No, I don't think so. Killing isn't Sal's style. He could have killed me easily and didn't. He finds other ways to solve problems."

"Could he have ordered Vinnie to do it?"

"He wouldn't have done that. Same reason."

"And if May had asked Vinnie to kill her?"

"No, again. Vinnie takes orders from Maggio and nobody else. His job was to look out for her, not to kill for her."

"What's the other possibility?" I ask.

"I don't want to think about that," Al replies.

"What am I missing, Al?" He looks at me curiously. "Something's missing. What are you hiding?"

"Nothing," he says.

"Bullshit," I say.

"Come on, Joe," he says wearily. "She was a wonderful lady. Why suddenly go out of your way to besmirch her name?"

"And how would I be doing that?" I ask. I am now positive there is something hidden. Something I need to know.

His eyes flare angrily and he stands up. I think he wants to take a swing at me. But then the moment passes. He puts out his hand and we shake. "Nice seeing you, Joe. Keep in touch. When I get out of here, I'll buy you a beer."

I shake my head. "When you get out of here, Al, the last thing you're going to need is a beer."

He laughs and gives me a little salute and shuffles off toward the ward, lighting another cigarette as he goes and trying to keep those damned slippers on.

CHAPTER FIFTEEN

I take a cab home and when I get to the apartment house, I find Russ Parmalee waiting for me at curbside, leaning up against his studio cruiser. He gives me a little flick of a salute as he puts away the small note pad he's been studying.

"Why do I have the feelng you are bad news?" I say, only half joking.

"What's your religion, Joe? Are you a practising pessimist?"

"Raving realist," I respond.

"Well, I may actually be here with good news. Or possibly good news. Do you know Tony Chung?"

"Never heard of him."

"He's an assistant art director. Kinda bald, kinda chubby. Got his break here about three years ago when they kept drafting everybody else into the army. A few months ago he got engaged and started spending a lot of money. Engagement ring, parties, dates, new clothes, down payment on a house. All money he didn't have which he borrowed from Guido the Grubber."

"Uh, oh," I say because everybody knows who Guido is.

"Obviously Tony had no concept of things like vigorish and weekly payments at 15% a week interest. So it didn't take long for Tony to be in deep, deep swampland with not only Guido but the people behind Guido."

"Which might include Sal Maggio," I venture.

"Which, in fact, does include Mr. Maggio because when the number gets up to about fourteen thousand dollars, Tony gets a visit from Vinnie DellaFerragio."

"Our Vinnie?"

"The very same. Our Vinnie makes all kinds of threats against Tony's persona and to prove that he is a serious man, he pulls out a gun and presses the barrel against Tony's forehead. Now this is where is gets interesting. A few months back Tony was working on that stupid Franchot Tone Burma war movie and even though he wasn't working props, he kept track of everything to do with the film. He's positive that the gun Vinnie was pointing at him was an 8mm Nambu Model 14."

I perk up. "Aha."

"Aha is right."

Just then the radio in the cruiser squawks and the deputy's voice comes in loud and clear. Sergeant Kleinschmidt needs him right away at the corner of Crenshaw and Washington. Something about a Lincoln Zephyr.

"We'll continue this later," Russ says as we both pile into the cruiser and take off.

At Crenshaw and Washington we both spot Kleinschmidt's car immediately. Black, obvious and ugly. Kleinschmidt is a few yards away, leaning against a building pretending to read a newspaper. He is bright enough not to be holding it upside down. The Lincoln Zephyr is parked at midblock. It is a street that boasts a couple of dozen stores. Good police procedure dictates that you do not go searching and risk alerting your quarry. You wait for his return.

Russ's eyes scan the area. He nods appreciatively. "They've really got it covered." He starts pointing subtly. "Johansson's got the hood up on that Merc and pretending to fix the engine. Nurse with a baby carriage up near the corner. Tall guy sitting on the end of the bus bench. Guy in shirt sleeves standing in the doorway of the State Farm office. Could be more out of sight."

Kleinschmidt leaves his post at the wall and walks over to us and starts talking out of the side of his mouth. "A black and white spotted the Lincoln about thirty minutes ago. We don't figure the car's abandoned. What we need you for, Parmalee---" He looks at me. "You, too, Bernardi. We got an old picture. You guys know what he looks like now. Chances are he'll go straight for the car but if he thinks something's wrong, he may try to walk away. That's where you come in."

"If he's here, we'll spot him," Russ says.

Kleinschmidt looks over at me. "I hear you've been hanging around with the wrong kind of people."

"Oh? Who would that be?" I ask.

"Sal Maggio."

I nod. "Yeah, he asked me over for dinner."

"Did you bring your taster?" Kleinschmidt asks.

"I tried to find one but all the cops I knew had already eaten."

"Ha ha," Kleinschmidt says mirthlessly.

Russ tugs at his shirt. "Sarge." Kleinschmidt looks. "Third building from the end. Just coming out of the doorway."

I look. It's Clancy all right. His arm is in a sllng and his right hand is heavily bandaged. I look up and see that the second floor houses a doctor's office. Oblivious, Clancy moves down the sidewalk to his car. His jacket is hanging loosely over his shoulders and as he walks, it slips off. He bends down to pick it up and as he raises his head, his eyes suddenly meet mine. At a hundred yards away, he recognizes me instantly. He freezes for just a second and then turns and starts to casually cross the street away from his car.

"We're blown!" I growl. "He spotted me."

Kleinschmidt dashes out into the street, blowing his whistle and pointing frantically toward Clancy who is quickly picking up the pace. Johansson dashes toward the opposite sidewalk to cut him off while the nurse pushes the baby carriage into his path. I assume the carriage is babyless. Another cop appears out of nowhere and throws a flying body block at Clancy who goes down in a heap. He tries to get up but now three of them are all over him. A handcuff is slapped onto his left wrist by a burly cop who clicks the other half onto his own wrist. Dave Clancy won't be going anywhere soon. As I approach he looks at me with a pleading expression and then he looks away.

I peer in through the large one-way picture window. We have driven to headquarters and now Clancy is sitting at a bare wooden table in the middle of an otherwise barren green-walled interrogation room. His good hand is raw and bloodied and apparently the other has a couple of broken bones. His shoulder has been sprained. His ankles are shackled and the sturdy chain has been drawn through a U-Bolt fastened to the floor. The chair is bolted down. So is the table. Clancy is immobile and it's obvious he is in great discomfort.

Russ and Johansson and I watch as Kleinschmidt enters the room and slams some paper work onto the table. He shows every sign of a man with violent propensities whose patience is at an end. There is a wire recorder in the middle of the table but Kleinschmidt doesn't turn it on. He starts asking questions. When Clancy doesn't answer him, Kleinschmidt moves in behind him and slaps him hard three times about the head.

Still Clancy stays mute. Kleinschmidt says they have him dead bang for felonious assault, maybe even attempted murder. The question is, what else is involved. Still Clancy will not speak. Kleinschmidt grabs him around the neck, choking him. I squirm uncomfortably. Even I didn't get this kind of treatment. I look to my right. Both Russ and Johansson are watching impassively. Neither is surprised or offended by what they are watching. Finally Kleinschmidt lets go.

Clancy gasps for air. "I want to speak to Joe," he says, almost a whisper.

Kleinschmidt slaps him across the face. "You'll talk to me, asshole."

"Fuck you," Clancy says.

Kleinschmidt hits him again and then again. Clancy glares up at him. Kleinschmidt raises his hand again, then stops himself.

"You want to talk to Bernardi? What for?"

"That's my business."

"Sure. You want to talk to Bernardi? Go ahead. But I'll be listening," Kleinschmidt tells him.

"I don't care what you do," Clancy replies.

Kleinschmidt goes out and in a few seconds he's coming in the door to the observation room. He looks at me. "You heard him."

I protest. "I'm not a cop."

Kleinschmidt nods. "That's the good news. Look, he wants to talk to you so go in there and let him talk. That's not a request." He looks at me hard.

I ponder it. "Sure. Why not? At least I won't be trying to beat his brains out." I move to the door.

"The wire recorder on the table," Kleinschmidt says. "When you go in, turn it on. Whatever he says I want a copy of it."

I nod and go out.

When I enter the room Clancy looks relieved. I switch on the recorder and pull the interrogator's chair up close to him.

"Okay. I'm here," I say.

"Joe, I'm sorry," he says.

"For what?"

"I put you through a lot. I thought maybe you were one of the bad guys. I was wrong. So I'm sorry."

"Okay. You're sorry. Now how about telling me what the hell is going on."

"I didn't kill Maggie.".

"Yeah, I figure that. But you come riding into town like some avenging angel ready to kill whoever murdered your old girlfriend and you almost succeed with Baxter. Lucky for you that milkman came along."

He gives me a genuinely puzzled look. "What do you mean, old girlfriend?"

"Don't bullshit me, Dave. I've checked you out."

He shakes head. "You're wrong, Joe. She wasn't a girlfriend, she was my sister."

I look at him incredulously and glance toward the mirror which masks the viewing window. I look back at Dave.

"That's right. My kid sister," he says. "I left home in '38 to attend Columbia. I had a free ride. The works. One thing I never was was dumb. The next year Maggie got herself in trouble. The folks put her into one of those homes for wayward girls. Not a home, she told me later. More like a prison. After the baby was born, Maggie left. Packed up her stuff and walked out the front door and never looked back. My folks brought the baby back to White River.

"So you were in contact with her," I say.

"Off and on over the years."

"So where did Dave Clancy come from?"

He shrugs."I was still in school when the war broke out. I was going to graduate in a year and I knew I was 4-F. Bad eyes and a busted eardrum. Had it most of my life. Anyway, I was already getting looks because of my name. Herr Baumann, they'd call me. I figured I'd have a better chance of getting work if they called me something else so I changed my name to Clancy. I was right. Nobody had a problem hiring a bright young Irish kid who was 4-F and not about to get drafted. I bounced around from paper to paper until I ended up at the Sun-Times in late '45."

"And then you wind up here in Los Angeles. What did she do, call you?"

Clancy nods. "About two weeks ago. She sounded bad. I knew she was scared and she admitted it. She said she had a chance to become a movie star but now she wasn't sure she wanted it. She was all confused. She said she was in trouble and could I come. I said I would but when I asked her what kind of trouble, she wouldn't answer. She'd tell me all about it when I arrived."

"Which was when?"

"The night she was killed. She'd given me her address. An apartment in the Pacific Palisades just off Sunset Boulevard. I sat outside her building waiting for her. It was long past midnight when I guess I fell asleep. When I woke up the sun was shining. I figured maybe I missed her so I went around back to her unit. It was pretty classy. Overlooked the Riviera Country Club. All of a sudden I'm a little uneasy, asking myself how she can afford a place like this. Anyway I knock on her door several times. No answer. So I went for breakfast. That's when I bought the paper and read about her murder."

"Dave, I did the math. So did the cops. We know when you left Chicago. You should have been here days before she was killed."

He nods. "And I would have been," he says, "but I broke an axle in a little town in Colorado and I was stuck there for three days while they waited for a new one to be delivered. The receipt is in the glove compartment."

"Okay. So, about Brick Baxter," I ask him

"She'd told me she'd been seeing him," he replies.

"I know. I've seen the letter you wrote her."

"When the news broke that she'd been pregnant, I thought it might have been him. I also thought it might have been you the way the papers were playing the story. But then you showed me how it wasn't you and I knew it was Brick."

"So, would you have killed him?" I ask.

"I wanted to. The son of bitch gets her pregnant and then kills her to cover it up. Yeah, I would have killed him. Gladly."

"You don't know that he killed her, Dave," I say.

"No?" he says angrily. "Then who else?"

I shrug. "You said yourself you went around back to her unit. Anybody see you? Anybody try to stop you?"

"No."

"That's my point. Anybody could have been seeing her. Anybody could have been paying her rent. It didn't have to be Baxter."

He glowers at me. "You're saying she was a slut."

"No, just a confused young kid trying to make her way."

Clancy's eyes start to tear up. "She was a sweet kid. She never hurt anybody. I should have killed him. I'm going down anyway. What's the difference?"

"Assault and murder are two different charges," I remind him.

He nods. "I guess." He looks at me shaking his head sadly. "You were a good friend to her, Joe. I'm sorry I put you through all this."

"And you were a good brother, Dave," I say and reach over and give his good arm an encouraging squeeze.

I feel sorry for Dave. For a smart guy he has done a very dumb thing and unless he is very, very lucky he's looking at five years minimum, maybe more, in Folsom State Prison. I think about sibling ties and wonder at the strength of them. My siblings were strangers, wards of the state. When I walked away I forgot them completely so maybe the adage is true. About the thickness of blood.

Russ is driving me back to the apartment house and he, too, feels a bit of compassion for Dave Clancy which is unusual for a hard nut realist like Russ. I wonder if maybe he has a sister but when it gets to personal things, Russ reveals next to nothing. He has let his guard down only once with me. He is worried about his future. We have all heard the rumors that the studio is in financial trouble and that it may be sold. Russ worries that he will not keep his job or be able to catch on elsewhere, given his checkered past in the Navy. His relationship with Buford DeSalle is close and some people have said it is because Russ tried to help "persuade" the previous owner to sell the studio. Maybe true, maybe not. But at the moment, Russ is displaying a frightening disregard for law and order as we discuss Vinnie the Muscle.

"I don't think there's any doubt the son of bitch killed her," Russ says. "Probably on orders from Maggio. Anything for his little girl."

"You may be right but the cops will have a hard time proving it."

"Maybe not so hard if we work things right." He looks at me for a second with a wide grin on his face. "Remember how those two cops tried to frame you by planting the gun in your apartment?"

"Oh, come on, Russ," I say, knowing what he's hinting at.

"Hey, it's not like we'd be framing an innocent guy, just making sure that justice is served. We stick the gun where the cops can't miss it and make the phone call. The rest takes care of itself."

"Are we sure it wasn't Brick? I mean, maybe he got a hold of the gun somehow and---"

"It wasn't Baxter. Kleinschmidt checked in with the doctor right after putting Clancy into a cell. You'll never guess, buddy. A couple of years ago, Baxter had a procedure called a vasectomy. A lot of states use it to semi-sterilize repeat sex offenders and other kinds of degenerates. Baxter couldn't have knocked up Maggie Baumann if he'd wanted to and if that's so, he's got zero motive. No, no. Vinnie's our guy. No question."

We pull up to my apartment house. Reluctantly I agree to get the gun and then we will decide how best to use it. I am still a little squeamish but I see Russ's point. The last thing I want is for Maggie's killer to go free.

I am outside my apartment door when I hear the phone. I hurry inside and get it on fifth ring. It's Lydia.

"Joe, I'm glad I caught you."

"Catch me any time, Lyd. I don't mind," I smile.

"Yeah, last night was great, wasn't it? God, how I've missed you, Joe."

"It's mutual."

"Look, about tonight. No can do. The slave driver's talking merger with another realtor and we're going to be working at least to midnight getting the books in order. Can we push off until tomorrow?"

"No problem," I say. "I'll call you."

"No, let me call you," she says. "Love you, Joe."

She hangs up. Okay, so I'm at loose ends for the evening. Maybe I'll take in that Charlie Starrett western or maybe stay home and listen to Amos 'n' Andy. Either sounds good. I might even catch upon my sleep.

But first I have to go across the hall and see Mrs. Crimmins about her chafing dish.

CHAPTER SIXTEEN

Vinnie the Muscle has a small apartment on the top floor of a building on Vermont Avenue. The building is owned by Sal Maggio and Vinnie stays there free. However, most of the time he resides at the mansion in Bel Air. Security is high on Maggio's list of requirements and Vinnie is high on Maggio's roster of mugs so Vinnie doesn't get a lot of time off. When he does he usually has a lady friend visit him at his Vermont address. Sometimes even two lady friends. Vinnie is a man of voracious appetites.

It is Wednesday shortly after noon hour. Russ and I are in my Studebaker which Russ has helped me pick up from its parking spot at Union Station. We are sitting outside the apartment and Russ is wearing the uniform of a Southern California Telephone Company serviceman which he borrowed from studio wardrobe. In his lap is a SoCalTelCo tool box. Beneath all the tools, still wrapped in sealskin, is the 8mm Nambu Model 14.

"If the door lock's not tough and I don't run into any hangups, this won't take more than fifteen minutes," he says. "Remember, any sign of Vince or someone who might be one of his buddies, lean on the horn three times."

"Got it."

He opens the passenger door and slips out, then walks quickly toward the apartment house entrance. He strides like a man who knows what he is doing and I pray that he does. In his pocket is a lockpick set which he claims to be very adroit at using. I am once again fascinated by the similarity between law officers and criminals. Both players in the same arena and often playing by the same rules. Two sides of the same coin and I think, if the coin gets old enough and the images get worn down, who is to say which side is which?

My eyes scan my surroundings. It's a downscale neighborhood, not yet shabby but definitely headed in that direction. There are not a lot of cars parked on the street and those that are seem to be relics from the early thirties. Across the street an organ grinder is shuffling listlessly along with his monkey perched on his shoulder. Few people pay him any mind. They've seen him before. You'd think he'd wait until the local kids were out of school but then kids don't have pennies to put in the monkey's cap. I think maybe this is an occupation that doesn't have much of a future.

True to his word, Russ is now emerging from the building. He sees no need to rush. When he hops in the car, he smiles. "Just for the hell of it, I stuck it in the toilet tank. Kleinschmidt ought to get a kick out of that."

I shake my head. Russ is a guy who loves to live on the edge.

We drive a few blocks and pull over to a phone booth. I have the honor of making the call. I ask for Kleinschmidt but I get Johansson instead. No matter. I muffle my voice and give him the address and the apartment number. Just a patriotic citizen doing my duty. I hang up and since I have the time, I call Lydia at her office. She answers brightly.

"It's me," I say, "ready for a wild night on the town or maybe just a quiet roll in the hay. Your choice."

"Oh, Joe," she says with real disappointment in her voice. "Tonight's no good. All that work we did last night. Never got finished. We're going to be at it again this evening."

"Hey, that boss of yours is a real Simon Legree. How about if I come over and talk to him?"

"Won't do any good," she says.

"How about if I punch him in the nose?"

"And I lose my job? No, thanks. Joe, tomorrow evening. Without fail. I'll call you, promise. Ooops, have to go. Other phone line is ringing." And she is gone. Now I am slightly annoyed but what the hell, it isn't her fault. I tell myself this is a good lesson in patience and humility.

I get back in the car with Russ and we park a block away from Vinnie's apartment. We know we will be here for some time but it's something we don't want to miss.

An hour later the neighborhood kids are just coming home from school. The tots are playing potsy on the sidewalk, the older ones have organized a stickball game. The Good Humor truck appears but the kids ignore it. In this neighborhood who has a dime to waste on ice cream? And then the first black and white appears at the head of the block. It drives slowly past Vinnie's apartment building. Another squad car comes from the opposite direction. It, too, slows passing the apartment. Within seconds the stickball game vanishes into thin air. A couple of minutes later Kleinschmidt shows up in his unmarked car. There's another right behind him. He and Johansson get out and start into the apartment house. They reappear after thirty minutes. Johansson walks across the street and takes up a position in a candy store. A uniform comes to Kleinschmidt who gives him an order. Pretty soon the squad cars are pulling into alleys on opposite sides of the street. The stakeout has begun.

It is nearly six when Vinnie appears, oblivious to the snake pit he's walking into. He gets as far as the front entrance when two cops who have been lurking in the doorway grab him and wrestle him to the ground and throw the cuffs on him. Kleinschmidt appears along with Johansson and they take Vinnie by the arms and shove him inside.

I look over at Russ. He winks at me. "Show's over, my friend. Let's get out of here before we're spotted. Our presence might raise some embarrassing questions." I agree and unobtrusively we leave the area.

I drop Russ at the studio. He has paperwork to catch up on. Then I head for home. I am pretty sure I will be hearing from my two buddies with the badges since the last time they saw that gun, Johansson was preparing to hide it in my toilet. It's just possible they might suspect me of being involved with the surprising discovery in Vinnie's apartment.

On a whim, I decide to drive by Lydia's place of business. Maybe I can charm her boss into letting her out early. But when I get there, there is no boss. There is no nobody. The doors are locked. Everyone has gone for the day. I hope this means that the workload remaining was not as demanding as first thought but I have a nagging feeling that such is not the case.

When I get back to my apartment I find a postman in the foyer. He has just driven up with a special delivery letter addressed to me. I tear open the envelope. It's from the studio notifying me that I am no longer on suspension and ordering me back to work. This is excellent news and I wonder who went to bat for me. Maybe Kleinschmidt had a crisis of conscience or, more likely, he realized that his clumsy attempt to pin a murder rap on my rear end was going nowhere. Either way I'm pleased not only for the vindication but because for the past week I have been bleeding money.

Inside, I call Lydia at home. There is no answer. I call Tyler Banks Theatrical Management and ask for Banks. The sweet young thing on the other end of the line tells me he has left for the day. Is there a message, she asks. Yes, I say, but it is unprintable and unspeakable. The euphoria that I had been feeling only an hour before is gone. I hang up the phone and sink slowly onto the sofa where I put my head back and begin to stare at the ceiling.

The next morning I drive to the studio. Although the studio had been quick to toss me overboard at the first sign of indiscretion, Bruno, the ex-Nazi storm trooper, is at his post. As usual he gives me the cold Nordic once over and demands to see my studio pass. I decide that enough is enough with this jerk so I flip him the bird and roar past him onto the lot without a backward glance. I can only hope that if he is stupid enough to complain to Russ, he'll have his ass shipped back to the Munich beer hall where he came from.

Surprisingly Phyliss is at her desk and more, surprisingly, ready for work. I learn later that in my absence, she was assigned to an executive who actually made her type and file. She is delighted to be back under my tolerant wing and I know she is praying I stay at the studio forever. She has saved the morning paper for me and points out a small item at the bottom of Hedda's column. It reads, in totality: "Joe Bernardi reinstated to his post at Continental Studios". I marvel at this. My public vindication has taken up less than a half- inch of space. My excoriation dominated the front pages for days. My respect for the press has been waning for months. Now it has hit rock bottom. I am depressed beyond words. These are the people I have to deal with to earn a living.

There are a couple of dozen telephone slips on my desk,

neatly arranged in the order of calling. Also several letters. Most seem to be from people that I have pissed off over the past year and are now undoubtedly telling me how distraught they are over my troubles. Heh Heh. You bet. Phyliss brings me coffee and says she forgot to tell me that the kid in the mailroom who is after my job has showed up twice to measure for curtains. I'm not sure she's kidding.

As I lean back in my chair, sipping the coffee which is hot and not half bad, I look out the window and see a familiar car pull up in front of the building. Within five minutes a familiar figure that goes with the familiar car is bulling his way into my office.

Kleinschmidt sits down in my visitor's chair and says, "Tell your girl I take my coffee with three sugars, no cream." I do so. As Kleinschmidt watches me carefully he leans back. I lean back. We stare at each other for a few moments. "A very smooth move, Bernardi," he says. "Very smooth."

"What's that?" I say, all innocence.

"If I had any doubts about who planted the gun, finding it in the toilet tank erased them."

"Don't know what you're talking about," I say.

"The murder weapon which we found in Vince DellaFerragio's apartment. You're telling me you didn't put it there?"

I solemnly raise my hand. "I swear on my mother's grave." I have no idea who my mother is or whether she is dead or alive but I sound as sincere as hell.

He studies me carefully for a long time. Then he says, "What about your buddy Parmalee?"

"Ah," I say brightly, shaking my head, "that would be telling."

Kleinschmidt nods knowingly as Phyliss hands him his coffee mug.

"You said murder weapon. Does that mean you have a ballistics match?" Kleinschmidt nods. "Just out of curiosity," I say, "where did you and the big Swede find the gun in the first place?"

"On the soundstage about twenty feet away from the body, half hidden under a paint tarp. Vinnie shot her and for whatever reason I can't figure he just tossed the gun away. Stupid. Very stupid."

"You got a confession?"

"We got nothing," Kleinschmidt says.

"We can give you someone who Vinnie threatened with that gun a few months ago."

"Oh, and was this guy able to read a Japanese serial number on the gun while he was being threatened? If he saw a gun, it doesn't necessarily mean it was this gun."

"He killed her," I say.

"Yeah, I know, but we need more. His lawyer's looking for him and we're walking Vince around the city from one division to another without logging him in but we can't do it forever."

"Fingerprints?" I ask hopefully.

He shakes his head. "All smudged."

We fall silent for a minute or two before I dredge something up from my memory. It was over a year ago. An old timer chatting me up in a bar. He had a script. True life drama based on an actual case. He intrigued me with the key element but not being a screenwriter I forgot about it. Until now.

"Did you check the cartridges?"

He looks at me funny. "The what?"

"The cartridges. In order to load a gun, you have to handle the cartridges. About seven or eight years ago in Waco, Texas, there was a case where the killer had wiped the gun clean but they found his prints on the bullets. The judge let it in and the guy was convicted."

Kleinschmidt is sitting up straight now. "Yeah, we could check them out."

"Another suggestion. Let me talk to him."

Kleinschmidt frowns suspiciously. "What for?" he says.

"Because I'm not a cop and I'm not bound by the very few rules you seem to go by. Maybe I can get him to say something he shouldn't say because it's me, not you."

He shakes his head dubiously.

"What have you got to lose?" I say.

A couple of hours later I find myself in the West Traffic Division on Venice Boulevard. Kleinschmidt's tech guy has fitted me with a wire to record my conversation. If Vinnie finds it, I hope that someone will come to my rescue before he kills me.

He is sitting alone in a small holding cell at the rear of the building. The usual amenities are in evidence. A sink, a toilet, and a rock hard cot. Vinnie looks up at me as the jailer lets me in. The jailer closes the barred door shut and says he wlll be right down the hall.

Vinnie greets me affably.

"What the fuck do you want?"

"I thought we should have a talk," I say.

"Fuck you," Vinnie says. The breadth of his conversational skills astounds me.

"Move over," I say. He's hogging the whole cot. He repeats his favorite phrase.

"Your funeral," I say. "I'm just trying to save you from the chair, but what the hell, if you don't care, neither do I." I start to move toward the cell door.

"What the hell are you talking about?" he says.

"I'm talking about a conversation I had with May the night she was killed. She nailed you good, asshole, and if I want, I can see that you fry like a piece of bacon."

Grudgingly, Vinnie moves closer to the end of the cot giving me room to sit down which I do.

"What did she say?" Vinnie demands to know.

"You know what she said. That you killed Maggie Baumann on orders from Maggio because May had begged her father to have it done."

Vinnie shakes his head violently. "Bullshit," he says.

"No, Vinnie, that's what you say. It makes perfect sense. Maggie's being groomed for the part May thought she was going to get. With Maggie dead May gets the part back. Would Daddy say no to a little murder? No, he wouldn't. If Daddy told you to put one between her eyes, would you refuse? I don't think so."

"Your'e wrong," Vinnie says and I can see the fear building in his eyes.

"And the best part, as far as the cops are concerned, is they not only get you, they get your boss as well for giving the order. Oh, and Vinnie, if you think wiping the prints from the gun is going to save you, think again. Even as we speak the lab people are checking the cartridges in the gun for your fingerprints. You did load the gun, didn't you, Vince? And you didn't wear gloves, did you, Vince? No, I didn't think so."

"I didn't kill her," he says quietly, now pretty much terrified.

"I don't believe you and neither will anyone else. Now I came here to see if we could work something out that didn't involve fingering your boss who, I think, would be very grateful to be left out. Maybe grateful enough to fund yours truly with a decent cash gift."

"May lied," Vinnie squeals. "The old man didn't give any orders and I didn't shoot her."

I rise from the cot. "Fine. If that's the way you want it---" I start for the door again.

"May did it."

I turn and look at him.

"May did it", he says again. "May shot her. Yeah, it's my gun but May used it."

I return to the cot and sit down.

"I told her not to do it," Vinnie says. "But she was drunk and she didn't care. I'd seen her like that before. Bombed out of her mind. Didn't know what she was doing."

I nod. "Let's have all of it," I say.

"She knew the kid was pregnant because she'd come to May looking for the name of a doctor who could, you know, fix things."

"Abortion."

Vinnie nods. "May also had a pretty good idea who got her that way."

"Leo Blaustein," I say.

He shakes his head. "DeSalle."

I had always considered the possibility but it seemed a long shot. I am actually surprised.

"No question?"

"No question. Now I know how bad she wanted the part in this new movie. She also knew the kid was working on the side with the director. Not much happened around the studio that May didn't know about. Anyway, I'm pretty sure she went to DeSalle and told him how much she wanted the part and if she didn't get it, she might have to tell the world what's been going on between him and the pretty little stand-in".

"You know this for sure?" I ask.

He glares at me. "I put it together. About some things I am not as stupid as I look. Anyway I think DeSalle tried putting the screws to the director but he got nowhere and suddenly things are getting nasty. A lot of threats are made. None of this I know for sure but I am reading between the lines. You capishe?"

"I capishe," I say.

"Anyway, all of a sudden she's got my gun and she's waving it around and she tells me to get the hell away from her or she'll use it on me, too. I know she could pull the trigger any second, that's how nuts she was, so I get out of there fast. Next thing I know the kid is dead and May is shedding phony tears and sucking up to the director."

"That's it?"

"That's it," he says.

I get up from the cot and walk over to the door. I turn and smile. "I have good news, Vinnie. You're not going to get the chair after all."

I call for the jailer and leave.

That afternoon, Kleinschmidt allows the lawyer, Arthur Baxendale, to find Vinnie and take him home. Ballistics has determined that the 8mm was the murder weapon and fingerprints on the cartridges prove that it was Vinnie's gun. But the case against him is still weak and Kleinschmidt feels, as do I, that Vinnie told the truth, the whole truth and nothing but the truth. It is not a closed case. Not yet. There will be a lot of meetings and court appearances and interrogations but as far as Kleinschmidt is concerned, the murder of Maggie Baumann has been solved.

CHAPTER SEVENTEEN

That night I sleep fitfully. Half the time I am dreaming of Lydia and she is laughing and smiling a lot and then suddenly she is gone and I can't find her no matter how hard I look. The other half of the time I am seeing May Britton with a grotesque smile on her face and blood gushing from the slash across her throat. I am satisfied that May killed Maggie but a nagging question keeps hammering away at my subconscious. Who killed May? I see shadowy figures hovering over her body but their faces are obscured.

Shortly before eight o'clock, I awake with a start. The sun is streaming through the bedroom window and though I would like to stay hunkered down and let the rest of the world go to hell with itself, I climb out of bed. I have places to go and people to see. Let me correct that. I have a place to go and a person to see.

I am parked at curbside in front of the real estate office, leaning nonchalantly against my car, when Lydia drives up. As she gets out of her car she spots me and she freezes. Then, trying to ignore me, she heads for the office doorway. I hurry to cut her off.

"We have to talk," I say.

"Not now, Joe."

She tries to brush past me. I grab her arm. She tries to pull away.

"You're hurting me," she says.

I say, "Baby, you've been hurting me for years."

"Look, I have to go to work---"

"No, we're going to talk. Now."

"You're going to get me fired," she complains.

"Lots of people out of work these days, Lyd. It's not fatal. Why are you jerking me around?"

"I'm not. I----"

"Quit the bullshit," I say angrily. "Last night. The night before. I don't know where you were but I sure know where you weren't."

She looks away. I can see her eyes moistening. She looks back at me. "Let's get coffee," she says.

We take my car and I drive us to The Egg and I. Phil tries to interest us in his newest creation, the Hawaiian Neapolitan, which is an omelet with pineapple, mango, sausage and garlic. If Phil isn't careful he is going to "create" himself right out of business. Lydia and I settle for just coffee.

We're silent for a minute or two before she finally says, "I don't want to hurt you, Joe."

"That's nice," I say. "Then why don't you stop trying."

"Tyler and I are going to get married."

I try not to let my jaw slip open.

"He's already married to someone else," I remind her.

"He won't be. He's getting a divorce."

"Really?" I say. "And when is this momentous occasion scheduled to take place?"

"Soon," she says.

"Meaning?"

"At the end of summer."

I smile humorlessly. "Why the rush?"

"Don't be snide, Joe."

"Sorry. Just curious about the wait, that's all."

I look past her to the wall where a glossy photo of Jean Hersholt is staring down at me. Hersholt is best known for playing kindly Dr. Christian who solves everyone's problems. The inscription on the photo reads: "Good Luck". I think I am going to need it.

"He always spends the summer with his wife and his children. They have a cabin in Lake Arrowhead. It's a tradition. He doesn't want to interfere with that and I can understand."

"Can you? I can't. He's ready to toss them all overboard but he'll feel badly if they have to miss family time hiking and fishing and murdering bears."

Her eyes are getting wet again. "Joe, you have to understand. I love him and he loves me. Sure, it's going to be tough but we're going to see it through. I'm sorry I'm hurting you. In many ways I love you, too, and I hate hurting you but I can't help it. This is what I want."

I think I see Hersholt whispering 'tsk-tsk' and shaking his head sadly but it's probably my imagination. What do I say to her? That this shadrool has no intention of marrying her? That summer will turn into Thanksgiving and then the Christmas festivities and the kids need to stay in school and shouldn't be uprooted and on and on, one month after another, one excuse after another. Is she so infatuated that her brain has turned to oatmeal? I despair, not just for me, but for her. Heartache is in her future and there is nothing I can do to stop it.

I nod and say I understand and I wish her luck. I mean it because she'll need it. I drive her back to the real estate office and let her out. I watch as she walks up to the door and goes in. And then I drive off. Unless something drastic happens I am pretty sure I will not see her again and maybe that's for the best. As much as I love her I could never compete with an idealized love she could never have. I have learned this life lesson from watching Barbara Stanwyck movies.

I drive to the studio, do my little 'screw you' ballet with Bruno, and learn from Myrtle Figg, the wardrobe mistress and queen of gossip central that there's going to be a funeral mass for May today. A private affair. No one is invited. I determine that I will show up, invited or not.

Shortly before noon, I drive to the corner of Pico and Beverly Glen and park in front of St. Timothy's Catholic Church. It's not actually a church. Not yet. They started construction in 1943 and it is still only about three-quarters finished. A small building off to one side is serving as a temporary church until construction is complete.

I walk up to the main entrance of the little building and let myself in. Compared to what is being built, it is very small. Martha was right. It is a private affair. There are no more than eight people in attendance. A mahogany coffin is situated at the foot of the center aisle, directly in front of the altar. There are flowers everywhere. From the loft above an organist is playing softly. I spot Sal Maggio at the end of the front pew, his back to me. The others in attendance seem to be members of his entourage. For some reason Vinnie, who is sitting next to his boss, turns and sees me. He whispers in Maggio's ear. The old man responds and Vinnie gets up and starts back toward me.

I wonder if Vinnie is on Maggio's shit list for having ratted out May to the police. It didn't seem so. I found that encouraging. If Maggio isn't mad at Vinnie, chances are Vinnie won't be mad at me.

"Not now," he says.

"Look, I just----"

He takes another step toward me. He's not angry, just matter of fact. "Mr. Maggio says not now."

I look past him. A priest has appeared on the altar. No, not a priest. He wears the garb of a bishop. I think that perhaps Salvatore Maggio may be a substantial donor to this church. Whether his largess will help him find his way into heaven is another matter altogether. I nod to Vinnie and leave.

I make my way back to the studio. Bruno must have complained to Russ because when he sees me coming he forces a smile and waves me through without the usual ballbusting. Phyliss is at her post and while I don't consider doing the daily crossword work, I am encouraged that she is available if I need her. She tells me that Leo Blaustein called and that I have been assigned to publicize Kingman Krug's new project, "Treasure of the Klondike". He suggested I get together with Krug as soon as possible. I learn that Russ has driven to a location shoot in Malibu where the female star's ex-husband has shown up drunk and nasty and is threatening everyone in sight. I feel sorry for the ex-husband. If he's not careful, black eyes, a broken nose and perhaps bone fractures are in his future.

I wander over to Krug's office and find him chatting with Gail Russell, the beautiful raven-haired ingenue with the piercing blue eyes. Ever since "Salty O'Rourke" with Alan Ladd I've been smitten and "Angel and the Badman" which came out a couple of months ago only solidified my crush. They are just wrapping up and Krug introduces me. She smiles. I smile back but I am tongue tied and manage only a feeble 'Nice to meet you'. She leaves and Krug flops down wearily on his sofa.

"A dozen yesterday. Eight so far today. Every pretty face in Hollywood and you know, I think some of them can actually act."

"She can," I say nodding toward the door.

"The best so far," he says, "but the little girl from the other picture, she was what I wanted. A new face. Fresh. Unspoiled. Like Laughton discovering Maureen O'Hara. Serendipity, my friend."

I nod in agreement though I am not sure what serendipity means.

"So, Kingman," I say, "you must be flying high. You escaped the other picture and here you are with your favorite project well in hand. Too bad May Britton had to die for it happen."

He gives me a hard look. "I do not need to succeed on the misery of others. Naturally, I mourn her death and strangely I am sorry we didn't get to finish the picture. It might have turned out better than my critics had predicted." He lies well, this man.

"Do you think Brick Baxter is also sorry? Maybe not, considering the deal he has going for him at Republic."

Krug shakes his head. "Deal? He has no deal. When this newspaper reporter beat him silly, Herb Yates reconsidered and hired Buster Crabbe."

"Oooh. Bad news for Brick. I think he would have done anything to get that part. I mean, anything. What do you think, Kingman?" I ask pointedly.

"Do you mean do I think he might have killed May to shut down the picture? I doubt it."

He reaches into the humidor on the coffee table and takes out a big ugly Havana grown panatela. He lights up and the smell is equally ugly. The Cubans have fooled the world into thinking this is a luxury. Next they will be exporting cane sugar and telling you it's a terrific way to lose weight.

"You doubt it why?" I ask.

"Because down deep the man is a simpering little boy. He wouldn't have the courage."

"But you would," I suggest.

He blows smoke in my direction. "Of course, but only if I were certain I would not be caught."

"You have no alibi for the time she was killed."

He laughs. "I do not and that is just my point. Without an alibi I risk arrest and conviction. Therefore I would not commit such a clumsy murder."

He stands up. "And now, Mr. Bernardi, if the interrogation is over, I have work to do."

I get up and head for the door. He stops me as I'm about to go out.

"Out of curiosity, what do you think of Larry Parks?"

"Who?"

"The guy who played Jolson."

"Not bad," I say.

"Harry Cohn's got nothing for him right now and I think I could borrow him cheap."

"I think you can do better," I venture.

He shakes his head ruefully. "Not on this budget."

I go out and give it further thought. Larry Parks and Gail Russell. He could do a lot worse.

I hang around for a while, shuffling papers. A copy of Krug's screenplay is on my desk and I am going to have to read it sooner or later. I opt for later. Russ drops by and I ask him how things went in Malibu. He just smiles. Our leading lady is happy and relieved and her ex-husband is being treated by the best doctors at Santa Monica Hospital. He fell down a long flight of stairs while being pursued and Russ can produce a dozen witnesses who will swear to it. Aside from a broken jaw and a dislocated elbow, he's in pretty fair condition.

I consider paying a visit to Brick Baxter but on reflection, I think Krug is right. Down deep Baxter is a sissy boy. He never could have killed May, and certainly not in the vicious way it was done. I think about my boss, Buford DeSalle. According to Vinnie, he'd been sleeping with Maggie and had gotten her pregnant. Vinnie'd gotten that tidbit of information from May who'd gotten it from Maggie. Was it true? I had no idea but that was one hornet's nest I was not about to jam a stick into.

I decide to quit for the day and head home. I wonder what is so special about home. There will be no Lydia to look for, now or ever. I am tired of reading empty and badly written books and tired of listening to "Gangbusters" and for a brief moment I think about going to some bar and getting plastered. But ever since I was mustered out of the service, I'm tired of that, too.

It's close to six-thirty. I am slathering butter and marmalade on a slice of pumpernickel bread. I have already polished off a can of Campbell's chicken noodle soup and for dessert, I am looking forward to three stale chocolate chip cookies. It is all filling and best of all it's cheap but now the cupboard is bare and like it or not I will have to go grocery shopping in the morning.

There is a knock on my door. When I open it, I find myself looking at Vinnie.

"Now," he says.

The Packard is parked at the curb. Vinnie and I get in. Baldy is behind the wheel. We pull out into the street. Am I being taken for a ride? I don't think so but you never know. Baldy heads north toward downtown and within minutes, we are pulling up in front of the Ambassador Hotel, home of the Cocoanut Grove nightclub. Crowds of people are milling about and Baldy lets us off a half block away. As we near the hotel, a limousine appears and pulls to a spot being guarded by metropolitan police who pull temporary barricades out of the way. A man steps out of the back seat and waves to the crowd with a big smile. The crowd responds with a lot of whooping and hollering as he knifes his way through them to the front entrance. His face is familiar. I think he might be an actor but no film comes to mind. Vinnie and I make our way through the crowd and find ourselves in the lobby. Even more people are milling around.

Off to one side is a large sign on an easel stand. The Cocoanut Grove is closed until nine o'clock for a private party. It is a fund-raising event for the Congressman from the 12th District, Richard M. Nixon. His photo confirms that he is the man from the limo. I vaguely remember his victory last November. The campaign was loud and dirty on both sides. Immediately there was talk of him running for the Senate. I have heard that he is a Quaker and an honest man but frankly I don't care. Politicians from Germany and Italy and Japan and Great Britain and the United States caused a six year world war. I have no use for any of them.

Vinnie takes me to the cocktail lounge and seats me at a banquette in the rear that has a "Reserved" sign on it. Vinnie removes the sign. "Wait here," he says and he goes off. A wait-ress approaches. "Would you like a drink, sir?" she says. "Yes, I would," I say, "but I may have to ask permission." She gives me a funny look and wanders off.

A few minutes pass and then Vinnie returns walking two paces to the left and behind Sal Maggio. I am sitting on one end, Maggio slides into the middle and Vinnie takes a position oppo-site me where he watches me warily. He may have heard of the jackknife I carry in my pocket. He seems ready to spring into action at my first false move.

"I thank you for coming to my daughter's funeral. A nice ges-ture. But as you saw, it was for family only," Maggio says.

"You mean the men who work for you."

"They are my family now, Mr. Bernardi."

He offers to buy drinks and I accept. I have a feeling I am going to need at least one. I order a gin sling. Maggio opts for a robust Bordeaux. Vinnie opts to keep his eyes on me.

"The man outside, the one we're here for tonight. You know him?" Maggio asks.

"I've heard of him," I say.

"A good man," Maggio says. "The way he's going after those Commie rats. Man has balls." I didn't doubt it but I say nothing. "Ever since the war's over, the country's going to hell with itself. Nixon, he's got the right idea, even if he is a Republican. First time in my life I'm giving money to a Republican. Like I say, he's got balls."

Politics makes me nervous and I know that's not why I'm here so I try to change the subject. "To May," I say, raising my glass. Maggio follows suit. We sip.

"I find it interesting," Maggio says, "that the police no longer consider you a suspect in my daughter"s murder."

"I've been cooperating with them," I say. "They believe I was not involved."

"Even though there is ample evidence that you might have done it. They seem to regard her death with total indifference. Why do you suppose that is? Because her father is man who often deals with the underbelly of life? Or maybe it's because my dear Vincent here---" He gives Vinnie a hard look---"convinced them that she was a cold-blooded killer. As such, well, who really cares who killed her. Someone did the state a favor."

"I care, Mr. Maggio," I say.

"Do you, Mr. Bernardi? I remember you assuring me that you were going to work to uncover the identity of my daughter's killer. Do you remember that?"

"I do. Vividly," I say.

"And what do you intend to do about it?"

I take a swig of my drink. "I'm doing what I can, Mr. Maggio, but I'm not a trained detective. I don't have access to reports and files."

"But you did promise to discover the man who murdered her."

"Yes, but----"

"I'm going to hold you to that promise, Mr. Bernardi. Tomorrow I am taking Angelina's body to Chicago. She will be buried next to her mother and her two brothers. I will visit some friends and conduct some business and then in four days I will return. I expect you to give me the name of the guilty party."

He waves his hand at Vinnie who immediately gets up. Maggio slides out of the banquette.

I am in a panic. "Mr. Maggio----" I say.

"Now I must pay my respects to my good friend, Richard Nixon, who is a great patriot and a man with a vision for America. You have four days, Mr. Bernardi. Don't waste them."

He leaves the cocktail lounge without looking back, Vinnie trailing behind him.

Dread courses through my veins. Four whole days. Fate has dealt me a really ugly hand.

CHAPTER EIGHTEEN

Four days. He might as well have given me four hours. There is no way I am going to solve his daughter's murder in four days or even four weeks. I have no clues, no leads and if there is any forensic evidence, Kleinschmidt isn't sharing it with me. And here's a bulletin for you. I'm not a detective. It looks easy when Sam Spade gets on a case and stumbles onto the one clue he needs to bring the killer to justice. The only thing I have stumbled upon is Maggie Baumann's body ten days ago and I wish I hadn't.

Still, there is one person I am pretty sure I need to talk to but if I do, I might be back on the unemployment line by the end of the day. Maggie, May and Buford LaSalle. They all seem to be tied together in one gigantic knot but how each one relates to the others, I have no idea. If Buford had gotten Maggie pregnant he is in deep but digging into his motive and alibi, that's Kleinschmidt's business, not mine. Blaustein will keep his mouth shut no matter what and Brick Baxter is a total dead end.

And so I keep coming back to one guy, the one person who might have the key that would unravel the mystery. It is possible Al Kaplan killed May but my gut says no. My gut also tells me he is carrying around a dark secret and the centerpiece of that secret is May Britton.

Early the following morning I drive to the hospital but I am too late. Al has been released. The business office will not reveal his home address. I call Russ at the studio.

"Hang on while I dig out his employment application," Russ says. After a couple of minutes he is back on the phone. I jot down the address he gives me. Then he laughs.

"What's so funny?" I ask.

"Under next of kin, he lists May Britton. Weird."

I don't think it's so weird. I had done the same thing with Lydia.

Russ asks what I'm up to and I tell him. He volunteers to go with me. Maybe a little "official" presence will get Al to open up. I decline his help. I am pretty sure a low key one on one is the best way to go.

Al has a room in a private home in a seedier part of town. It's certain his rent is next to nothing and I wonder what he spends his money on. Or maybe he has a bank account worth tens of thousands of dollars. His landlady says he is not in but she has a good idea where I can find him.

It's only two blocks away so I leave my car parked and hoof it. He's sitting at the end of the bar, hunched over, his right hand clasping a glass of whiskey while his eyes are staring straight ahead, unfocused, because as far as I can see, there is nothing to focus on. The place is called Burt's and the guy behind the bar may or may not be Burt but at this time of the morning, he and Al are the only two people in the place.

I settle onto the stool next to him and order a beer. He turns and glares until he recognizes me and then he just looks away.

"I went looking for you at the hospital," I say.

"They can't keep you forever," Al says. He sips at his drink. It's a dark rich color and it hasn't been cut with soda or water. From what his landlady told me he's probably been here at least forty minutes but he shows no signs of falling off his bar stool. There is, however, a slight fuzziness in the timbre of his voice.

"How'd you find me?" he asks. I tell him. He nods his head knowingly. "Right. Parmalee the cop. Knows all. Sees all."

He sips again. A little more this time.

"You think this is the best way to pass the morning?" I ask.

"Best one I know," he says.

"Seems a shame after all those years of staying dry,"

"Staying dry isn't all it's cracked up to be," he says.

I sip my beer. Al drains his glass and raps it hard three times on the bar. It's a secret signal to the barkeep who brings the bottle and refills his glass. No words are exchanged and Burt or whoever he is goes back to the other end of the bar and continues washing and drying the glassware.

"Tell me about Buford DeSalle," I say.

Al looks at me, half amused. "Southern gentleman, not too bright, pompous asshole, first class hypocrite."

"Tell me about Buford and Maggie Baumann."

He shrugs. "Way I heard it, he knocked her up."

"And where'd you hear it, Al?"

"Around."

"Around where?" I ask.

"Just around."

"May tell you?"

"She might have."

"She must have been pretty pissed," I say.

"You think so?" He's amused.

"If not pissed, then what?" I ask.

"May never let personal feelings get in the way of good business although in DeSalle's case, there were no personal feelings to fuck things up."

I give him a long look. He's dancing around something but I can't pin him own. I am, however, not a total dolt so I make a stab.

"What about blackmail?" I say.

"Where'd you hear that?" he says sharply.

"I think I'm hearing it from you."

He shakes his head and takes a healthy swig from his glass.

"You're crazy," he says.

"No, I don't think so, Al. Look, I'm trying to find out who killed her. I think of all the people who knew her you'd be the one most willing to help me out but frankly, it looks like you don't give a damn."

Al stares at his drink. Finally he says, "She was a good woman. Deep down she was a good woman. You're trying to make her look like a-- I don't know. Why can't you just leave her be? She's dead, Joe. Leave her alone."

"I can't, Al. You know I can't. Tell me about DeSalle."

He's still staring at his glass which is half full. He pushes it away.

"She wanted that part, Joe. She wanted it so bad." He looks up, unfocused, remembering. "I was with her in her dressing room. I'd brought her flowers. I did that a lot. She got a kick out of it. I went into the bathroom. Right away I hear a loud knock on the door and then I can hear voices. His. Hers. Loud."

"DeSalle."

"That's right. I'm getting every other word. I go to the door. I'm not about to bust in because I like my job and besides it sounds like she's got control of things. So I listen. You're right. She's been putting the screws to him."

"About Maggie?"

"She's already dead and the autopsy has just come out.

May's got DeSalle by the short hairs. She threatens to tell his wife. DeSalle is scared shitless. His old lady runs the studio and runs him. If they do a blood test on the fetus, she'll crucify him. He has tried to bully Krug into giving May the part but Krug won't budge. Nothing works. Money. Additional commitments. Whatever. Krug won't have her in his picture. May's drunk and nasty and now she gets nastier. All of a sudden I hear like a struggle. May screams and I hear her fall to the floor. DeSalle is out of his mind, screaming at her. He's going to kill her if she doesn't keep her mouth shut. I hear a couple of slaps and May is saying No, No. And then I hear the door slam and DeSalle is gone."

"And May?"

"She's okay but still pissed. Maybe even more so."

I can only stare at him in disbelief though I know he is telling the truth. "Jesus," I mutter quietly under my breath.

"Yeah," Al says quietly.

A few minutes later, I'm walking head down, hands jammed in my pockets, headed back to Al's boarding house. When I get there Russ's cruiser is parked behind the Studie. He gets out and walks toward me.

"What are you doing here?" I ask.

"Thought you could use some backup," Russ says.

I smother a laugh. "Thanks but even I can handle Al Kaplan."

"Where is he?" Russ asks.

I point in the direction of Burt's. "Having breakfast. Ninety proof without chasers."

"He have anything interesting to say?"

I tell Russ what Al told me. About May and DeSalle and the blackmail and the threats.

Russ looks at me, disbelieving. "What's he saying? That Mr. DeSalle killed May? That's nuts."

"You think so?"

"C'mon, Joe. The man runs a movie studio. He's worth four or five million minimum. He's gonna risk that over some lush of an actress? Not a chance."

"And if May talks to his wife?" I venture.

Russ's eyes harden. "Forget it, Joe. I'm not going anywhere near this. You shouldn't either. The man signs our paychecks."

I shake my head. "You don't mean that."

"The hell I don't. I like my job. I plan to keep it. And no offense, Joe, but guys who do what you do, there's a lot of them floating around looking for work. If I were you I'd hang on to what I've got."

It's a low blow. I don't like it much. "Thanks," I say, hardly masking the sarcasm.

"Don't get all pissy on me," he says. "Just telling it like it is. Besides, didn't he have an alibi for when she died? Out meeting with the foreign press people? Something like that?"

It could be. I don't remember. Then I look past his shoulder as a black and white metro squad car approaches and pulls to the curb. Two uniformed cops get out and approach. Russ sees my look and turns. The taller of the two wears a name tag that reads 'Greenberg'. He speaks.

"Russell Parmalee?" he says.

"That's right."

"Mr. Parmalee, are you---"

"That's Chief. Chief Parmalee," Russ corrects him.

Greenberg hesitates for a moment while his partner looks me up and down. Greenberg nods. "Okay Chief---" He bites off the word with a smirk. "Are you familiar with a man named Oliver Carnivale?"

Russ shakes his head.

"He's in Santa Monica hospital. The doctors think he may lose an eye."

Russ nods. "Oh, that guy."

"He's pressing charges, Chief." He emphasizes Russ's rank again. "Aggravated assault."

"That's a load of crap," Russ fires back. "He was trespassing on a closed movie set. The only force I used on him was in self-defense."

"That's not the way he tells it," Greenberg says. "We need you to come with us."

"Not likely," Russ says coldly. He shifts his weight subtly, getting ready for trouble.

Greenberg shakes his head. "Don't make this tough. We can handle you and if we can't the next time it'll be a half dozen guys and you'll also be looking at resisting arrest."

Russ hesitates, then says. "Okay, I'll follow you in." He turns to me. "Joe, I'll catch you later."

I nod. "You need anything? A lawyer?"

Russ laughs. "A lawyer? Jesus Christ, Joe. I'll be out of there in twenty minutes." He switches his attention to Greenberg and scans his uniform for a rank which he doesn't find. "Okay, Patrolman," he says. "You lead and I follow. Try not to get lost."

He and the cops get in their respective cars and drive off. I start to slip behind the wheel of the Studie when I look across the street at the Pontiac coupe parked at curbside. Behind the wheel is Vinnie. He gives me a smile and a little salute. He doesn't seem to care that I've spotted him. I wonder how long he's been tailing me and how long he plans to keep it up.

CHAPTER NINETEEN

few minutes later I'm making a beeline for the studio. Vinnie's on my tail. I know he's operating on orders from Maggio because the last time Vinnie thought for himself it was a choice between chocolate and strawberry. Does Maggio not trust me? Does he want minute by minute reports on what I'm doing? Is Vinnie there to protect my ass if I get in over my head? Whatever it is, for the moment it's immaterial because I am turning into the main gate and Vinnie is peeling off looking for a parking spot on the surface street

I think maybe I have May's killer in my sights which is good. I don't like who it is and that is bad. What's the old adage? If you shoot the king, you better make sure you kill him. I have no substantive proof against DeSalle. Just circumstance here, circumstance there. Little pieces that seem to fit. On the other hand he has a rock solid alibi if you are to believe a few dozen foreign press representatives he was schmoozing with that night. The whole night? Or just part of the night? I don't know. I think I need more information and I need it quickly because Sal Maggio is going to want the killer's head on a pike and if I don't deliver---- Well, we don't want to think about that.

In search of proof I park my car and go looking for Martha

Brodsky, our head of casting. Last time we chatted she blew me off. (Figuratively speaking). This time I will get answers.

Her anteroom is crowded with olive-skinned dark-haired actors. All are south of 25. A couple are still sporting teenage acne. Most are dressed like like East L.A. gang members. Half are seated, a few are leaning against a wall, several are pacing the floor, mouthing melodramatic lines from scripts they are holding in their hands. Ben Hecht has nothing to fear. I hear a few lousy hispanic accents wafting up from the assemblage. This is a film I probably will not go to see. Gwendolyn, Martha's secretary is doing her best to ignore them. Martha's private door opens and a piece of beefcake with greasy unwashed hair comes out looking totally pissed. Gwendolyn refers to her list.

"Enrique Morales!" she calls out.

I sidle up to her. "I've got this one, Gwen," and I start for the door, cutting off a skinny kid who can't weigh 110 even soaking wet.

"Go back and sit down," I tell him.

"She called me," the kid whines.

I raise my voice so that all can hear. "And I'm her husband. I want a few minutes with my wife so sit down and shut up!"

Even as I enter her private office, I hear the mumbling and whispering. Within hours it will be all over the lot. By tomorrow Louella will be leading with it. Martha will have a lot of explaining to do to her fellow Sapphists.

Martha looks up from her desk. She's wearing harlequin glasses with a loopy thing to make sure they don't fall in her lap as she looks down her nose at the actors she has brought in. The lenses in her specs are wide and thick and I suspect she may be almost blind when it comes to close work. She peers at me over the top of the frames.

"I don't want you," she complains.

"But I want you, babe," I say pulling up a chair.

"You're wasting my time, Bernardi," she says. "I'm busy."

"Not for me you're not," I say. "I have questions, you have answers. If you work this right, I'll be out of here in five or six minutes." She reaches for the phone. "Who are you calling? Security? Russ isn't here but he should be back in a half hour. I can wait. Then he and I can both hear what you've got to say." I swing my feet up on her desk. She replaces the receiver.

"What do you want?"

"Who pressured you into hiring Maggie Baumann?" I ask her.

"Nobody. I---"

"Don't yank my chain, Martha. I'm way ahead of you."

"She was my idea. Nobody else's. Now get the hell out of here." She's furious and she's spooked. A good combination. I reach in my shirt pocket and take out a small piece of paper. I hold it up so she can read it.

"You see this phone number? It's the one I use to call my good friend Sgt. Aaron Kleinschmidt of the LAPD. If I call him now he will come here to talk to you and he will ask you the same question I am asking except that the good sergeant is liable to arrest you for impeding a police investigation or worse, accessory to murder after the fact. One way or the other, Martha. I don't care which."

She glares at me, the hatred oozing from every pore. Finally she says, "She was suggested to me by Leo Blaustein."

"Suggested." I don't like the word and she knows it.

"Strongly suggested," she amends.

I can see this is going to be like pulling teeth from an angry crocodile.

"Try again. I'm still way ahead of you."

She hesitates. "All right, he ordered me to put her on payroll."

I shake my head. "You're one of the three best casting directors in Hollywood. You don't need to take orders from an empty suit like Blaustein."

"Thanks for the compliment but you don't know jackshit, Bernardi. I told him I don't hire bimbos who can't act. He says he knows that. Put her on the Blue Satin picture as a standin for Britton, he tells me. No acting, I warn him. I don't care if she's the next Harlow. Hiring actors is my job. Lining up bimbos is yours. Don't ever confuse the two."

"Guess he didn't care much for that," I say.

"Not much."

"I like your term 'lining up'. Interesting. As if he weren't doing it for himself but someone else."

I look her square in the eye to see if she'll flinch. And she does.

"Are we through here?" she growls in annoyance.

"Not yet, Martha. Who was he lining her up for?"

"I have no idea."

I twiddle the paper with the LAPD phone number between my fingers. Now, suddenly, the bravado is gone. She looks genuinely concerned. Maybe even frightened.

"For Christ's sakes, Joe, leave it alone," she says.

"Who, Martha?"

"Damn it, Joe, are you crazy? The man is psychotically self-protective. Leave him alone."

"Leave who alone, Martha?"

"You know who!" She practically screams it.

"His name," I demand.

She shakes her head violently.

"Did Blaustein mention his name?"

"No more, Joe. I'm through. I don't feel like getting mugged in a dark alley like Sam Harvey."

I react sharply. "What's that supposed to mean?"

"Joe, I said I'm through," she tells me. "That phone number in your hand. Call it. I've got nothing left to say." She turns the phone and pushes it toward me.

She fixes me with a hard stare and she doesn't look away. I decide she's been wrung dry. I get up and head for the door. I turn. "I'll send in Enrique Morales but he's all wrong. The little guy's a total wuss." I go out.

I trudge across the lot toward my office. I have my answer in so many words. The studio old timer who discovered Maggie in the Van Nuys diner was Buford DeSalle. He'd strung her along, promised her a career, paid her rent and boffed her brains out. You're a kid from South Dakota. He runs the studio. How can you say no? I know that when Martha gets on the witness stand, if it ever comes to that, she will finger DeSalle. She'll have no choice. But for the time being I wonder if this will be enough for Sal Maggio. The pieces fit. The blackmail. The possible scandal that has be shut down before it starts. But the picture is still muddy. There are still loose ends.

I mull Martha's reference to Sam Harvey. What was she trying to say? That Sam was in Buford's way and met a violent end, that this is the way Buford operates and woe to anyone who stands in his way. If true I don't blame her for being scared. I think that maybe I am insane if I pursue this any further.

As I am about to step into my office, Russ's cruiser drives by and I watch as he parks in front of the security office and goes inside. I do a one-eighty and head for Russ's office. He needs to know what I know and I need his advice on what to do about it.

He's at his desk with his checkbook out. The way he's writing the check I can tell he's not happy. He looks up at me.

"You never had kids, did you, Joe?" I confessed I hadn't. "Good move," he says. "I had a four year marriage and when I'd had enough I walked out. The bitch I never missed but I felt bad for my little girl. I started sending checks. Nobody makes me do it. I just do it."

"I never knew you were married, Russ."

"It's something I try to forget." He slips the checkbook back into a desk drawer and takes out a studio envelope. He slips in the check and starts to address it. "Hey, look at the time. I said twenty minutes. So it was forty. The cops tried to jerk me around. That lasted about three minutes. I made them see the righteousness of my position."

"Yes, you do have a certain gift for persuasion, amigo, but right now we have other things to worry about. Or more specifically, I do."

He leans back in his chair. "I'm listening."

I have been standing. Now I sit. I tell him about Sal Maggio and the box the old gangster has put me in. I remind him of my conversation with Al Kaplan and I tell him what I learned from Martha Brodsky. Anyway you look at it, I say, it keeps coming up Buford DeSalle.

He just shakes his head. "Blaustein, maybe, but not DeSalle. It can't be, Joe. I checked his alibi with four different people. He and his missus were hanging out with the foreign press from about seven-thirty to well past midnight."

"He could have ducked out. The hotel's only a few minutes from here."

"Right. He goes to the valet to get his car. He didn't. He calls for a cab to take him to the studio. He didn't. Joe, he's alibied. Live with it."

"Then he hired someone," I say.

Russ almost laughs in my face. "Oh, sure. He's so upset by May's blackmail over a sexual fling that he hires somebody who can then blackmail him over a first degree murder charge. Yeah, that makes a lot of sense."

"I know, I know," I say weakly. "But still---"

"Still nothing." Russ says. "We're missing something, Joe. Someone we don't know about. A jealous rival. An old boyfriend. Maybe even Al himself. Look, I know you're up against it with Maggio and if you want, we'll go see him together when he gets back. I won't say we're friends but I sit in on some of these union talks and we get along. Maybe I can get him to back off."

I nod but I'm not convinced. It'll take more than talk to assuage Maggio. I get up and go to the door. I turn back.

"What if I can prove it's DeSalle and I tell Maggio?"

"Then I think that maybe in a couple of weeks the studio's going to have a new owner," Russ says.

A few minutes later I drive off the lot and head for home. I look around but there's no sign of Vinnie. I don't know whether to be relieved or nervous.

CHAPTER TWENTY

My apartment is quiet. Deathly so. For supper I have eaten a bowl of Grape-Nuts and a four day old banana. I also brewed a pot of coffee and now I am sipping my second cup as I stare at the Bridge of Sighs in Venice. It's a framed print that was hanging on the wall when I moved in. I've been too lazy to get rid of it. I think about the poor bastards who trekked over it to spend their final years in a cell and I am aware that others have had worse troubles than mine.

The sun is disappearing over the western horizon and I have not turned on the lights. Dimness slowly turns to darkness. I step out onto my smallish balcony and look down into the court-yard below. The Finneran kids from 1D are carousing in the swimming pool and they force me to smile. The water's icy cold because the pool's not heated. Never has been. Never will be. The landlord's a cheap s.o.b.. Nothing's ever taken care of but the rent's rock bottom so I stay. And cold or not, the kids play.

I sit in the camp chair and look out over the slate gray sky turning to ebony. My mind has been turning over for hours. What am I missing? I try to connect Kingman Krug or Brick Baxter to May's death and it just doesn't compute. I try to picture Leo Blaustein wielding a knife. It's almost laughable. The man's a simpering coward hiding behind a facade of bluster. I can't rule out Al Kaplan but my gut says no because if ever a guy was destroyed by the death of a loved one, Al is it. And so it keeps coming back to Buford DeSalle and his convenient alibi.

Something else is bothering me. Something Al said but I can't remember what it is. There are so many pieces, some that fit and some that don't. Maggie is murdered and the cops try to lay it on me because I'm convenient and maybe because they think I did it and they are going to help the evidence along. But then somebody murders May and goes to a lot of trouble to fit me with a similar frame. DeSalle? He leaves behind a bloody bone-handled knife but I'm not sure he knows I carry that kind of knife. Few people do.

And then it hits me. Not hard. It's a small annoyance that is wriggling its way into my brain and I remember what it was Al was bothered by. How did I learn where he lived? From Russ who has the employment applications for everyone who works at the studio. Including me. And I think back. I'm at Lydia's. The police suddenly show up and I cannot figure how they got there. No one knows she is my ex-wife. I do not talk about her. She is a non-person except to me. Except for one thing. On my employment sheet, I put her down as my next-of-kin even though we were divorced. Lydia Grozny, I had written down, along with her address.

And then I remember something else. I'm on Stage 5 and May orders me to come to her dressing room that evening for a "chat". Only one other person had heard this invitation outside of me and that person was Russ Parmalee. Anonymous flowers arrive and I am identified by a delivery boy. A bloody knife matching my own is left behind by someone who knew how to match it. Russ? No, not Russ. But even as I think it to myself, I know it is true. Russ, the man of many faces and many moods. A man used to taking orders. A man frightened for his future and willing to do whatever he has to to keep his job. I think about his volatile temper and those he has maimed, acting perhaps on orders from above. And now I think about Sam Harvey and Martha Brodsky's veiled hint that all was not as it seemed in Sam's convenient death that paved the way for DeSalle to buy the studio. Given his history how many companies would hire Russ Parmalee and put him in charge of security? I would bet not many but Buford DeSalle did. Is it an act of charity from a man who preaches God's love and the purity of forgiveness? Or is it something else?

Suddenly it all starts to make sense. May died on a night when DeSalle had an iron clad alibi. Couple that with a frameup directed at a person the cops had already tried to finger for another murder and it all came together like peanut butter and jelly. Frame Bernardi. It won't take much and then the case will shut down and soon be forgotten. No poking around. No embarrassing questions. The slide is greased for a one way ticket to Folsom.

I stand up. I can hear Mrs. Finneran below screaming at her kids to get out of the pool. Their Irish Setter helps by barking. Then the dog jumps into the pool. Her problems have compounded.

I step back into my darkened living room. I can see well enough to spot my car keys on the table by the doorway. I pick them up. I have somewhere to go. Something to check on. If I am right, Sal Maggio will no longer be one of my troubles.

On the way to the studio, I think and rethink my logic. It keeps coming up the same way and I curse myself for not seeing it sooner. Russ Parmalee, my friend and ally, has been using me from the first. He has kept himself close to learn whatever I learn and I am forced to surmise that had I gotten too close, he would have dealt with me the same way he dealt with that Navy non-com in San Diego or the poor jerk who walked onto the set in Malibu or worse, Sam Harvey who only wanted to hang onto the studio he'd founded decades earlier.

I drive past the main gate without turning in and go around to the back of the studio. As I approach the rear gate I douse my lights and look for some sign of Scotty. I don't see him. I drive in, turn down one of the alleys and park in the deep shadows of Stage 6. From the glove compartment I take out a small penlight. For the first time in my life, I wish I had a pistol to go with it. Off to the left I can see lights and activity and I remember that one of our films is picking up some missed shots on New York Street. I walk in the opposite direction, toward the security office. I doubt Russ will be there. More likely he'll be hanging out with the shooting company.

I'm right. As I approach the office, it's dark. I try the door. It's locked. I take out my knife and jimmy the lock. It's a newly acquired skill. I let myself in noiselessly and turn on my little penlight so I don't bang into the furniture. I sit down at Russ's desk and try the drawer where he keeps his checkbook. It slides open easily and I take it out. I leaf through the stubs going back about three weeks earlier. That's when I spot the deposit entry. $7500. The day before May was killed. I stare at it for the longest time trying to decide what to do. I can't take the checkbook. I could call Kleinschmidt and tell him everything I know. Maybe he can get a warrant for the checkbook but if he does, what does it prove? Maybe Russ had a lucky day at the track or collected a long overdue debt from some friend. He's sharp. He'll have a story ready and dare the cops to disprove it. And then I think, maybe I don't have to prove it. I think that maybe what I have will be enough for Sal Maggio.

I get up from the desk and turn to go out. In the dim light I see him standing there quietly in the doorway, leaning against the jamb, eyeing me carefully.

"Find anything interesting, Joe?" Russ asks quietly.

A chill seizes my body. I search for something bright to say but the words don't come. I have been caught and there is no believable response.

"What's so fascinating about my checkbook, Joe?" he asks stepping into the room. He flips the light switch. The overhead fixture glares down at me. I feel naked and defenseless. Russ is in full uniform, his .38 Smith and Wesson in its holster. I can't take my eyes off it.

"Come on, Joe. You and me, we could always talk. So what are you dolng here?" he asks. He steps closer to me. I see a look in his eyes I have never seen before. They are ice cold. Nearly demonic. I sense that inwardly he is coiled up like a cobra, ready to strike.

I finally find words. "There was something I had to check out."

"And what was that? Something in my checkbook? What could possibly interest you in my checkbook?"

"Nothing, really," I mumble unconvincingly.

"Nothing? You come looking for something and you find nothing? Pretty disappointing." I nod.

Now he is very close, invading my space. I try to back up but the desk is in the way.

"And what was that something you came looking for?" he asks.

I don't answer and suddenly he has rammed a ham-like fist

into my gut and I double over in agonizing pain. I fight to keep my breath. I feel the bile rising in my throat and then I gag and vomit spews from my mouth. Russ steps back in disgust as I sink to my knees gasping for air.

I look up at him, fighting to get the words out. "People know I'm here," I manage to say.

"Bullshit," he says, almost laughing. "Who, Joe? Who knows you're here?"

"Can't tell you."

"I'll bet you can't," he says. He reaches down and grabs me by the shirt front and pulls me to my feet. "Let's go," he says.

"Where?"

"For a walk. I need the air." I shake my head vigorously. "Come on, Joe, don't make me hit you again." He shoves me toward the doorway and follows. He doesn't pull his gun. He doesn't have to.

We're out on the street. It's well past eleven o'clock. It is eerily quiet. The company on New York Street has shut down. He points. I walk in that direction, away from New York Street. He follows closely behind me.

"I haven't decided yet whether to kill you. I think maybe I won't. I think maybe you're scared. But hear this, Joe. You cry out or yell for help and I'll put a bullet in the back of your head and I'll do the same to anyone who tries to help you." He waits. "Did you hear me, Joe?"

"Yes, I heard," I say.

We continue to walk without speaking. We skirt "jungle park" where we have twice filmed programmers starring an Olympic runnerup as a great white hunter. The pictures are lousy and so is the actor. Johnny Weissmuller has nothing to fear. To my right the studio is constructing a huge swimming pool. The hole has been dug. The equipment has been left in place. It'll be another week before it's completed. DeSalle seems to have a penchant for imitation. If MGM can do it, so can we, except that we don't have Esther Williams. In fact we don't have anybody yet.

I try conversation to distract him.

"Seventy five hundred bucks seems a little cheap for a human life, Russ. Is that the going rate?" He doesn't answer. I try again. "How about Sam Harvey? Did he come a little higher? I'd guess yes. I mean, he was worth a whole studio, right, Russ?"

"Left, Joe," Russ says, pointing.

Conversation has gotten me nowhere but I note that he has not offered a denial. I turn. We're heading to Stage 5, the place where all of this began. The irony doesn't escape me. Russ still hasn't pulled his pistol from its holster. I try to calculate my chances if I run. How long will it take him to pull the gun? Will he fire if I am fleeing? Can I outrun him? If I outrun him where can I hide? It's all iffy but I don't think I have a choice. He says he hasn't made up his mind but I know that he has. He plans to kill me and I'm pretty sure he has figured a way to get away with it.

"Up the steps," he says as we reach the sound stage.

I turn toward him. "Russ----"

"Move!" he growls.

I start to climb the steps but I deliberately trip and fall. I reach down to break my fall and clumsily roll to one side. In that moment I am able to slip my hand into my trouser pocket and grab my knife which I conceal in the palm of my hand. I get to my feet and go to the door. It's not locked. I open it and step inside. Russ is right behind me.

The stage is not totally dark. There are two work lights casting a dim glow on the still standing sets from "Jezebel in Blue

Satin". No one has yet bothered to take them down. The night-club set is deep in shadow, the bandstand deserted, the dance floor empty. The tables and chairs are as they were. The cameras and lighting equipment have all been removed, but otherwise all is the same.

"Stop right there," Russ tells me. I do so. "Now drop the knife." I hesitate. "The knife, Joe. On the floor. Now."

I think about it but not for long. I let the knife go.

"Good man," he says. "Now turn around."

"No," I say.

"Joe---"

"If you're going to shoot me, you're going to have to shoot me in the back. You might have trouble explaining that."

I am standing very still, waiting for the shot. I hear him moving and I know he is coming up behind me. He is very close. Instinctively I drop down low and throw myself backwards as hard as I can. I feel myself slam into his legs and he falls. In that moment I scramble to my feet and dash toward the nightclub set, past the bandstand and through an archway that leads into a darker unlit section of the soundstage. I listen for a shot that never comes and I duck down behind a rolled up tarp against a far wall. I try not to breathe.

I hear him cursing. "Jesus H. Christ, Joe. What are you try-ing to prove?" He's on the move now, but I don't know where he is and I am damned sure not going to pop my head up to look. "You should have tried outside. You might have had a chance. Inside here, hell, Joe, the stage is soundproof. You have no chance. Not smart, Joe. But then you never were." I think I hear his footsteps but they don't seem close. Not yet.

"Why couldn't you let it be, Joe? She killed your pal, Maggie Baumann. She got what she deserved whether it was me or the state, what's the difference? The bitch deserved to die. You want a laugh? For once I thought I was one of the good guys. You know, avenging angel. That kind of shit."

I realize now he is getting closer. Has he seen me? Is he playing with me? I hunker down more, trying to bury myself in the cement floor. I feel something hard under my leg. I reach down. It's a crowbar. I grasp it.

"Joe!" he calls out and I realize he is right on top of me, on the other side of the tarp. If he has seen me, I'm dead. If he hasn't I've got a chance. I peer over the tarp. He's less than five feet away and looking in the other direction. I spring to my feet, lashing out as hard as I can with the crowbar. He hears me and starts to turn as the crowbar slashes down on his arm. The pistol in his hand clatters to the ground and skitters away as he cries out in pain. I slam into him, knocking him to the floor, and stumble toward the pistol which lies several feet away. I grasp it and roll over on my back, holding it with two hands as I point it toward Russ who is on his feet, lunging toward me. I squeeze the trigger but it won't budge. I squeeze again. No good. Russ lifts his leg and kicks out, slamming his boot into my face. I lose control of the gun. I try to scrabble away but he's faster than I am.

"Joe, don't fight it." The pistol is in his hand. He removes the safety and points the barrel at my face. I turn away, covering up. My last thought is of Lydia and I hear the shot exploding in the empty cavernous stage. I wait for the pain. It doesn't come. I look up. I have been splattered with blood. Russ is standing over me, a look of startled disbelief on his face. His uniform shirt is oozing blood. He falls to his knees. Another shot rings out. His body jerks and then he falls forward and is still.

I raise my head and look up past him as Vinnie steps out of the shadows by the nightclub set. He is carrying a .45 automatic.

He approaches and looks down at Russ who appears to be very, very dead. Vinnie kicks him in the ribs and I hear a faint groan. Vinnie points the .45 at Russ's face and pulls the trigger. Suddenly Russ has no more face and I am covered with more blood.

"You heard?" I ask him.

"I heard," he said. "Get out of here. Go home. You were never here tonight." I look past Vinnie. Baldy has appeared, gun at the ready. When he sees it's not needed he puts it away.

"What about him?" I ask pointing to what's left of Russ.

"Preston and I will take care of it."

I look at Baldy. Preston? It doesn't fit but I'm not complaining. I struggle to my feet. My heart is still racing and I feel a little dizzy.

"Can you drive?" Vinnie asks.

"I'll be okay," I tell him.

Vinnie nods and then he offers me a grudging smile. "You did good. Very good." Before I can acknowledge the compliment, he says, "Now get the fuck out of here."

I don't have to be asked twice. I head for the exit. Vinnie calls after me. "And remember. You were never here."

I look back and give him a little salute and then I walk out.

It isn't until I get home that I can finally relax and when I do, I fall asleep in a chair, still wearing my blood soaked clothes.

CHAPTER TWENTY ONE

Forty eight hours have passed and the studio is abuzz with the unexplained disappearance of security chief Russ Parmalee. His car is parked in its assigned space but his office is empty and a thorough search of the studio grounds has failed to turn up any sign of him. The police have even recruited bloodhounds but to no avail. Many think that Parmalee has gone off on a bender though he is not known as a drinker or a party goer. Others see something more sinister in his absence. They point to the fresh blood found on the floor of Soundstage 5 as proof that foul play may be involved though there is no evidence that the blood is Parmalee's.

Meanwhile, life goes on at the studio as normally as possible under the circumstances. The giant swimming pool is near completion. Where once there was a huge dirt hole, concrete has now been poured and painting has begun. Three contract screenwriters have been assigned to write swim-fest scenarios and presumably the best of the lot will be filmed. Martha Brodsky has started to line up a bevy of attractive female swimmers, some also-rans in the national championships, some from overseas, others natal extras from one of Billy Rose's Broadway extravaganzas. Studio gossip pegs the favorite as the Bulgarian national champion who swims like a dolphin and brutalizes the language like Akim Tamiroff. The babe from Bucharest is no Sonja Henie.

I am at loose ends, trying to concentrate on my work but unable to focus. Like the others I wonder what has happened to Russ but I have an advantage. I know he is dead. I am also pretty sure his body is not going to pop up unexpectedly because if I am really honest with myself, I have a pretty good idea where Vinnie stashed it. Not certain knowledge. Just a hunch.

Krug has signed Gail Russell for "Treasure of the Klondike" and I am trying to keep busy preparing press kits. A press conference is tentatively set for the day after tomorrow to make the announcement. Larry Parks is out since Harry Cohn has suddenly decided he's going to do a sequel to "The Jolson Story" and he doesn't want his new found star to be sullied by appearing in a Continental picture. Ronald Reagan has risen to the top of Krug's list. This I can't believe. Ronnie is a nice guy but if he could act as good as he talks he'd have an Oscar on his mantlepiece. I also hear rumors that those Alaska-Canada location shots have been tentatively moved to Lake Tahoe.

Besides being at loose ends, I am also very irritable. Earlier that morning I had spent a very uncomfortable fifteen minutes in the office of Buford DeSalle. He was upset about the disappearance of his security chief, naturally. He feared that something more tragic might be involved. He wanted me to contact all my sources to find a lead, if possible, on Russ's whereabouts. He also asked me to start thinking about an obituary press release if worse came to worst. He suggested that any unsavory details about Russ's earlier life might be best ignored and that I concentrate on the excellent work he had done for Continental in his short career. He described Russ as a sinner who had found his way back into God's bosom. I was afraid at one point that he was going to drop to his knees in fervent prayer, dragging me along. Thankfully, it never came to that and I left his office, my knees intact. I was seething. Several times I'd had a chance to tell the hypocritical bastard what I knew but I couldn't find the courage. When I got back to my office, my self-respect level was just about zero.

My phone rings. I answer it. It's a UPI guy looking for the latest. I tell him there is no latest. I do this all day long. And all the while I am getting more and more angry. Buford DeSalle wants me to describe Russ Parmalee as a modern day Galahad when he is no such thing. Quite the opposite. But I am going to do it because it's my job. Or is it? It's one thing to hype a dog of a movie as a potential award winner. In my profession it's done all the time. But to whitewash a psychotic killer? That is a different matter.

And then there is Sal Maggio. Vinnie has told him everything and he is pleased. But he is also no fool and he knows that Russ almost certainly did not act on his own. He is due back tomorrow and I wonder if I will be summoned into his presence and told that my job is not quite done. I would be hard pressed to disagree. For whatever reason, cowardice or something else, I know the truth and I do not bring it out into the open. I seriously wonder what kind of man I have become.

A few years earlier I was brimming with ambition and integrity. I had worlds to conquer and books to write. Then a war came along and turned me into a card carrying cynic. I became convinced I had nothing to say. I was content to write puff and nonsense about third rate actors, egomaniacal directors and illiterate screenwriters. Any respect that Lydia might have had for me was lost. I had become nothing and now, for the first time perhaps, I was facing it.

It's well past seven o'clock. I have to get away from myself and since my stomach is growling, I wander over to the commissary. It is nearly deserted. I spot a screenwriter I know and strike up a conversation. But my concentration is nil and after a few minutes, bored, he takes off. I order a sandwich and coffee. I eat half the sandwich and drink three cups of coffee as my thoughts keep coming back to Buford DeSalle. Finally, I get up and go back to my office.

I am now clear about what I must do. I slip two sheets of paper into my typewriter with a sheet of carbon paper in between them, I start to type. When I am finished I take the original and jot a short personal note at the bottom, put it in an envelope and address it to Sergeant Kleinschmidt. I fold the carbon copy and slip it into my jacket pocket. I leave the office and start toward the Palace. On the way I put the letter to Kleinschmidt into a mail box and continue on. As I near the Palace, I look up to the third floor. The lights are on. Buford DeSalle is working late as I knew he would be.

I enter the lobby and the old timer is behind the desk reading a book called "I, The Jury" by a guy I never heard of. I can never remember the security guy's name but like Scotty, he's been around since Sam Harvey turned his first roll of film. We chat for a moment. Where's Russ? No idea. Not like him. No, not at all. I sign the register, name and time, and head for the elevator. I'm sort of amused by the old guy and even more so by the so-called security he represents. The building has underground parking which can bypass the lobby, two side doors and a loading platform in the rear for deliveries. Patton's Third Army could infiltrate the place and the old guy would never know.

The doors open on the third floor and I step into the fancy anteroom, dimly lit as the sun goes down. The lamp on the reception desk is lit but no other. The mahogany walls and dark brown plush sofas and easy chairs sop up what light there is. No one is seated at the reception desk and it is quiet. Deathly so. I look toward DeSalle's private office. Light seeps from the partially ajar door. I walk toward it.

He is seated at his desk poring over some papers. For a moment he is unaware of me but as I approach the desk he looks up, perhaps surprised but not startled.

"I thought you'd call first," he says.

"About what?" I reply.

"About Russ. You have something for me?"

I shake my head. "I'm not here about Russ," I say. I take the folded carbon copy from my jacket pocket and lay it on his desk. "I'm quitting, Mr. DeSalle."

He frowns, puzzled. "Quitting? What for?"

"I think you know," I say. I point to the letter. "It's all in there."

"I don't get it, Joe. You have a home here. All that business about the Baumann woman, we know you weren't involved. All that's been settled."

"Not quite," I say.

He shakes his head. "Look, if it's money---"

"It's not money. I suggest you read that, Mr. DeSalle." Again I point to the letter.

He picks it up and unfolds it. He starts to read and a frown crosses his face and then the frown turns to anger. He looks up at me.

"What the devil is this? Blackmail? Murder?" He rises from his chair and leans forward. His face has taken on a reddish hue and fury flashes from his eyes. "Are you out of your mind? How dare you write these lies about me?"

"You should know that the original of this letter has been sent to Sergeant Kleinschmidt of the LAPD," I tell him.

"My God, son," he says, seemingly bewildered. "You are crazy. You have no proof of any of this."

"The police will find it now that they know where to look and who to look at."

He comes around the desk and I back up a step. He's considerably older than me but he's a bear of a man and I've never seen him angrier. He reaches out and lays a giant paw on my shoulder. A sadness has now crept into his eyes.

"Joe," he says. "Joe, what have I done, what have I said that would lead you to write these lies?"

I shake my head. "Do you deny that you got Maggie Baumann pregnant?"

He hesitates. Finally he says, "I don't know. It's possible. The flesh is weak, Joe, and my marriage to Percy---to my wife is not conventional."

I'm surprised. "She knew?"

"She never knows but then, she never asks. I think if she were to find out, she would feel obligated to do something."

"And May was threatening to let her find out."

His rage returns. "Damn your soul, I did not have her killed! I did not acquire this studio over the dead body of Sam Harvey. I loved Sam as I would have loved a brother. Your accusation is monstrous!"

"Buford!"

A woman's voice cuts into the silence following his rant. We both turn to look. Persimmon DeSalle is standing in the open doorway. She steps inside.

"Percy----" DeSalle starts to say.

Persimmon looks me dead in the eye. "I'm disappointed in you, Mr. Bernardi. I thought you were part of the team."

DeSalle says, "He's made some outrageous accusations, Percy. I---"

"Yes, I've been listening, Buford." She continues to stare into my eyes.

"I told him---"

"And I heard what you told him. Buford, I think you should leave."

"No, I think---"

She raises her voice only slightly. "I want you to go home. Go downstairs, get the car, drive home. I will be along shortly."

"Percy, this matter---"

"Now, Buford." She says it sharply and breaks off her gaze at me and looks sharply at her husband. DeSalle starts to speak and then thinks better of it. He starts toward the door and then turns.

"How will you get home?" he asks.

"Why, Joe will drive me." She smiles at me sweetly. "Won't you, Joe?"

I say nothing. DeSalle goes out, leaving the door open.

Persimmon walks around the desk and picks up the carbon copy of my letter to Kleinschmdt. She reads it carefully and then lays it back down on the desk. She looks up at me.

"I wish you hadn't written this, Joe," she says.

"It was sort of a necessity," I say flippantly. "May Britton was dead and while Russ Parmalee might have slashed her throat, he's not the one who killed her."

"And you think my husband gave the order?"

"I do."

"And how do you suppose the police will go about proving that?"

"I have no idea," I say. "I've done what I had to do and now

I wash my hands of it. I'm done with Buford DeSalle and I'm done with this studio."

She nods. "And you seriously think my husband had the balls to order her killed? I mean, you are talking about my husband, the Bible-thumping holy man who has made a career of nailing every pretty face from here to Ashtabula but who deep down doesn't have the guts of a housefly? Is that who you are talking about, Joe?"

She looks at me hard and she doesn't flinch. Her language does not match the genteel lady of the South that I had always believed her to be. I had always known she was smart and strong but now I perceive something else and it is not pretty.

"I think I see," I say.

"Of course you see," she says. "We couldn't let that unprincipled slut of an actress jeopardize everything we had worked for. Buford would have paid her off and then paid and paid and she would have been a part of our lives until hell froze over."

"And Sam Harvey?" I say.

"Sam Harvey was a man not smart enough to realize the party was over, at least for him. We made him a very generous offer. We offered to keep him around for a couple of years in a consulting capacity. His son Will was all in favor of the sale but the old man refused to budge."

"And so you hired Russ Parmalee."

"Not I, Joe. Buford had advertised for a driver-bodyguard. Mr. Parmalee answered the ad. Buford scanned his resume and hired him. I took the time to dig a little deeper and I liked what I found. I anticipated that there would be times when we would need a man of Mr. Parmalee's skills and disposition. Obviously I was right. When the purchase of the studio was made final, our first corporate hire was to hire him to head security."

"And spending the evening with the Hollywood Foreign Press the night May was killed, that was your idea," I say.

She half-smiles. "Can you believe I practically had to force the man out of the house at gunpoint? Buford loves his fellow man as long as he isn't a wop, frog, spik, kraut or a mick. A perfect alibi that Buford was oblivious to but which I knew he might need. But then Buford is oblivious about so many things."

"You seem to have no trouble sanctioning murder, Mrs. DeSalle," I say.

"My husband believes that the Lord will provide," she says. "I prefer a more pragmatic approach."

"You won't get away with it," I say. "None of it."

"But I will, Joe," she says, "unless Mr. Parmalee suddenly appears out of nowhere and then it will be our word against his and given his background and my husband's spotless reputation as one of the Lord's dedicated Christian soldiers, I don't think we have a lot to worry about."

"I'll talk to Kleinschmidt. I'll swear----"

"Swear to what, Joe? Anything I say here I'll deny. As for you, I am sympathetic. The press labeled you a killer. Your exoneration went unnoticed. You want justice. Of course, you're lashing out against others. That's why you are making these terrible unfounded accusations."

She comes around the desk and leads me toward the open doorway. "You needn't resign, Joe. Buford and I like you very much. You are a talented young man and we don't want to lose you. If it's a question of money, we can handle that."

I'm standing in the dimly lit anteroom now. I can't believe what I am listening to. This woman is as cold as a Siberian river. Murder is a problem solving device. If I were a religious man, which I am not, I would swear she was Satan incarnate.

She steps toward me, away from the door. I see a movement in the shadows behind her and suddenly a figure leaps forward. She starts to turn just as a man's arm swipes through the air from left to right with a vicious backhand stroke and I hear a faint gasp as her arms reach up to her throat. She looks back at me with eyes wide in horror as blood gushes from her neck. For a moment she is suspended and then she crumples to the floor and I watch as she dies.

I look toward her assailant. Al Kaplan is holding a huge knife with a blood covered blade that must be 12 inches long. He is staring down at her and there is no pity in his eyes and when he looks at me, there is no remorse. His arm falls to his side and he lets go of the knife. I know I am in no danger.

He crosses to the receptionist's desk and dials "O" on the phone. "This is an emergency," he says. "Get me the police." He turns to me. "Get out of here, Joe."

I shake my head.

"This is my business, not yours," he says.

"I'll stay," I tell him and I sit down in one of the over-stuffed easy chairs.

I'll stay and I'll tell the police what I said to Buford and his wife and what they said to me and maybe it will help Al and maybe it won't. I hope it will.

CHAPTER TWENTY TWO

Over a month has passed since the cops grilled me about the death of Persimmon DeSalle. There was no question that Al Kaplan had wielded the knife but I was constantly being referred to as an accomplice. It went on like that for two days and two nights of relentless hammering of my psyche, bright lights burning my eyes and threats of bodily harm designed make me shiver in my penny loafers. Oddly enough, I was saved by Sergeant Kleinschmidt who convinced my tormenters that I was a harmless doofus that happened to be in the wrong place at the wrong time. When I tried to thank him for his intervention, Kleinschmidt told me to get lost. I was pleased to see that our relationship was improving.

I am now driving through the Colorado Rockies on my way to White River, South Dakota, where I plan to talk to a little seven year old girl named Penny. I am going to tell her about her wonderful mother who loved her and missed her and every day had wished she could be with her. All of this is a lie but I tell myself that she will be better off with this kind of memory than the one her grandparents have been feeding her. Maybe Paul and Dorothy will try to stop me and they may succeed. Maybe I am unfairly judging them. I'll find out when I get there. All I know is, for Maggie's sake, I cannot turn my back and do nothing.

It is slow going because I am in no rush. I do about a hundred miles a day, then check into a roadside auto camp or a tourist court. I have brought my trusty portable typewriter and have managed to unblock myself long enough to write chapters three through six of my unfinished novel. Each day it comes more easily and I look forward to each stop. Slowly I think I am regaining my self-respect. Last night I stayed at a place that called itself a "motel" which was a lot like a hotel with all the amenities at about a third of the cost. I think these places have a future.

Tomorrow is July 4th and I plan to stop in Steamboat Springs. All along Highway 40 billboards have been advertising a gala Independence Day celebration and I am in the mood for some patriotic kickback. In a way I am celebrating my own independence. I have left Continental Studios. I have no job and no prospects but thanks to a grateful gangster I have no money problems, at least not for the foreseeable future. Most of all, I am secure in my independence from Lydia.

We have not spoken since that day in front of the real estate office but I know she is hurting and her pain is my pain. But not the way it used to be. Tyler Banks has had his photo in the papers twice in the past several weeks. Once on his return from a cruise which he enjoyed with his wife and two children. The second pictured him at the groundbreaking ceremony for the new Valley Crest Country Club being built in the west San Fernando Valley by real estate entrepreneur Sean Flaherty. Tyler Banks, shown smiling arm in arm with his father-in-law, has been tapped to be the club's first president. I wonder if Banks has dropped Lydia altogether or whether he continues to maintain the fiction of an imminent divorce. If she has been reading the papers, Lydia could not possibly believe such a thing. On the other hand there are men who claim that they can turn bilge water into champagne and women who will believe it. Not only believe it but drink it.

Shortly before my last day at the studio, I learned that Gail Russell had pulled out of Kingman Krug's epic picture. Something about a crappy screenplay, I believe. An offer immediately went out to Priscilla Lane. DeSalle, too busy to grieve for his dead wife, pulled the plug on technicolor and moved the location shooting from Lake Tahoe to Big Bear in the mountains north of San Bernardino. And Ronnie Reagan, newly elected as President of the Screen Actor's Guild, pulled out due to the press of union duties. Kent Taylor was offered the role and jumped at it.

The swimming pool set on the back lot was finished in record time and plans were made to start shooting "Swim, Baby, Swim" with the Bulgarian water princess. There was still no sign of former security chief Russ Parmalee.

As for Vinnie he is belatedly celebrating a career move he had made a year earlier. Two weeks ago, Bugsy Siegel was sitting in his living room when someone had the bad manners to fire a well aimed shot through a picture window at the back of Bugsy's head, popping out one of his eyes and erasing most of his facial features. Although gunsels from the Genovese family in New York were at the top of the suspect list, Vinnie underwent perfunctory interrogation. He was released after an hour.

Only one thing remained on my plate. Dave Clancy. He wasn't a bad guy. I think maybe if I'd had a sister like Maggie, I'd have done exactly what he did. But the cops didn't see it that way and neither did the D.A. Maybe they were so fed up with everything that had happened that they took it out on Dave.

Instead of charging him with assault, they indicted him on a charge of attempted murder and he was being held without bail.

I paid a call on Sal Maggio who greeted me at his front door like a father being reunited with a long lost son. He had already thanked me for everything I had done and to demonstrate that gratitude had written me a check for $5000. I was not too proud to accept it. He also wrote a check for $1219 for a new Chevrolet to reimburse the guy in the seersucker suit for totaling his car.

Over a bottle of chianti I told him about Dave Clancy and asked for his help as a personal favor. Perhaps his attorney, Arthur Baxendale, could find some way to get the charges against Dave reduced to simple assault and perhaps see that he received probation. That would serve the cause of justice. I doubt that Sal was big on the cause of justice but he promised he would do what he could and I took that to mean that Dave would be out on the street in a matter of days.

Later that day I paid a call on Brick Baxter who I found at a car dealership in Van Nuys. He was filming a commercial to be shown on a television station, KTLA, which had just started broadcasting a few months earlier and is now desperately trying to sell ad time to anyone with a few bucks to squander. It all looked pretty silly to me. Brick pounding on the hood of a Buick Roadmaster to show how tough it was while the car dealer, wearing a goofy top hat and an oversized bow tie, kept bragging about the fact that they were practically giving the cars away.

When I was finally able to pull Brick away for a few minutes, I told him what I had done for Dave Clancy and that I hoped he would let the matter drop and not bring a civil suit against him. I realized immediately that Brick had never considered the idea, probably because he didn't know he could, but now that I had alerted him to the possibility, he seemed to think it was an excellent idea. I suggested that it was a very bad idea because if Brick pursued a case against Dave, I was prepared to let all of the film and theater community in Los Angeles know that Brick was a raving heterosexual who posed as a homo to get work. He blanched visibly and begged me to keep quiet. He was happy to let Dave return to Chicago in peace.

And so I tool along in the gorgeous Colorado mountains, looking forward to waving an American flag and singing "God Bless America" and at peace with myself for the first time in years. In my suitcase is a work in progress which I believe will turn my life around. I also have a set of glamour glossies of Maggie Baumann to give to her daughter as well as a letter signed "Mother" which I dictated and which Phyliss hand-wrote professing love and regret. I hope I am not making a mistake.

At this stage of my life, I cannot deal with another crisis.

So why do I feel one is coming?

THE END

AVAILABLE NOW

The second in the "Hollywood Murder Mystery" series...

WE DON'T NEED NO STINKING BADGES

When Joe Bernardi is ordered by Warner Brothers to fly to Tampico to get Humphrey Bogart out of a Mexican jail. he has no idea of the kind of mess he is about to be embroiled in. Set against the background of the filming of "The Treasure of the Sierra Madre", this tale of extortion, blackmail, double-dealing and murder will keep you on the edge of your seat and keep you guessing, Here is just a sample:

uddenly I am aware of a murmuring in the crowd and people shuffllng about. I look up to see two cars pull to the curb, very close to the set. The first is a stunning 1935 12 cylinder white Packard formal sedan. No one pays much attention to the second one. John Huston stands up and Bogie and Tim turn to look as a gaunt looking man perhaps in his 30's gets out of the Packard and pauses, taking in his surroundings. There is a small but distinct scar alongside his left eye which droops badly as if in a permanent wink. He is wearing a light double breasted gabardine suit and a snap brim fedora and there is no question in my mind who this man is. Three men emerge from his car, three others from the second car. All six are wearing pistols on their hips.

Walter leans in close and half-whispers, "What? No Fredo?"

"Who's Fredo?" I ask.

"His brother. He never goes anywhere without him."

As the man walks toward the set, people move out of his way including the private security people hired for the duration of the shoot. He hardly seems to notice as his gaze looks everywhere.

Huston rises to intercept him.

"Can I help you?" Huston says.

"I don't think so," the man says. "I do not see Mr. Drago."

"He's back at the hotel," Huston says.

"I had hoped to see him here," the man says.

"This is a closed set and we're in the middle of filming so why don't you and your companions go elsewhere."

By this time Bogie and Tim have moved up behind their director and I force myself not to smile. That look in Bogie's eyes, I've seen it in a dozen films. He's itching for a brawl. I look at the American crew. They're not sure what to do, all except for Jimbo Ochoa who has inched forward and is intently studying the faces of the six men backing up El Jefe. The local Mexicans are inching backwards very cautiously. They know what they're dealing with.

"You know who I am?" the man says.

"I know and I don't care. Take your men and vamoose, Jefe. There's nothing here for you."

El Jefe smiles a mirthless smile. "I did not come to make trouble, Mr. Huston. I am an admirer of your films. The one about the black bird, it is one of my favorites. No, no. I came to offer my sympathies about the troubles you have been having. These incidents, they are a shame. So costly and so avoidable."

I lean in toward Walter and whisper, "I think your son could use a hand." The elder Huston grabs me by the elbow and holds me back. There's a twinkle in his eye.

"Johnny can take care of himself," he says.

And sure enough, Huston steps forward until he is right in the man's face. I'm too far away to hear every word because

John is keeping his voice down but I think it goes something like this. Take your phony apology to Mr. Drago. I don't care. And if you are not off my set in thirty seconds I am going to fire all of your men that I hired and then I am going to call the federales in Mexico City and invite them up here for the next eight days to meet the stars, get drunk and watch the filming. Do I make myself clear?

Or words to that effect.

For a moment, no one moves and I wonder if John hasn't overplayed his hand. But at that moment I hear the wail of a police car approaching and the Chief's squad car pulls to a stop, boxing in El Jefe's car. Santiago gets out, hefts his gun belt and approaches.

"Do we have a problem here, Senor Huston?" he asks.

"I don't know. Do we?" John looks El Jefe square in the eye.

El Jefe considers his options and then shrugs. "A pleasant conversation, that is all. We were just leaving." He looks at Santiago and then toward the Chief's cruiser. "If you wouldn't mind moving your car, Chief."

Santiago stares him down, "I'll move it when I am ready to leave." They lock eyes and it is El Jefe who looks away with an amused smile. Santiago turns to John.

"I know the trouble this man is bringing to you. If you would like to press charges, Senor Huston, I think now is the time."

John nods. "You're probably right, Chief, but that's not a decision I can make. You'll have to talk to Phil Drago."

Santiago shrugs. "Yes, I have talked to Mr. Drago. It is like talking to my dog and expecting a reply." He shoots a dirty look toward El Jefe and then turns again to Huston. "I do not see Mr. Drago here."

"No, he's still at the hotel."

"I see. Then I will inform you. An hour ago, two boys who should have been in school were playing in the rock quarry outside of town and came across a dead body. All identification including the man's wallet was removed but from his dress and his grooming I know he is not local. I need someone to come with me and perhaps to identify him."

John hesitates as he looks around, scanning the crowd. "I know of no one missing, Chief, and frankly, we're in the middle of a scene and I can't spare anyone to go with you."

I hear this and step forward. "I'll go," I say.

John looks at me and nods gratefully. "Here's your man, Chief" he says.

"Gracias," Santiago replies and leads me toward his cruiser. He pauses for a second as he reaches El Jefe. He looks the bandit leader square in the eye.

"Do not test me, Jefe," he says. "I tell you this only once."

We climb into the squad car and drive away. I look back and watch as El Jefe and his men get in their cars and leave.

ABOUT THE AUTHOR

Peter S. Fischer is a former television writer-producer who currently lives with his wife Lucille in the Monterey Bay area of Central California. He is a co-creator of "Murder, She Wrote" for which he wrote over 40 scripts. Among his other credits are a dozen "Columbo" episodes and a season helming "Ellery Queen". He has also written and produced several TV miniseries and Movies of the Week. In 1985 he was awarded an Edgar by the Mystery Writers of America. "Jezebel in Blue Satin" is the first in a series of murder mysteries set in post-WWII Hollywood and featuring publicist and would-be novelist, Joe Bernardi.

TO ORDER ADDITIONAL COPIES

If your local bookseller is out of stock, you may order additional copies of this book through The Grove Point Press, P.O. Box 873, Pacific Grove, California 93950. Enclose check or money order for $12.95. We pay shipping, handling and any taxes required. Order 3 or more copies and take a 10% discount. 8 or more, take 20%. You may also obtain copies via the internet through Amazon, Barnes & Noble and other sites which offer a paperback edition as well as electronic versions. All copies purchased directly from The Grove Point Press will be personally signed and dated by the author.

CPSIA information can be obtained at www.ICGtesting.com
Printed in the USA
LVOW06s1642301213

367456LV00001B/258/P